OUR ESSENCE SURVIVES

Copyright © 2021 by Katherine Murie Webster.
All rights reserved.

No part of this book may be reproduced, distributed, or transmitted in any form or by any means, electronic or mechanical, including photocopying, recording, or by any information storage and retrieval system, without the express written permission of the author, except brief quotations used in a review.

(This book is a work of fiction using resources readily available. Parts have been creatively fictionalized in varying degrees for various purposes. Names, characters, places, and incidents either are a product of the author's imagination or are used factiously and are not intended to reflect truth. Any resemblance to actual persons, or real-life historical figures, living or dead, should be plainly apparent to them and those who know them. Especially if the author has been kind enough to have provided their real names and, in some cases, events and locales of any said person. All events described here in this fiction the author has taken certain liberties as is their right as an American. This book does not represent personal views. It is written to connect the reader to the past)

Printed in the United States of America

CHAPTER I

"Therefore I went about to cause my heart to despair of all the labor which I took under the sun."
(*King James Version*, Ecclesiastes 2:20)

The wooden handrail creaks a harsh, high-pitch grievance as Friedrich Josef Klucke yanks upward. Anger accumulates with each step like heavy, sticky mud collects on boots. His cadence slow and methodical. The indignant day mindfully ferments as he climbs the brewery stairway.

Up top, Friedrich carefully pours tobacco from a small cotton bag onto an off white, paper-thin sheet. Tugging the drawstring bag closed with his teeth and slipping it back into an overall chest pocket. He taps tobacco evenly, rolls paper tight around it, licks the paper's edge, presses a seal and introduces the hand-rolled cigarette to his lips. Striking a lucifer, Friedrich ignites a lantern before making tobacco glow.

Below, they linger. His employees. Not Christoph's. Not Conrad's. His! They linger longer than their usual propensity. Prolonging this day. Friedrich unbuttons his overalls. He takes a long drag and blows smoke out of his nose. *They even allow him time to smoke.* He looks at his cigarette and takes another puff. Down below they circle around each other in small groups cackling like seagulls about Christoph's announcement. A declaration Friedrich cannot understand. He grabs the pocket watch chain and flicks his wrist, provoking it to wrap around his hand. The watch drops precisely, face up, into his palm. *Half past five*. Tucking the watch back, he hooks his thumb into the waistcoat pocket. He takes another puff and waits.

Simpler times come to mind. At the age of ten. Following his father, Christoph, around the brewery. Standing on top of the world above the copper brew kettles. Here, on this established spot. Joyful times watching colorful deep reds and oranges reflect off metal. Watching ships' masts on the Odessa merchant quay sway jubilantly. Standing precisely where Father merrily bid each employee "Gute Nacht!" Tonight, Friedrich's heart lacks civility to do the same. The swaying masts just sway. The feierbend week's end feels terribly mute as he puffs the cigarette gone and watches the sky colors fade into darkness. On this spot where today's sunset hues streaming through old dirty, arched, unglazed windows give a stark reminder of times long gone.

Albert climbs two steps at a time towards him. "See you at the malthouse later, brother!" Obviously showing no ramifications.

"Ja." Friedrich twinges envy as his little brother quickly exits.

Employee after employee ascend. Some comment about Christoph's decision. Some just make their way out the brick building that now feels like a prison. Most are oblivious of Friedrich's mediocre "Good night!"

"Tough break." An employee slaps Friedrich's shoulder.

"Guten Abend, Boss," one employee says.

"Gute Nacht," is Friedrich's mechanical response, getting lost on one word, boss. It sticks to his mind like a licked seal on a handmade cigarette. Reality sets in that next week or even the next time they greet one another, he will not be their boss. His father, Christoph Josef Klucke, made that quite clear today saying, "Starting Monday, Conrad, my son, will step up and run the brewery." *Conrad?* Friedrich wants to shout! *Conrad is not my father's son!* His mind seethes. *Conrad is not his flesh and blood. Conrad never stands here, on this spot.* Friedrich solidifies a feet apart stance and clasps hands behind his wiry body. *Conrad has never bid good night.*

Side by side Christoph and Conrad proclaimed change. Abrupt, out of the blue, spewing forth discordant words that still burn in Friedrich's ears. *Why? Why Conrad?* How can Father disregard him? His oldest, biological son, who keeps the brewery running and the vats heated at the right temperature? Why does Father ignore him? The one who knows Father's step-by-step brewing process by heart? For ten long years, Friedrich has been Christoph's head brewer. All the while having the impression that someday this brewery will be his. How? How can Father ignore Friedrich's devotion to a perfect golden lager every batch? His father's blatant neglect for Friedrich, a legitimate choice, fuels anger deep inside. Today, in one brief moment, Father took Friedrich's future hope away.

"Well, that's all of them." Old trusty Hans wobbles up the stairs, saying, "All is well down below, lanterns out and all." Hans' body and gas lantern sway to and fro rhythmically.

Friedrich removes a boiler man cap and runs a hand through his mousy, bowl cut hairstyle that needs a trim. "You go home, Hans, I'll close up."

"Nein." Hans states, "I will keep you company while you make sure all is well."

There is no desire to check if all is well, much less engage small talk. Even less, talk about Father's visit today. Summoning no aversion or excuse, Friedrich allows. "Danke!" Forcing a good nature thank you, thirsting instead for a mind-numbing drink to help forget this day.

"My pleasure." Hans' supportive hand touches Friedrich's shoulder. "Sorry to hear about Conrad taking over."

"Ja." Friedrich lowers and tilts his head left towards Hans, "Things change?"

"Not sure I like all the big ideas Mister Klucke and your brother have in mind."

Friedrich pronounces each word, "Conrad Klucke is not my brother!" Breaking free from Hans' touch and stomping up a small platform beside a large wooden fermentation vat.

"Oh?"

"Conrad is Martha's child."

Hans' bewildered look prods.

"Martha is Christoph's second wife, and Christoph is Martha's second husband." Friedrich rattles off forthrightly. "Martha is not my mother."

"Oh, I see." Hans' face turns sympathetic. "That must make it harder to swallow."

"Ja." Friedrich softens his voice seeing that Hans might understand.

"If I remember correctly, the saccharometer read 1.010 specific gravity this morning."

Friedrich likes the fact that Hans is keeping on task and not dwelling on present conversation Friedrich lifts the cover and takes in the aroma. The wort in the open vessel smells like banana, cider, and bread. The classic sweet, fruity and yeasty fragrance that emits each final batch. "Smells like the reduction was perfect once again," Friedrich boasts.

"Yes, the sugars have converted nicely." Hans reaches for the brew ledger to confirm the measurement and his own memory.

"No need," Friedrich stops him. "This Jung bier will be ready Monday."

"Yes," Hans agrees.

Friedrich wraps a friendly arm around Hans' shoulders. "Come, Hans, I would like to show you something."

Friedrich leads on. Downstairs. Past wooden kegs filled under his supervision. Full of maturing lager made from his instruction. Through a narrow passageway glowing brightly from lanterns they carry. Leading to his private space.

Digging inside his two-sizes-too-big waist coat pocket. *Father can hand down his clothes, but not what is important to him,* Friedrich thinks. He finds the key to unlock the southwest corner room.

"I have always wondered about this room." Hans reverently awaits unveiling.

"This is my experiment room!" Friedrich waves a gas lantern invitation. The incandescent glow reflects off several amber and clay jugs. Illuminating his creative treasures. He feels like a research chemist as they enter his laboratory where new beer recipes come to life. A sanctuary to start out each workday. Early, before anyone arrives. Challenging himself. Sometimes disappointed when a batch doesn't match expectations. But always Friedrich finds deep pleasure trying and tasting these new brews.

"I see you have been busy," Hans says, setting the lantern down.

Friedrich takes a British dimpled glass pint mug, acquired at the beer fest last year, off a shelf. That year Father's old recipe lagged behind ribbon winners presenting new flavorful beer. A festival fueling Friedrich's new passion. A desire to examine new possibilities. Extracting essences out of just about anything. Changing the basic recipe his father swears by. Friedrich is not opposed to change, just the change Christoph and Conrad announced. He grabs another mug. A gift from Eldora, his wife, on their first Christmas as man and wife. It fits Friedrich's hand perfectly. He pulls the cork off a small jug and dispenses fine amber liquid into each mug. "Wet your whistle on this, Hans."

Hans grabs tight and gulps down a good portion. "Well, that is no rot-gut. It tastes," licking his lips, "like mama's apple pie."

"Cinnamon!" Friedrich smiles with pride. "I don't make skullvarnish."

"Ja, cinnamon, that's what it is!" Hans agrees, taking another quaff.

After a big inhale, the spicy, sweet cinnamon essence fills Friedrich's nostrils. In one long pull, it is gone. "Ah, that's how to know a good beer, you inhale it." Wrapping first finger and thumb around upper lip and pushing residue foam off his mustache. "Like a good cigar. All flavor and taste come from the whole experience. The way it looks," filling his mug again. Placing mug to nose, he says, "The way it smells." Taking in a big gulp. "The taste and feel on the tongue." Friedrich ruminates, licking his lips. "I enjoy the experimenting challenge. Adjusting proportions to accommodate small batches. I declare this is a good batch!" Holding his mug high like a cheer before finishing its contents.

"I couldn't agree more." Hans mimics Friedrich. "You should enter beer fest this year."

"Nein, Father thinks this is a pleasant hobby. Not good business."

"Yes, he is pretty stuck on the original recipe."

"Here, try this one."

"You have another? It will be my honor." This time Hans sniffs and postulates, "Ginger?"

"Ja, I thought perhaps it could ward off hangovers." Friedrich chuckles.

"Ah, ginger is known to ward off a queasy stomach." Hans empties his mug. "Well, if I may? I will have another one of those."

Friedrich obliges a brimful.

"You have plenty of books. When do you find time to read?" He looks at his mug. "And make fine beer?"

"Early in the morning."

Hans puts his mug down and examines Friedrich's book on roses. "What other experiments have you tried?"

"Some normal variations, poppy, tobacco."

"Poppy?" Hans says, "defeats the purpose. I would rather stay awake and drink. Poppy is too calming."

"Ja," Friedrich agrees. "What about henbane?"

"That is potent stuff. Doesn't that cause hallucinations? Isn't it hard to find? I heard it was banned in 1516. Isn't it still?"

"One can use it for personal use like the Vikings did. I found some out in the countryside and now grow my own," Friedrich states, pointing at the windowsill where a broad leave plant grows. "Haven't experienced hallucinations. I might be using too little or perhaps it is a Viking myth."

"Perhaps." Hans grins. "This room must get splendid light."

"A sight for sore eyes during the day." Friedrich pulls a clay bowl forward. "Rose hips are my current favorite addition. There are so many uses for roses. My wife, Eldora, loves the smell of rose water." He twiddles the dried berries. "I am currently adding them to a dark porter."

"Why? Dark beers are just fine the way they are."

"It should add a tart punch and provide a dryer beer." Friedrich pushes the bowl back. "Just working on the right measurements."

"I think dark beers are dry enough."

"Sounds like you agree with my father." Friedrich sarcastically states further, "No need changing recipes."

"I guess I do." Hans smiles, handing Friedrich an empty mug, saying, "One more before I go home to the Missus."

"Ja."

"Sure wish you were going to continue as boss. Don't know your brother, I mean, Conrad much."

"Much like the old man." Friedrich wishes it wasn't true. Father has groomed Conrad into an exact replica. Two of a kind. They think alike. Agree together on management and distribution changes. Plans that leave many workers out in the cold without a job. Changes Friedrich fears will place the brewery in stagnation like Father's ancient recipe. Christoph and Conrad hate any intrusion into their comradery.

Friedrich's chest tightens as his head reverberates Father's words. *'Starting Monday, I will step down as your employer. Conrad, my son, will step up and run the brewery.'* Harsh words that reject all Friedrich's efforts. Paying no never mind to his expertise. Degrading Friedrich in front of every employee. Words that inhibit ambition.

Friedrich misjudges the table's height, forcibly slamming his mug against the table's edge. Powerful enough to free it from his grasp. Shattering at his feet. Shock overflows his body. Friedrich can't fathom why, of all days, today is the day to drop his favorite stein. He kneels down on one knee and stares at the pieces.

Hans rushes to help clean up.

Automatically going through the motions, throwing away a prized procession. Friedrich's mind flitters between sharing his horrible day with his wife and a longing desire to drink this day away.

"I sure like the way you're one of us, working as we do, amongst us." Hans brushes his hands before grabbing both lanterns, allowing Friedrich free hands to lock up.

"I don't plan to change that," Friedrich says, knowing the disturbing truth. Friedrich will always be Christoph's, now Conrad's, hard worker. Like a drone worker bee. Securing his private treasures behind a door, hidden, never seeing the light of day but what shines through the window. Owning this brewery or one like it isn't his future. Hope has been extracted, leaving him nothing. Father, being a prominent man, will make sure of that. Friedrich can hear Father saying, *"If you don't work for me, you work for no one."* His experiments, new ideas, are all for naught. Things will never change in Friedrich's favor.

Silently, they walk back where Friedrich's dreams began fifteen years ago.

Hans snuffs one lantern and exchanges his leather apron with an overcoat.

"Well, it will be nice to continue closing down the brewery with you," Hans says, picking up his wooden lunch box. "Especially if you're sharing the good stuff." Hans winks. "Gute nacht!"

Friedrich nods. "Gute nacht, Hans!"

Friedrich clicks and tugs the brewery's padlock. Turning the lantern flame down, watching the light flicker out on his callused working man hands. Left standing alone, outside. A strong urge for obliteration consumes him. He walks down the dimly lit alleyway, setting his heart on strong drink to drown out Father's words.

CHAPTER II

"Surely there is a future, and your hope will not be cut off."
(*King James Version*, Proverbs 23:11)

The huge mirror reflects a broken man. Many patrons sit, backs to the wall, behind long wooden tables. The full bar is buzzing. The hum overwhelms Friedrich's ears. But not one familiar face. He feels a twinge of disappointment that his employees are missing. *Doesn't anyone care?* Friedrich can't imagine that everyone went home because they do care. That they worry about Conrad's plans. What Conrad has in store for them and the brewery. Still, why is there no one, not one person, here to talk about how unfair Christoph is to him? Friedrich wonders, *what is the possible topic of discussion?* No matter. He came to drink. Friedrich plods closer to the mirrored bar.

"Over here!" Albert waves exuberantly, sitting half on, half off of his barstool. Over in his usual corner. Albert looks as if something lit him afire. Never a good sign. *What is Albert's intemperate state gravitating towards now? How much can Albert drink in such a short time?*

Flicking his watch out. *Quarter past six.* Later than Friedrich thought. Yet, it doesn't seem like enough time for intoxication. Perhaps Albert's drunkenness is fueled by Father's announcement. More likely though, it is some schnapsidee. Some crazy idea roaming Albert's mind. Friedrich doesn't care. It matters not to him. But something is up with Albert. Friedrich is sure of that. But right now, Albert and time can just keep ticking without his care.

The barkeep places a beer down. "Your regular stout, Friedrich?"

"Heavy wet. I'll take a whiskey chaser too."

"Yes. Care to play a tune or two?" The barkeep wipes his hands.

"Nein, not tonight." He rejects the idea, shaking a negative.

"It would calm down all this talking," the barkeep says, insisting, baiting Friedrich to ask why all the hubbub. He reaches below the bar where the violin rests.

No matter how true music equals less talking and more drinking, Friedrich refuses. More drinking is good business. But tonight, his heart feels heaviness. Father's speech put a darkness inside. One that matches the dimly lit surroundings and the stout set before him. They say that the more a man drinks of it, the heavier and more stupid he becomes. Yes, Friedrich is feeling the effects of doing too much for Father and thus being the fool for it. Soon this drink, and the ones following, will make him forget. Drinking is what he wants to do. "Nien, I wish to only drink tonight."

"Did your watch," Albert's chair wobbles, "tell you yo'ass late?" He slurs. "You are," Albert snubs out a cigarette, "late."

"Didn't know I was on the clock." Taking his hat off. He puts an elbow down on the bar. His hand smooths hair and rests below the ear, turning his glace towards Albert.

"Brother, you look ten years older. Why do you do it? Why must you be such a meater? Stand up to Father!" Albert reaches over and grasps Friedrich's beer and quickly swallows it empty.

"Like you?"

"At least I don't spend all my time trying to please the old man." Slamming the mug down, he wipes the back of his hand across his peach-fuzzed face. "You know that it doesn't matter. Father sees Conrad as his only son. We matter not. Not since…"

"Martha," Friedrich finishes, motioning for another beer. Plainly Friedrich has some catching up to do. Mind numbing, pain reducing catching up. Enough to drown Father's words ringing loudly inside his head.

"Juss bring us a piccher," Albert stammers.

The barkeep fills their mugs and sets the pitcher down. He fills two shot glasses and sets the whiskey bottle nearest Friedrich. "I'll put it on your tab, Friedrich."

"Danke!" Friedrich nods affirmation. He places the other elbow on the bar and hovers over his beer and whiskey chaser like an eagle over his catch. Albert won't get his drink again. "Out with it!" Friedrich provokes Albert to start talking. *More talk and less drinking.* Leaving more for Friedrich.

"Out with what?"

"Whatever is brewing." Friedrich gestures to the noisy crowd.

Albert whispers, "Gold," and then even more quietly, "theee found gold. In theee Americas."

"That is old news."

"I'm planning to go," Albert says, raising his voice and shot glass. "I am going to dem Americas," he says, and drinks it gone. Lowering his voice again, "Theress still plenty of gold." He nods his head up and down. "Their President saysso. Look at this." Tapping his finger on a well-read news article.

Friedrich reads:

> *"It was known the mines of the precious metals existed to a considerable extent in California at the time of its acquisition [1848]. Recent discoveries render it probable that these mines are more extensive and valuable than was anticipated. The accounts of the abundance of gold in that territory are of such an extraordinary character as would scarcely command belief were they not corroborated by the authentic reports of officers in the public service who have visited the mineral district and derived the facts which they detail from personal observation." President*

James K. Polk's State of the Union Address, December 5, 1848.

"Like I said, old news."

"There are still rumors of them finding gold. I will find gold. Be riiich!" Pounding a fist to his chest. "Make myselfth a name! No more being an unseen shadow of Fautther."

Friedrich surprises himself by finding all this intriguing. After today, gold might be something worth looking into. If nothing else, to avoid being a shadow himself.

"And you!" Albert gestures, waving his stein about. "You, should fleeee wivth me."

Friedrich pours the last drop of beer into his tankard. "What will Father," stammering the words out, "and Eldora…," though Friedrich includes Father, Eldora is the only one that matters on what they "… think?"

"Eldora, sweet Eldora!" Albert turns, teetering towards Friedrich. "I knowth tat livving under the same roooff asours Fauttherss wears her down as well as it does you, brother. I know, becausith wearses on meee. Today Fautther made it clear tat we inhereth nothing. You and Eldora havvtha come with me. Especially now, you're going to be a fautther yoursself soon."

Friedrich sighs, pouring himself a shot. Albert's words have a truthful bite. They make sense. He throws the whiskey shot back. It warms his throat. It feels like another. That one goes down nicely. He rolls a cigarette and thinks. *Perhaps Albert is on to something. Something worthy to think on.* Albert reminds Friedrich of the days when Friedrich himself dreamed big. About owning a brewery. He gulps beer and ruminates the flavor briefly before tilting back another cleansing whiskey shot. He smoothly strokes his mustache. Perhaps, in America Friedrich can establish his own brewery. He puffs on the cigarette. Father will not be able to stop that. Albert struggles pouring another shot, missing the mark. "Here, brother, let me help." Friedrich fills the shot glass, lifts it to his lips and rewards Albert's previous offense by downing its contents. "Enough for you," he says, slamming purposefully. Yes, Albert's words do make sense. Maybe they won't by morning when the alcohol wears off.

"Ahh, juss one more?"

"Nein, it is time to go home."

Albert teeters onto Friedrich.

Friedrich wraps an arm around his brother's midsection. Yes, Albert's words, Albert's questions make him think. Eldora deserves better. It is time to provide a place for her and the child she carries. Time to make his own decisions about the future. It would be a way, as Albert pointed out, to get out from under Father's shadow.

"Oh, sweet Eldora," Albert mutters, staggering beside Friedrich. "She'll wanth to venture to them Americas wifh mee."

"Not like this."

"We'll see." Albert threatens, looking up at Friedrich.

"None of that, you'd best let me tell her." Friedrich did not realize what he had said until it was out. Somewhere, deep, deep down, like the sediment at the bottom of a fermentation vat, he has settled. Settled on going to America.

"You will come?"

"We will see. Right now, it is between you and me."

A grin spreads over Albert's face. He puts his finger to his lips. "Shhh!" Is cut off as he trips over his own feet.

Securing Albert's arm around his neck, Friedrich contemplates. Today's development has been unbearable to think on. But tonight's conversation holds promise. An awakening of hope. Perhaps the swaying jubilant masts alongside the Black Sea quay were bidding Friedrich farewell.

CHAPTER III

And for the precious fruits brought forth by the sun, and for the precious things put forth by the moon,"
(*King James Version*, Deuteronomy 33:14)

The outside door rips free her grasp and slams against the mud-brick house. Stucco falls to the ground. Elizabeth Hess struggles awkwardly against the wind to restrain further damage. Time and time again the door escapes capture. "Just a little more," she coaxes, grunting, pushing, and pulling. A wind lull favors her efforts. Elizabeth perseveres to latch the door open as the hook slips into the eyehole. "There!" She states out loud, facing the sun. Elizabeth stands firm, placing hands, thumbs out, on narrow hips and takes a deep breath. "Cacat! Shit!" She exclaims, bearing the winds full authoritative impact through her nose and right down into her chest. She bows her tall lanky body over, hoping to gain some semblance of breath.

Elizabeth straightens, turns, and re-enters the hovel they call home, for now. Just in time to watch Johannes wipe the kitchen table. "You missed a spot!" It still surprises Elizabeth that Johannes, only two years her younger, can't do a better job and keep crumbs in control. Crumbs land on the hard packed dirt floor.

"You sound just like Mama, Bethie," Johannes remarks.

"I get to sweep, right?" Elizabeth's littlest sister Mags' sad eyes look up and point at Rosie. Rosie's chubby fingers hold the broom firm. They clinch tighter as Elizabeth flashes a stern look, stating, "That is what Mama said."

Rosie pushes the broom on the hearth, making smoldering coals wax and wane.

"We will only have to re-sweep," Johannes states, throwing the rag into a bowl, spattering soapy water onto the table.

"Like we will have to re-wash the table?"

Johannes ignores Elizabeth and yanks on the living room rug. The rug they all helped make. Many hours cutting old clothes into half-inch-wide strips. Sewing, end to end, making three long narrow stripes. Rolling the stripes into a ball so as to make it easier to braid. All taking turns braiding more strips so Mama and Elizabeth could hand sew them into a tight coil. Producing a suitable rug and place to sit and make more rugs. A heavy rug that slightly budges as Johannes attempts to stomp out. She turns and grabs it from behind her, leans forward with all her might and drags it. It stops abruptly on the threshold.

"Rosina Jacobina Hess." Elizabeth uses her whole name. Just like Mama would do. Expressing annoyance in a similar Mama tone. She gives Rosie a withering look and nod towards the door and says, "Help your older sister." A perfect Mama imitation.

"Yes, Mama!" Rosie snots off. The broom bounces to the floor. A tongue sticks out at Mags in passing.

"I'm not your Mama!" Elizabeth states blatant defiance. "Mama would slap that tongue off."

"No, she wouldn't," Johannes says, still wrestling the rug.

That being true, in all Elizabeth's eighteen years Mama has never slapped anyone's tongue. Threatening with words, *"Put that tongue back in your mouth before I slap it off."* Yes. But never once following through.

"I don't want to beat rugs. Maybe you can beat rugs and I can dig in the garden and pick potatoes," Johannes suggests.

"Mama told you to do the rugs, I heard her," Mags utters.

Johannes and Rosie jerk the rug together. The threshold releases it. Chickens squawk as the huge rug disappears. Rosie's voice becomes fainter with each word, "Don't kick my chickens," as the two trail off.

"There you go, Mags, broom is all yours." *So is the house,* Elizabeth thinks. A part of her is jealous since rarely does one have the house all to themselves. But today is a day to enjoy outdoor chores. Picking up the broom and presenting it, she adds, "Do the best you can."

The shoe box by the door barely gets a side wise glance as she exists. No time to lace up boots. A smile creases and pronounces Elizabeth's high cheekbones. "I'm off to the garden!" No one voices care. The cool dirt pathway invigorates her feet. The wind lifts hair off her back as she skips. An excitable giggle exudes. Outdoor love overpowers the task ahead. Feeling the autumnal sun drench body and soul. *Autumnal.* Such a fancy word for autumn. Just one of the many recent word gains. Too many to recite presently. All in preparation for a possible journey to America. Never knowing when such a word may prove useful, but relishing the knowledge. Her current favorite word being bucolic, meaning country life. Yes, bucolic! Where Elizabeth can be free to go barefoot.

"Bucolic is country," Elizabeth sings, "and country is free to roam. Without shoes, if you please," twirling, arms outspread, "to dig your toes in the dirt while you pluck potatoes," she voices. Long brown hair strands follow her to a stop. The momentum continues draping the hair across her face. A quick toss, into the wind, places it back where it belongs, on her shoulders and down past her hips. "Bucolic is country and country is for me."

Down the path, just a little way, is Papa's rock. The sun-kissed granite behemoth beacons her to sit, just for a moment. It warms her bum. The Mican Mountains outline the distance, surrounded by a tranquil haze. Elizabeth can imagine spending a lifetime doing only this. Sun shining warmth, happy and carefree. Alone. Just her thoughts. Like so many times Papa sits, prays, and completes sermons right here, upon this rock.

Looking down the road, no one. Elizabeth hopes Papa and the littlest Hess, Henry, will soon return with favorable news.

"Quit your dawdling, Elizabeth Magdalyna Hess!" Mama hollers.

"Yes Mama," Elizabeth stands slowly, trying to savor a moment more. The trees down by the Donau River's banks glow vibrant green. Putting one foot up on the solid rock, she neatly folds her bloomers. Counting each fold out loud, "One, two, three, four." Lifting the other foot and repeating an exact count uniformity. Skipping closer to Mama, she sings, "once upon a time in a valley low and kind is a family, an archaic family, old fashion, but archaic family, who hope to travel and see all America's beauty."

"Where's your babushka?"

"My kerchief is on my neck," she replies. Elizabeth knows Mama would appreciate a more American word, perhaps softening her irritation. Singing softly, she continues, "To America where things are new and modern," finishing, "with beauty everywhere."

"Put your kerchief on," Mama shouts, adding, "before the sun burns a hole in your head."

"Yes, Mama." Elizabeth gathers her calico skirt and plops down. Wiggling toes and shins into the cool earth.

"Are the girls' chores in order?"

"Yes, Mama." She releases her grip, allowing the skirt to fall.

"Don't make me tell you again to put your headscarf on. Why didn't you tie up your hair?"

"I didn't have time, Mama." Dutifully Elizabeth slips the scarf over her head remembering days, fun days, playing. Without a thin silk babushka supposedly preventing a hole to burn through her head.

Glancing up to breathe deep and glad the wind doesn't take her breath away this time. An eagle effortlessly soars across the sky. She marvels how easily it glides around in this horrendous wind! Having no worries. Being reminded that Henry, much like the eagle, is worry free and has little restraint.

"Elizabeth Magdalyna Hess," Mama sternly encourages, much to Elizabeth's chagrin, "pay attention to your work."

Being the oldest has restraints. Elizabeth thinks, *you grow up amazingly fast and before you even are aware, you are Mama's helper. Just like that. Barely remembering anything else. Then marry and have children of your own.*

"The potatoes are small this year," Mama tells her, "be sure to look closely. We need all the potatoes you can find."

Elizabeth stuffs potatoes into an earthy smelling gunnysack. "Too bad we can't grow them as big as Aunt Dorca's."

"She was exaggerating a tad, Bethie, dear."

"Didn't she say her carrots were as big around as her wrist? That she was going to have enough carrot tops to supply tea and stew for the entire village all winter?"

"Town, Bethie dear," Mama corrects, "They don't have villages in America, they have colonies and towns."

Elizabeth disagrees. She knows that there are Indian villages throughout the Americas. It isn't her place to correct Mama. Mama hasn't read, "The Discovery, Purchase and Settlement, of Kentucke," over and over again about a million times, appeasing her brother Freddie, Wiggy and Henry's bedtime story demands. Where Daniel Boone instills a pioneer passion. Where he mentions towns, colonies, forts, farmsteads and villages.

"I can't imagine drying that many carrot tops."

Elizabeth picks up an unusual tuber. "Look at this one."

Mama gently puts forth her hand to receive the heart shaped spud. "Let us plant this one in the winter barrel."

Brushing off the dirt from her knees, Elizabeth wonders why Mama procrastinates after all the encouraging haste.

"You know," holding the potato firmly, "we," waving the red Belgium between Elizabeth and herself, "are from same roots." She grabs a knife from a pocket that lies just south of her V-shape apron ties. Tied tight, accentuating her disproportionate figure that has borne eight children. "We are from same family," and with precision, honed from many practiced years, she cleaves two equal parts. "We all are from the same family," she reiterates as she points the knife towards the house, road, and Elizabeth's brothers working hard to harvest. "Though, someday, we all will go our separate ways," Mama says, placing two heart halves apart in the hay. "Someday, you will marry, have children and settle down. Plant yourself, so to speak."

"I want to see all that the world has to offer first," Elizabeth refutes, outreaching arms. Thinking it a more realistic goal, since she feels eighteen is way past acceptable marriageability age. Cascading towards spinster.

"That is a dream, Bethie. Woman unaccompanied in their travels are looked down upon."

"Then I will travel with you and Papa."

"I welcome that, but I hope to settle down in Oregon and do no more travel. Besides, God may have other plans for you." Mama grabs Elizabeth's arm and taps gently as they return to their work. "One does not know when, where, or how their life may go."

No control of the future unsettles Elizabeth.

"When the day comes for you to be planted, I will miss you very much." Moisture pools around Mama's eyes. "I will always carry you here," putting hand on heart, "as I hope you, my sweet Elizabeth, will always carry me in yours." She grabs the pitchfork.

"Oh, yes, Mama, always," she confirms, gazing at her siblings. A deep desire swells in her to never miss them, to stay with Mama, Papa, and them forever. To always be near her younger siblings and care for them. Keep them safe like the day Reverend Johannes Boneskemper came to a nearby town, Braila. He preached reformation that

Papa took to heart. Elizabeth has never seen so many people as were at rally square that day. That day Elizabeth spent all day outdoors playing instead of working. Looking for lucky four-leaf clovers with her siblings. Scratching furrows and planting pretend seeds. Playing horsey, a game where Elizabeth pretends to be a horse. Her siblings would take care of her in exchange for a horsey ride. The same city Papa and Henry will soon return from. The same city they all will depart from. But only if Papa returns with the good news to go to America. "Won't it be great," Elizabeth says, shoving a few more potatoes into an already full sack, "to travel?"

"If we are ready," Mama replies. She stops exposing potatoes to the sun. Elizabeth can see that Mama contemplates just that, doing her own daydreaming about taking a lifetime voyage. Traveling across a vast sea to America. "It should prove to be a grand adventure," she says. "Jakob, dear," Mama requests, "bring Bethie another sack."

"Imagine, a land free and empty." Elizabeth looks up at houses lined up, side by each. A hillside covered with houses, fences and yards close to one another. Where Johannes and Rosie beat rugs on a line between their small shed and small barn. Small, like all the rest in the line. All having yards harboring many different animals. In the Hess family alone, everyone has their animal to take care for. Their own household contribution. Being the oldest, Elizabeth tends to the horse. Jakob milks two cows. Johannes cares for five sheep and sheers them once a year. Rosie feeds the chickens and geese. Ludwig and Karl feed the pig and sometimes rides it like a horse. Little Mags mostly cuddles the cats. Henry gets to feed the dog, so the dog favors him. All this prods Elizabeth to add, "A country, not crowded. Ready to Explore."

"Well, what do you, child, want to explore?"

This is a subject that she has given great thought to. Without hesitation, "There is so much God-given country to see," she says. "So many experiences awaiting. Descriptions of such I can bestow on my future students."

"Oh, that's right, you want to be a teacher. You will be a fine teacher with what you already know." Mama assures.

"Yes. But I want to enrich their minds about faraway places they may never get to see. Like Romania. The trip Papa plans will give me plenty of stories. Stories about buffalo and wolves visible for miles. What they look like. What they are like. And so much more." Excitement spills out in her words.

"I doubt that, very much, since Aunt Dorcas claims the grass in America goes up to her chin. One may never see animals that wish to stay unseen."

"Maybe the grass isn't that tall. You did say that Aunt Dorcas tends to hyperbolize."

"Hyperbolize?" Mama questions, raising her eyebrows.

"Exaggerate! Hyperbolize!"

"Oh, you and your words," she says, relaxing her face giving Elizabeth a sidewise grin. "Perhaps she does at that. One thing is for sure, it will be an adventure that will make men and women of you all. It will make you strong and suitable husbands and wives."

"Who wants any of that?" Jakob deposits two empty bags. He hoists the full one up onto his shoulders and carries it off. Elizabeth wonders when Jakey, just a year younger than her, became stronger than all of them put together.

"You will, someday, Jakob," Mama assures.

"Never!"

"I think," Elizabeth says, "there will be plenty of consuming labor and no time to find a spouse."

"There is always time to find a mouse," Freddie interjects, not understanding the conversation.

"Mouse? I want it," Wiggy is ready to fight for it. He excitedly looks up from the menial task scrapping around for potatoes. Freddie and Wiggy always make finding potatoes a treasure hunt game. A mouse will increase the booty.

"Someday, my children, you will all have your own spouse, not a mouse. That means wife, Freddie and Wiggy." Mama prophesies.

"I would rather have a mouse," Freddie and Wiggy simultaneous voice.

"I would rather rob from the rich and give to the poor, like Robin Hood," chimes Karl, three years older than Freddie.

"What about exploring the wilderness like Mister Boone?" Jakob says, giving Karl a strange look. Like Karl must be out of his mind.

"That is Colonel Boone," Elizabeth reminds. "If I remember correctly, Colonel Boone had eleven children."

"Well," Jakob says, "that explains it all, that is why he took to the woods."

"Oh, Jakob," Mama admonishes.

"What? Children are annoying." Jakob says, pitching up potatoes.

"Annoying," Freddie and Wiggy repeat together as if they were twins. Being the closest in age, only nine months apart, explains their parallelism.

"You all are children," Elizabeth points out.

"Mark my words," Mama remarks, "you will all go your own ways. Find a spouse and have children. That is how it is."

Elizabeth hopes America will give her the chance to be Elizabeth Magdalyna Hess before becoming Elizabeth someone else.

"Mama! Betzie! Mama! Betzie!" Henry's exuberance slams into Elizabeth with all the force a nine-year-old can muster, knocking Elizabeth backwards. "We go! We go! Papa says!"

CHAPTER IV

"There is nothing better for a person than that he should eat and drink, and that he should make his soul enjoy good in his labour. This also I saw, that it was from the hand of God."
(*King James Version*, Ecclesiastes 2:24)

Awakening thoughts swirl Friedrich's mind, *America holds a fresh start. It allows freedom from Christoph Josef Klucke's shadow. It allows Father to cast it solely towards Conrad. Will Eldora want to start anew?* Friedrich is unsure. America holds opportunity that nourishes welcomed change. Quietly propping himself onto his elbow, he looks fondly upon Eldora. Resting head on hand, he watches her sleep. Her long, light brown hair drapes over her right shoulder. Early morning sun kisses her restful cheeks. Her skin glows irresistible beauty. Unable to suppress an urge, his back hand caresses her soft complexion. Eldora's eyelids open. Her green eyes glisten as he whispers, "I a-Dora you." She grins at his loving pun. "Picnic day, me Dora?" Friedrich knows she will not refuse. It will be a perfect opportunity to approach the subject of embarking on a new adventure together.

"Were you reading my mind?" She asks, combing her fingers through his hair. "You know I never can say no to a picnic. It is the only time for us."

"It is a beautiful fall day. I will have Charlotte prepare us a meal."

"And my favorite drink, hot apple cider?"

"With a cinnamon stick." He gently rubs her abdomen. "I still cannot believe a baby is in there."

"Careful, your happiness is showing." Eldora smiles.

More than ever, Friedrich desires to provide a better life. A child needs room to roam. In Friedrich's mind, America will provide that opportunity.

"You are going to be a great father."

Friedrich vows just that.

#

"Here." Eldora points.

Friedrich places the blanket down. The seagulls mull around. Their calls sound closer than they are. Friedrich doesn't worry about them as much as the crowd gathering. "I hope the square meeting doesn't ruin your appetite. Charlotte outdid herself."

"There is nothing that this view can't remedy. Perhaps, we will overhear something of interest."

Friedrich doubts that.

"Shall we start with the cider?"

"First, you must have a seat." He lifts high her arm and motivates a graceful pirouette. Eldora's blue dress swirls and billows. It neatly deflates and sighs upon the blanket.

"Why, thank you."

"My pleasure."

"What a view. Not a cloud in the sky."

The Black Sea shimmers an invitation to sail abroad. Passengers bustle about while ships await. Hope lingers that they will soon do the same. Friedrich sits beside his wife and uncorks a jug. Steam rises with sweet apple cider aroma. A glance up before filling their cups, he wonders, *Will she want to travel?*

A cinnamon stick goes in each cup before he presents a toast, "To our good fortune to have such a grand day."

They sip and admire the clear view. Eldora twirls the cinnamon stick and expresses, "We must travel on that body of water someday."

"I couldn't agree more," Friedrich boldly states. "Soon. We should travel to America."

Eldora faces him.

"What do you think?" His eyebrows lift.

Her face gives no indications.

A distant voice preaches, "You don't have to be a man of the cloth as myself. Your beliefs and actions will speak for themselves. That is what America needs. Good, God fearing people."

"Here Sir," a girl hands Friedrich a handbill.

"It is preordained!" Eldora slaps his thigh. "It cannot be any clearer."

#

The savory smell of senfbraten awakens Friedrich's appetency. Strong, like his appetite and desire to leave Odessa and start anew. His hand slips comfortably into Eldora's.

Everyone radiates Sunday finery. Even Martha's fine china gives a customary Sunday panoply display. Friedrich looks at Eldora's blue dress, past her bosom, right into her green eyes gazing his way.

"Conrad, will you do the honors?" Martha requests, gesturing her son to say the dinner prayer.

Eldora squeezes Friedrich's hand as Conrad voices the familiar blessing. To have such a woman is a blessing no words can express. A woman willing to embark on a new adventure. He squeezes back.

As Conrad finishes, a ringing, firm, "Amen," echoes throughout the room.

"I believe this meal needs more illumination," Martha announces.

Without hesitation, Conrad jumps up like an obedient soldier, putting match flame to candle on the wooden candelabra. It gives a warm glow.

"Perhaps we can consider a bay window, like the Gorche's," Martha continues, glancing Father's way.

Father says nothing as Charlotte places one huge, boiled potato onto his plate.

Friedrich reflects on how Charlotte is more like a mother to him. Many years have gone smoothly with Charlotte taking charge after his mother's death. Charlotte has always been here to fill Father's plate, clean his house, tend his garden, take care of the children. Just as Mother would have. As far as Friedrich is concerned, Charlotte is more than a housekeeper. More like a mother than Martha could ever be.

Charlotte places a tiny potato on Christina's plate. Friedrich watches his little half-sister poke at it like a strange, unique garden bug. Charlotte and Christina bring this dreary house sunshine. *It will be hard to leave them,* Friedrich thinks regretfully.

"It is so nice of you, Phillip and Disa, to join our family meal today." Father aggressively smears butter all over his potato, making no eye contact with Eldora's cousin Disa or her husband.

"So kind of you to invite us. It is always a pleasure to dine with your lovely family." Phillip stops cutting his potato into neat quarters, skin and all, to look at Father. Father rudely ignores Phillip.

Friedrich pulls a finger around his starchy stiff collar.

Albert fidgets, tugging his lapel. Pulling and smoothing his tie. Nervously looking about acting like the day he brought home a cat. Calling the cat his own. Refusing to let it go. Friedrich waits until the proverbial cat is out of the bag. Each sip of dinner wine certainly increases Albert's courage.

"Well," Phillip proclaims, "what does any one of you think of the goings on across the ocean?"

"We plan to see for ourselves," chimes Disa, scraping peelings off her potato. She glances mischievously at Eldora.

Disa's look gives Friedrich pause. *Has Eldora shared their plans?* If so, it only confirms her excitement that equals his own.

Hearing news that Rauser's plan a trip to America delights Friedrich. Hopefully, they can plan to travel together.

Albert offers while chewing, "They are… finding… tons of gold… everywhere. Gold beyond belief! Gold as big as this bun and bigger," Albert says, grabbing one from the platter, holding it high. Taking a bite, he continues, "I plan to go… strike it rich… get some of that gold for myself."

"Slow down, child," Charlotte chides, placing the pork dish down. "Chew, then talk."

"I am not a child! I am twenty-one years, now," he says, spewing forth pieces of bread.

"Hand me your dish, child of twenty-one." Charlotte reaches out.

A true statement by age, but not by stature. Albert is short like their mother. But slenderer, like a boy. Strong, though, like a man. Friedrich could attest to that, when Albert predisposes himself to work.

Charlotte forks a slab of pork onto Albert's dish and hands it back.

"Perhaps we can all travel together?" Friedrich speaks, decisive. He squeezes Eldora's hand tightly. "You and Eldora are like sisters. It would be a pleasure to travel together," Friedrich proudly suggests. Eldora squeezes back approval.

"What a great idea!" Albert approves.

Father's places his fork, tines down, at the edge of his overflowing plate. "I have a dozen or more written materials, papers and articles in my study that may change all of your minds. Many stories of young people, like yourselves, being persuaded into worthless ventures," Father says. "America is a place full of hornswoggling, film flams and chicanery. All to extract your funds. It is all an evil elaborate scheme to finagle workers into a new country."

"The Mormons are immigrating in droves," Phillip pointedly says. "How can a country so willing to let people with different religions and esteemed beliefs into their country be so devious?"

"America is a place where one can start their own community, raise their children how they see fit, and have their own convictions," Friedrich adds.

"An article was written about Mormons perishing from exposure and disease. It is one of many stories I have on my desk," Father states. He stuffs a bun in his mouth, making an obvious statement to end this discussion.

"I think it is worth the risk," Albert interjects. "For the hope of being your own man." He glances towards Friedrich, "Or being acknowledged as such."

Father almost chokes but manages to chew and swallow the mouthful and Albert's accusatory words. Father's reaction and shocked look makes Friedrich wonder how his father could not have known. To be so blind. To act like this is completely new information. Father glares at Albert, then directly at Friedrich.

Friedrich averts his eyes.

"You have all that you need right here." Father taps a pointed finger beside his fork. "I provide well for each and every one of you."

"I provide very well for my own, Christoph, thank you very much," Phillip retorts, adding, "It is a fine meal tonight, Martha."

Friedrich's stepmother looks about, apprehensive. Still Martha's small voice concurs, "Thank you, Phillip, for the pork tenderloin we have the pleasure of enjoying tonight."

"You're welcome. Glad I could provide. It is the least we can do in exchange for all the fine dinners in your home. Next time we butcher a pig, we will bring some bacon."

"You are too kind," Martha replies.

Father's stern diatribe continues. "Gold is a fool's dream." Folding hands over his plate, elbows on the table, staring at Albert. "You will end up down and out, without a way to get back home. This new country will cause you to do things you would rather not do just to survive. Things you will not want to attach our good name to," he expresses finality.

The table guests fall silent. Concentration is on Charlotte's delicious meal.

Conrad breaks the silence, slapping Albert's back, "That is what you do best, schinaglen's, it is right up his alley. Albert will flourish in such a peddler environment."

"I will admit a tendency to involve myself in things before knowing all that it requires. Nonetheless, I am going." Bold, truthful words backed up with more than his share of dinner wine. "Perhaps I will flourish, make a name for myself that will outshine yours, dear father," Albert states, unafraid, pushing aside his plate, indicating absolute resolve. "Excuse me!"

"No, you may not leave!"

Without looking up, Friedrich says, "What is wrong with dreaming of making your own way in this world? Making a bad or good name for yourself? Standing on your own two feet?"

"To start a new life of our own. Right, dear?" Eldora rubs her belly.

"Yes." Friedrich looks at her and sees only love and confidence emanate back.

Father wipes away butter from his lips. "I forbid it for your own good. I forbid you, Albert and Friedrich to go off willy-nilly. Your reckless disregard will, no doubt, dishonor our good name!" Father pounds the table with both fists.

Father's uncharacteristic manner allows Friedrich to channel Albert's determination. "You cannot forbid me, Father," he says, looking directly at Christoph. "Or Albert either, for that matter."

"Yes, you cannot forbid me." Albert firmly crosses his arms.

Defying Father together. Sharing Albert's exhilaration, right or wrong. Collaborating with his brother cements Friedrich's decision. Affirming that they will stand on their own honoring the Klucke name. He feels justified to side with his younger brother. He just does.

"I cannot believe that any one of you would leave all you have behind, all of this." Father outstretches his arms, hands open, palms showing. "Three square meals, a roof over your heads, a place to work. More than anyone could rightly dream of." Father's hand actions emphasize all he provides for them. "To leave it all behind, just for a chance to end up getting stuck in a snowstorm and resorting to cannibalism? Madness!" Father's face reddens.

"Christoph Joseph Klucke!" Martha scolds, "Not at the table! The horror of it!"

"Ah, yes, the Donner party. In the fall of 1846. Even after many were told it was dangerous to keep going, many decided to continue. It is all about choices." Phillip volunteers, amiably. His candid words signify that Father is not the sole source of accurate information.

"It is a choice to build a place of one's own honor." Friedrich looks to Eldora, confirming yesterday's firm decision.

"To build a life with your own principles," Eldora adds.

Friedrich remembers discussing just that. To stand up and be his own man. "To work with your own two hands and reap your own benefits." Friedrich emphasizes his last three words.

"All that I have will one day be yours and your brothers'." Father directs the comment towards Friedrich.

"That is not true!" Friedrich glares directly at Father, his voice expressing the marked truth that Christoph Klucke is biased towards one, Conrad. All others must stand aside. A stare down commences between them. Friedrich doesn't flinch or blink under Father's displeased gaze. Not anymore and never again.

"Suit yourselves!" Father breaks down. "Just know I do not support such foolishness. Such a trip is foredoomed. Footpads and muggers await you, mark my word." He slams fists again, making silverware clatter. Father stands and retreats to his study for his evening cigar, leaving an unclean plate. He leaves without excusing himself, something he never does, except today.

As soon as Father is out of earshot, Martha finally dares to ask, "What about you, Eldora? Are you really okay with going to America?"

Eldora lays her napkin down beside her plate. "I want what is best for my husband and our child. For them to be happy."

Friedrich loves that she understands.

"Prost, to America!" Albert raises a newly full glass.

"Prost!" Friedrich cheers.

CHAPTER V

"And lest thou lift up thine eyes unto heaven, and when thou seest the sun, and the moon, and the stars, even all the host of heaven, shouldest be driven to worship them, and serve them, which the Lord thy God hath divided unto nations under the whole heaven."
(*King James Version*, Deuteronomy 4:19)

They sprawl out around a glowing campfire like drunken squirrels on brandied plums. Dick cups an empty pipe with his thumb and first two fingers. The full moon behind casts Dick's shadow beyond the fire. Sitting erect on a fallen cottonwood log prevents cramped legs. *A much more comfortable perch*, thinks Dick, much more formal than his comrades, but less formal than his chair in his hometown, Taos.

    Taos is a place to hang his hat, but way too suffocating. More like a restrictive cage than a home. A town growing faster than Simpson's poetic words that Dick half listens to. The poet mountaineer rants on about mountain breezes and cold mountain springs freezing nether parts. Dick scoops tobacco into his pipe, packing it tight. Using the glowing end of a stick, he puffs and ignites the tobacco. Dark flavored tobacco enters his mouth, filling his taste buds. In truth, Dick rather likes not hanging up his hat.

His predominant hand removes his white, wide brim hat and tosses it. A thrill runs through him as it lands dead center his bedroll. Patting down wavy hair tufts and tucking some behind his ears leaves oil residue that he rubs into his hands. A reminder that it is time for a good washing. Which will involve getting his nether region wet. *Soon,* He thinks. Before fall weather is chased away by winter winds. When taking your hat off can cause whole body chills.

Dick makes a mental note, *A perfect evening, five beavers out of five traps. A great start to a month-long hiatus from responsibilities and confined city life.*

"There once was an old mountain man, he hunted and lived off the land. He always felt fine, when he danced in the moonshine. So, he danced and imbibed like he planned," Simpson finishes.

"Much like us." George pats his stomach.

"Great poem," Johan complements.

"Not bad, Sim old buddy," August adds.

"Pretty good for a poem," Dick lies, not even knowing all that he recited. "I remember a day, it was 1833." Dick leans forward, forearms to thighs. "I was picking cotton in Mississippi."

"That is a place too warm for my blood," Simpson says.

"We all heard that story," Johan mentions.

"Not all of you have," Dick insists.

"Spare us, please." George lies down placing hands behind his head.

"I'll be brief." Dick can feel inebriation slowing his words. Dragging out great descriptions. Dick didn't feel like being brief. They can listen or not. "It was a night much like tonight. Stars bright, temperature and air perfect. As I was lying in tall grass just a couple yards from the cotton fields I toiled and sweated in all day…"

"Shots of light crossed the sky!" George nonchalantly interrupts. He turns side wise to look across the fire at Dick. George sweeps his other arm up, "right before your eyes," and quickly slaps it back down.

"A perfect end to a hard-working day. An evening I will never forget," Dick elaborates, "stars shot across the sky with long white tails. One right after another," Dick says, not letting the thunder stealing, crusty old man George have the last word.

All but Simpson harmonizes, "Later you met an Indian."

"Now, now, mind your manners." Dick kindly reminds them, "If you don't mind, I would like to tell my own story." Dick takes a puff from his pipe. Pushing the pipe forward saying, "He was a son of a Ute Chief."

"A thieving, killing Ute," George says, raising up to his elbow.

Dick hears lead balls clink together in George's dirty buckskin pocket. His flintlock Lancaster lay close by, as always.

"Like those that attacked Taos?" Johan asks.

"I remember well." Dick intently watches flames lick the firewood.

"We lost a few good friends," George says.

Dick needs no reminder.

"Those Utes have a rampaging nature," George lays flat again.

For some Indians, Dick believes this to be true. But not his friend. "Ouray's nature has always been peaceful. He was born that clear, dark night that the stars fell. I was seventeen then and never felt more alive, content and…"

"Blessed!" reverberates from everyone around the fire.

"Yes, blessed." Dick's trapping companions sitting comfortably around the fire know this story all too well. "When I told Ouray my experience he said, 'It is a good omen. Good things are to come.'" Good things like this. Fire licked venison meals every night. Compadres that share his passion for the great outdoors. He feels blessed every day his eyes view starry skies, and his lungs fill with fresh air.

"And ever since you have been searching for that same bliss and freedom," George says. "Those days are gone for you and me, being married men and all."

George's words sting true and bring back memories of Dolores' demand to stay home. *She doesn't understand,* thinks Dick. This is bliss.

Being here by an open fire, hearing it crackle. Amongst friends, even the likes of those that interrupt his stories. A better life cannot be had. But George is right. Family responsibilities constrain.

"As far as I am concerned, there won't be any blessedness as long as those thieving killers are around," Johan says. "Besides, I hear Ouray stands for arrow. Arrows are for killing."

"Yes," Simpson agrees, "They are killing slackers that try their best to get as much as they can for nothing. Even going the extra mile to steal."

"Much like us." Dick implicates, tapping his pipe against the tree stump. Tobacco smolders on the ground. Dick prepares to ignore what is to come from his statement and call it a night. From his perspective, stray Indians who desire more cause trouble. Most Indians and white men alike are opportunists. Different kinds of people living together in this vast land of opportunity.

"You calling us thieves?" Johan sputters.

George gives an over the shoulder warning glare towards Dick to start no trouble.

Dick does not heed his warning. "In a way."

George shakes his head and lays back down.

"We work little trapping beaver, that are everywhere, and basically free for the taking. Then sell their pelts for profit." Dick adds, "Same as Indians."

"What we do is called business," Johan says, "what they do is rob us blind."

"All they want is as much as they can get for what they see is free for the taking," George adds.

"They take anything that isn't nailed down." August discourses.

"In other words, steal!" Johan reiterates.

"Soon, there will be no beaver, or other furs to take or steal," George mumbles.

"Yes, I am afraid it comes too soon." Dick stands and tap dances tobacco ashes dead. "Trapping beaver is the only reason for me to travel this far north and take a chance of getting my nether's cold. With that I say good night, tomorrow is another day to steal from the land," he jests.

The men shake their heads.

Johan takes out his jaw harp and plays a tune that tugs on Dick's heart.

"Good night, cut hand," George says, "you, Indian lover, you."

Just because Dick's hand is disfigured doesn't give George the right to call him cut hand. So, he returns the unpleasantry with another unpleasantry by replying, "Good night, crusty old man."

Simpson sings, *"The girl I've left behind me."* The words impose some truth on Dick. *"She said it makes no difference if you never return again; I knew by how she said it that she'd never change her mind, so we shook hands and parted, an' I left my girl behind."*

Shaking the harsh home life reality off, Dick focuses on George's words *'Indian lover'*. In all of Dick's one score and thirteen years he has never been called an Indian lover. He removes the hat from its resting spot and lies down. The moon shines brighter than the twinkling stars. He feels blessed any day or night that doesn't involve town chaos and lanterns obscuring the view. He is saddened that his wife forces compliance to restrictive ways. He is saddened that George's words make a soul wrenching mark. A man needs to be known. When you hear his name, it should conjure up Pioneer of the West, Trapper, Soldier, Guide, Scout, or even Rancher. Not a kept man or Indian lover.

CHAPTER VI

"a time to cast away stones, and a time to gather stones together; a time to embrace, and a time to refrain from embracing; a time to get, and a time to lose; a time to keep, and a time to cast away;
(*King James Version*, Ecclesiastes 3:5,6)

The ships rhythmic sway follows each wave slap against the dock. Swaying back and forth like Friedrich's mind and heart have been these last few months. Flip flopping between staying or leaving. Always landing solid on departure.

"Well, it is too late to turn back now." Father hands him a silver gentleman's cigar case.

"Ja." Friedrich's initials engraved above CJK, Christoph Joseph Klucke. Below Father's initials are JPK. His grandfather Joseph Peter's initials. A single case holding a single cigar.

"A cigar to celebrate your first born. You can hand it down to your first-born son."

Anger flares inside Friedrich. It is just a case. With one cigar. Holding little value. Hardly a consolation prize for being jilted. An heirloom to safe keep. For Christoph's grandson. Friedrich wishes to give a nonexistent thank you but decides instead to give an acknowledgement nod, saying weakly, "Danke," with no eye contact. He accepts Father's gesture, token, and primogeniture. Another hand-me-down that doesn't suit him.

Father gives him a quick, strong handshake. "Bode thee well." He encourages Martha forward.

Martha hands Friedrich a square shaped present. A neat, crocheted wrap tied in a bow box. "I made the wrapping myself," she proudly states. "It's a scarf, if you've haven't guessed. I hear that it can get very cold crossing the ocean."

"But," his father says and further requests, "you can't unwrap it until you are underway."

"Yes, you mustn't open it until you are on your way." Martha shakes a finger.

"Danke!" Friedrich slips it into his big overcoat pocket. It weighs down his right side substantially, leaving him quite unbalanced. "I promise." Giving the full pocket several taps.

Christina looks up at Martha and Christoph and asks, "Can I? Now, can I?" Getting two parental affirming nods, she lifts a rock using both hands. Looking so proud, saying, "This rock is for your garden."

"Thank you," Friedrich says, kneeling. Christina wraps arms around his neck. He picks her up, saying, "It will make a great addition to our garden. I will put it safely in my pocket." The above average weighted feldspar counter-balances Martha's present nicely.

Charlotte pries Christina away, "Okay, now, little Miss, let them catch their boat."

Sadness tugs Friedrich's heart as he gives them both tender kisses on their cheeks.

Conrad offers Friedrich his hand and shakes vigorous. "Try to keep Albert from running amuck." He smirks.

Friedrich assumes Conrad looks forward to having no competition upholding the Klucke name. Even though he isn't a at all related to the Klucke name. Conrad may have stolen his birthright, but not Friedrich's aspirations. He is ready to prove Father and everyone else his capability. To demonstrate he can soar triumphantly on his own. Accomplishing dignity and respect. Making Friedrich Klucke's name stand out.

Eldora finishes goodbyes and stands ever so close to Friedrich's side. Her rose water scent overpowering the oceanic stench. Their emotions in tune waiting as Albert, Phillip and Disa say goodbyes. They turn their backs to those they leave behind and walk somberly down the boarding platform unto the large clipper ship.

#

The Northwest wind snaps sails of the Wilhelmina II. Launching, what Friedrich estimates to be, 330 plus men, women, and children; almost as many cows; half as many stinking pigs; some sheep; a few horses; and too many squawking chickens into the great Black Sea. Friedrich's hand rubs across Eldora's back. Standing sadly together watching people become smaller and more distant. Odessa, Ukraine's Potemkin stairs appear like they push them into the Black Sea. People become dots on the quay and slowly, slowly, drift into a blur. There is no turning back or having second thoughts. The wind carries them away.

"Will we see them again?" Eldora nuzzles against his chest.

"Once we settle, perhaps." Friedrich knows Father seldom changes his mind. The possibility is highly unlikely.

"Oh, I think they will all come for a visit," Albert adds. "Once I'm rich, and make a name of my own, I will invite them with tickets for their own voyage," Albert bloviates. "That will impress them."

"He is stubborn." Friedrich looks over Eldora's shoulder at Albert.

"Stubborn, like all Klucke's." Phillip chuckles.

"I am sure Martha will soften his resolute," Disa reassures Eldora and the others. "Then they will soon be making plans for their own trip. Anyway, they will have to come see their grandchild."

"I sure wish my parents would have made the trip to see us off," Eldora says.

"You sent them a letter. It is the best you could do. It is a long trip from Kiev," Disa says.

"Not as long as a trip we are taking. I fear I will never see them again." Eldora's fingers wipe moisture away from the corners of her eyes.

"One never knows, dear cousin," Disa says, using a petite handkerchief to wipe her own eyes.

Friedrich is glad Eldora has Disa. He's not so sure on her husband's pig contribution. But it is nice to have family along.

"I think it is time to open this." Albert holds up a crocheted wrapped box. A similar package to the one Martha gave Friedrich. "You got one too, didn't you, brother?"

"Yes, I will open it later." Curiosity about the gift weighs down Friedrich's pocket and mind. But holding Eldora close is what matters right now. He knows the sad farewell affects her even more than it affects him. There is a time and place. "This isn't the time."

"Father said we could open it as soon as we were on our way. I can't wait." Albert unties the scarf unveiling a tea tin. He throws the scarf around his neck and opens the hinged cover and quickly closes it. Looking nervously about, saying, "Perhaps it is better opened when there aren't so many people around."

"That will be a challenge. We are on a crowded boat," Phillip comments.

"Why?" Friedrich's curiosity piques.

"Its contents cannot be discussed right now. I suspect that the gift is really from Father."

"Now you have me wondering." Friedrich himself suspects another token gesture that doesn't measure up.

"Martha does not have the means to fill the tin up with…" Albert hesitates, leaning closer. Unable to contain himself. Like Albert's October travel announcement so many dinners ago. Albert whispers, "Banknotes and coin."

Albert is not wrong. Martha does not have the means to gift money. Father does. The heaviness weighing down his coat indicates a substantial sum. Friedrich does not care how much. The anger towards Father is still fresh. Even after many months severing ties. Friedrich ponders this handout and wonders.

Eldora suddenly lurches forward over the rail, promptly vomiting into the water below.

Friedrich thought that morning sickness had run its course. Confliction attacks his mind. *Is this the right time to travel? Is this really the right thing to do at this time?* There is not a plan or a road map that leads him. He is taking his family into the unknown. The only guide is hope. "Are you alright?" Concern and sudden trepidation forms deep inside his mind and stomach.

"Yes," Eldora gasps, looking queasy, "just a little seasickness, I guess." Once again, Eldora retches over the starboard side railing.

It worries Friedrich. Eldora had to endure morning sickness that took a toll on her only to be stricken now with seasickness.

"Now, now, dear," Disa says, quickly handing over her petite embroidered handkerchief before Friedrich can dig his handkerchief out.

Eldora wipes and folds the filth inside. She tucks it between her wrist and dress cuff. Lifting her head saying, "I'm alright." A strong wind gust sends her hat flying, leaving her beautiful trusses unprotected.

"I will get it." Albert offers, pushing through the crowd. "Excuse me... pardon... excuse me...."

#

In a righted boat raised above the deck, Elizabeth dangles one leg over the edge. Below, caged animals protest confinement. The picturesque port view before her vanishes into a blurry horizon.

The crews heaving the sails song rings over and over in her head.

> *"We will pull, we will haul,*
> *Hearty, healthy, and gay,*
> *Heave a-way, a-way,*
> *Blow the man down,*
> *Like husky strong seaman*
> *To earn able and pay,*
> *Oh, give us some time*
> *To blow the man down.*
> *We will pull, the commands*
> *Of our skipper obey,*
> *Heave a-way, a-way,*
> *Blow the man down.*
> *We will haul till we hear*
> *The command to belay,*
> *Oh, give us some time*
> *To blow the man down."*

She looks over to the now sleeping Henry. *Poor child*, she thinks. His earlier exuberance caused him to miss leaving Ukraine's beautiful, majestic port. An amazing sight it was, and still is, from her quiet perch. Huge steps disappearing into waves. The shoreline barely a memory. Like the memory, only moments ago, when Henry announced, "Quiver, ye all, at the feet of Pirate

Henry the Great," high above chattering people and squawking animals.

The elaborate bon ton clothing styles below grace the ships topside. Such impressive splendor. Gingham and plain cotton dresses back splash Sunday finery. Elizabeth stops gawking and returns to study. Two Bibles precariously rest on her thin thighs. One German, the other Bible Noah Webster's English. She knows enough Bible verses that this proves a useful method to learn English better. Elizabeth reads, *"But pray ye that your flight will be not in the winter neither on the sabbath days,"* from the book of Matthew. She thinks, *It is a warm, sabbath, February day*, and continues, *"For then shall be great tribulation."* In her peripheral vision, a bright green ribbon appears. Almost as fast, an intricately embroidered hat slams into her chest. It startles her to grab tight. The movement necessary to achieve the catch causes The German Bible to fall at her feet. The wind flips the pages of Noah's version back and forth. Elizabeth's elbow stops them at Ecclesiastes 2:24: *"There is nothing better for a person than that they should eat and drink and find enjoyment in his toil."* Then, like some unknown force, the wind changes direction. A gust attempts to rip the hat free. Both hands wrestle against the wind to maintain a tight grip. She pulls it back close to her chest. The Bible pages turn and once again are elbow stopped at another verse. *"Behold, I have refined thee, but not with silver; I have chosen thee in the furnace of affliction."* Elizabeth closes the book without dropping it. "No more of that!"

"Little girl," a wee man says, looking up at her, "that hat is Eldora's."

"I am no girl," Elizabeth announces with spunk, like Henry displayed earlier. Or more like when Rosie does just before she sticks her tongue out.

The man makes his way up the Jacobs ladder towards her with hardly a waver. "The view up here is so much better." He climbs into the dingy and plops down comfortably beside her. "Only a girl," emphasizing girl, "ventures to such heights." Albert looks at Henry and says, "Or, a little boy."

"I will have you to know I am 18, old enough to marry." *Why did she blurt that out?*

"Hello 18, I am 21," he says, turning her way and offering his hand. "Was that a proposal?"

"No!" Elizabeth snaps. She notices his striking blue eyes while accepting his smooth palm.

"Ah, well then, pardon me." Albert says as he lifts and twists to give the back of her hand a gentle kiss.

What an odd fellow, Elizabeth thinks. *So pretentious.* Albert wears plain garments showing a hard-working man. His hands tell another story. They indicate a man who sits behind a desk. Elizabeth finds it an odd combination. Perhaps he hides amongst plain folk. A man with means kisses like so, on the top of her hand. It is more common to greet a stranger with a pretend kiss on both cheeks. This man bewilders her.

"Albert is the name." He looks expectantly.

Elizabeth still accesses him. A hand made crocheted scarf. Worn out tweed blazer. A handsome man that definitely hides his stature.

"And your name is?" Albert prods.

"Elizabeth."

"Hey, you two!" A sailor hollers up. "Get down from the yawl." He is wearing more buttons than Mama's button box contains.

"What?" Albert and Elizabeth say simultaneously.

"The ship's jolly boat." He says, giving a stern glare. Then the glare turns into a leer when the sailor gets distracted by a woman with beauty that outshines her bon ton style. He tips his hat and follows her, not enforcing his command and ignoring all others, including the intoxicated man following close behind.

"He must mean this boat," Albert offers, looking at Elizabeth.

"Yes, but I do not see the harm. It is so much better than standing down there."

"I concur."

Concur, really! Elizabeth thinks Albert is a very curious man indeed.

Albert stands and offers a helpful hand.

Not falling for that again. Elizabeth shoves the hat into his chest and says, "Here, take your wife, Eldora's hat?" Presuming Albert left his wife alone on the crowded deck.

"Thank you, my sister-in-law will be very grateful for its return."

Elizabeth gathers her books and stands. "I believe that the bawling seaman will return." *As soon as he is less distracted*, she thinks.

"You mean bellowing?"

"No, bellow means to shout in a low voice." She lowers her voice like a baritone in dramatic demonstration. "To bawl is to cry out loudly without restraint."

A disturbing look crosses Albert's face. Elizabeth feels it was too much, and she should have just agreed. Men do not like to be told differently. Especially men with suspected stature. Elizabeth is still not sure about Albert's status. His carriage is lacking rigidness. Still, some mannerisms hinder her determination. She will try to contain herself.

"Henry!" Elizabeth prods. "Time to wake up."

"He looks plum worn out. Let me help, here hold this," handing back the hat.

Thinking she was rid of its responsibility, Elizabeth places it between her and the books.

Albert gingerly lifts Henry, a soft objecting moan is heard as Albert hoists him up. Henry's head rests on Albert's shoulders. Albert whispers to Elizabeth, "What is poking my ribs?"

"My sword," Henry mutters.

Albert tucks the wooden object more comfortably between Henry and himself. And without falter, Albert maneuvers down the Jacobs ladder. Albert grabs the bottom round wooden rung and says, "I got you."

Feeling his steady hand holding strong and his eyes on her, Elizabeth musters up all the lady like mannerisms she can. While balancing two large bibles and a stranger's hat. On a ladder with two pivot points, wondering whose genius idea that was. Struggling, and twisting, despite Albert's efforts. The hat loosens. Elizabeth fears it will take flight and be lost forever. In her attempts to save the hat, composure lost. Wobbling precariously.

"Easy, steady," Albert advises.

She pauses, takes a deep breath, and gains some control. She makes up a rhythmic song in her mind. *Be meticulous. One hand in the middle, one foot in the middle, one step at a time.* It stabilizes her. It keeps her concentration on precise movement.

"You're doing fine," Albert encourages.

Pausing the song to say, "Thank you!" It causes her to slip and twist, freeing Albert's grip. She stumbles backwards when her feet hit the ship's deck. *How uncouth! How unrefined!* She Oscillates around and teeters ungracefully into a tall man's arms. He stops a disastrous fall. Elizabeth looks up into blue eyes. A deeper blue than Albert's. Like the ocean itself.

"Got you!"

The man smells pleasantly like freshly made rose water.

"Meet my brother, Friedrich," Albert introduces.

Friedrich tries to tip his hat while still supporting Elizabeth. Failing he nods.

"Friedrich, this is Elizabeth," Albert continues introductions. "She caught Eldora's hat."

"Thank you. A pleasure to meet you," Friedrich says.

"Thank you for catching me!" Elizabeth relaxes into Friedrich's steadfast attempts. Something about his eyes keeps her focus. Hearing Mama say the eyes are the windows to the soul. If this is true, this man's soul earnestly intrigues.

"Thank you for saving my hat," a willowy woman says, carrying her head high despite lacking covering on her light brown hair. Her hair is coiled concentric, like a braided rug. Except piled, one on another, forming a tidy bun.

Prim and proper, thinks Elizabeth.

Friedrich quickly adjusts Elizabeth's shoulders and releases. Bringing back equilibrium. Tugging an oversized vest that needs alteration, he says, "There you go."

"This is Eldora," Albert says.

"A pleasure to meet you," Elizabeth says, wanting to curtsy, but refrains. "I believe this is yours," presenting the hat. "Oh, I am so sorry," she says, trying to smooth out creases. "I must have crumpled it trying to save it from the boisterous wind."

Eldora's elegant dress clings perfectly to her slender figure with a slight bulge around the abdomen. The top dress coat has about 16 cloth covered buttons. Each button having the same color as the ribbon around the hat.

"Thank you!" Eldora receives graciously.

Friedrich places a hand sweetly into Eldora's.

"And this is Mister and Missus Rauser," Albert directs attention to a couple standing behind Eldora.

Mister Rauser pushes around and presents a hand to shake. "Pleasure to meet you, my name is Phillip."

"Pleasure to meet the woman who saved my cousin's hat," Missus Rauser moves in, almost pushing Phillip into the crowd. A gust threatens to expose light brown hair similar to Eldora's. Missus Rauser places a hand down onto a simple flat crocheted hat. A beautiful facsimile rose pin sticks above the hats other side. *A person needs more than one pin,* thinks Elizabeth, *in this wind.* "I am Disa. It is a challenge to keep your hat on in this horrendous wind."

"Boisterous wind, I hear!" Eldora smiles at Elizabeth. Grasping tight her hat against the slight belly protuberance. Making no attempt protecting herself from sun or wind.

"Nice to meet you, Mister and Missus Rauser." Almost bowing. Inadequacy floods Elizabeth. Never owning a hat, but agrees, saying, "It is hard to hold onto your hat, or anything for that matter, in this wind." Even though her kerchief has managed to stay where it belongs.

"Attention, Attention, please!" A loud voice announces.

The same man who told her to get down from the yawl, jolly boat or whatever they call it, is asking everyone's attention. Standing by what Elizabeth believes is the helm. To her, it is just a big wheel.

"May I?" Elizabeth says. Assiduously, she tucks books under an arm and reaches for Henry. Albert delicately places Henry into her arms, careful to keep Henry's wooden sword from poking Elizabeth in unspeakable places. Henry snuggles close.

"Captain Harrison wishes to welcome you aboard."

A good stout, fatherly looking man pats the sailor's shoulder. "This is Mister Drake. Some of you will come to know him as Shaun, my mate and right-hand man. He is to keep us all in order. There are seventy crew members to oversee three hundred and thirty-one souls. To assure we all act our parts properly." The captain pats Shaun's shoulder again. "Shaun and the crew know their business and shall attend to it, bearing their parts well. They shall require all of you to bear your part as well, which is small, but equally important. All law breakers will be disciplined. So, look after to follow the rules, do your part, and we shall have a creditable voyage together." He double taps Shaun's shoulder and moves aside to give him the limelight.

"These are Captain Harrison's Rules," opening a scroll, "listen and obey," Shaun begins. The ships passengers become spookily quiet. "On this fine day, the 28th of February 1850 and until we reach the end of our voyage on or about the 3rd of April." He holds the document firm, "these are the requirements:

> *Every morning at 6 bells all able shall rise. The fire shall be lit. Food and*

water given. Soon thereafter, cleaning of deck and quarters. Smoke house fire out at eight bells. All passenger's must be below for the night at ten o'clock, at which time one long whistle will blow. No tobacco or flame use below deck. Cooking is only allowed in smoke house front and stern. That is amidship. The smoke house must be kept clean. Days will be determined for washing. No washing is allowed below deck. All belongings, but essentials, must be stored in cargo hold. Access to cargo hold will be available once daily. No cards or dice allowed. No quarrelsome behavior will be tolerated. No pounding nails or damaging the ship in any way. No one speaks to the man at the helm. No one!"

Shaun points to the wheel.
So, it is the helm. Elizabeth gets confirmation.
"We run a clean, friendly ship and observe the sabbath," the captain voices strong and stern like when Papa means business. "There will be a gathering here every Sunday, starting today, at noon thirty." He steps forward, "All must attend. That is all. Dismissed."

The crowd's hubbub gradually resumes as the captain and the first mate step down. Many people escape the wind by going below deck. Elizabeth lingers, holding Henry close. The thought of going below causes her chest to tighten.

Henry awakes, wriggles free, and stands beside Elizabeth.

Abruptly, a man skillfully slides down a rope and lands at their feet. "Where do you think you're going?" He says, looking at Henry.

Elizabeth steps back. They were not going anywhere, having an instant urge to go somewhere. It is Mister Shaun Drake. Elizabeth fears chastisement for being on the forbidden spare boats. "Shaun, my mate and right-hand man." Elizabeth says. Immediately she questions herself on the reason to repeat the captain's words. Perhaps it was the shock of Shaun's sudden appearance beside them.

"Well, for you, darling, I can be Shaun, your mate and right-hand man, if you prefer." he winks.

Elisabeth blushes. "Sorry, Mister Drake," she apologizes.

"Not a problem. I can be anything you want." He turns to Henry. "But I came to talk with this young swashbuckler. I could not help but notice you swinging with determination that make-shift sword of yours." He kneels down, eye to eye with Henry, "You wish to be a future adventurer, do you now?"

"No, pirate, but a good one," Henry proclaims, fists on hips. "Like Robin Hood, rob from the rich and give to the poor."

"How commendable." Shaun suppresses a laugh, "But I have never heard of a good pirate."

"You will!"

"Well, then, let me shake your hand," Shaun puts out his hand. It dwarfs Henry's. "Hello, I am

Shaun, nice to meet you, 'Robin Hood of the seas.'"

"Pirate Henry, the Great," Henry corrects, moving to lift his sword high into the air.

"Excuse me," Shaun says and leans back, avoiding the sword. "Sir, Pirate Henry." Shaun stands. Pinches his hat and brings it to his chest and bows. Long, dark, thick, brown hair drapes over his back. A leather strap at the nap of the neck holds his top trusses tight and wrap around the rest loosely.

"The Great," Henry reiterates.

"And what is your name, young lass?" Tilting his head seductively, looking directly Elizabeth's way.

Nothing about this man gives Elizabeth ease. Not even his banter with Henry. "Elizabeth."

"Elizabeth," he repeats, placing the hat under his armpit. "A very pretty name for a very pretty woman." He digs deep into one of many large bulging pockets.

His pockets must weigh him down. It must prove difficult to do his job, thinks Elizabeth.

"This," Shaun says, "is what an imaginative lad like yourself needs." A small brass object with a tan leather strap appears. A quick parallel pull extends it out to about a yard. The main oak barrel is full of scratches. Shaun flips open end pieces. Presenting it open handed, palms up. A generous gesticulation. Encouraging Henry, "Here, try it."

Elizabeth swoops close, fearful that Henry will drop it. Backing off when it is obvious that he has control.

"What is it?" Henry's eyes widen with delight.

"A telescope, my lad. Go ahead, take a look." Shaun provokes. "Look through here," pointing to the front eyepiece. "Place your hands here and there." Helping him to balance the object. "Turn your hands opposite from one another like so," he says and again Shaun shows Henry how, "until an object comes into focus."

Henry treats it like a baby robin, naked to the world. The eyepiece swivels a little, causing Henry to readjust.

"Takes some getting used to." Shaun looks at Elizabeth.

The smell of chewing tobacco tells her he is too close. Wondering why this man, Shaun, doesn't have something better to do than to entertain a child. Elizabeth wonders about his motive. *Does Mister Drake have a hidden agenda?*

"You gotta grab it like a man," he instructs. "Here." Shaun positions Henry. "Tuck your elbows into your chest, to make steady." He pushes Henry's arms inward. "Focus there," pointing to the man at the helm. "Yes, focus on him."

Henry adjusts and wobbles some. The whole time Elizabeth is on-guard. Ready to grab the telescope. Hopefully preventing it from hitting the deck. All the while staying a distance from Shaun.

"I can only see his mustache or his ear or hair, not his whole face," Henry says. Wide eyed amazement looks at Shaun. "I think," taking another look through the scope, "I even saw nose hairs. Yes, I can see his nose hairs."

"Henry! Don't be impertinent," Elizabeth scolds.

"What?" turning her way. The telescope turning with him. Almost slamming Elizabeth. "I can!"

"That is improper."

"You like?" Shaun asks.

"Yes!" Henry smiles. "Very much." Henry repositions to hand it back exactly the way he received it, gentle and respectful.

Shaun collapses the telescope to about a foot long and tucks it into his other armpit. "Mighty handy tool for a pirate, don't you think?" Shaun massages his chin. "I have wanted to get a better one, a two draw. One that opens up twice, but not as long. Smaller, so it fits my pocket better. It will be able to see further as well. One might even be able to count those nose hairs." Shaun chuckles. "How would you like to buy this one from me?" He taps the telescope.

"We have no money for such things," Elizabeth says, touching Henry's shoulders to persuade movement onto the steps leading to the belly of the ship. Having a strong urge to follow the others below. This man gives her more trepidation than what awaits down there.

"Wait!"

"For what?" Elizabeth is weary of Mister Shaun Drake.

"Well, I think we can work something out."

"Not interested."

"Hear me out," Shaun says, grabbing her arm. Elizabeth yanks free.

Henry grabs Elizabeth's hand and stands firm, leaning towards Shaun. His pleading eyes melt her like butter on a warm, sunny day. For Henry, she listens.

"You are not the only ones with rules to follow. The one that gives me the most displeasure is having my boots shiny as a new penny."

Get on with it, she thinks, folding her arms across her bosom.

"I hate to shine boots." Shaun moves closer. His breath really reeks. Not of alcohol, like the stories and rumors she hears. "If 'The Robin Hood of the Seas' is willing to shine my boots for the rest of the voyage," Shaun says, presenting the telescope with both hands. "This fine telescope is his."

"Really? I can do that!" Henry says, looking at Shaun then at Elizabeth. With intense desire and with youthful innocence, he asks, "Can I? I shine Papa's boots all the time. Please, can I. Can I?" Henry tries to suppress jumping up and down, but Elizabeth can see his excitement, nonetheless.

"You do not need my consent." Deep down, she suspects he does. "You make the deal, you keep the deal, as Papa always says. You can check with him if you like."

"No, I can do this," Henry says with confidence. Henry seals the deal with a firm handshake. "And that is Pirate Henry the Great!"

Something about this exchange gives Elizabeth a horrible feeling deep inside her belly. A similar feeling the belly of the ship offers.

CHAPTER VII

"As we have therefore opportunity, let us do good unto all men, especially unto them who are of the household of faith."
(*King James Version*, Galatians 6:10)

The salty air invigorates. It restores Friedrich's soul. A respite above acrid unkempt bodies and soul-piercing baby cries. He conjectures the wee little ones' voice objections to the accommodations. The things everyone must endure day and night. Urine, foul breath, and vomit. Smells that can only be tolerated by chewing or smoking tobacco. Drunken sailor songs and occasional heartless, melancholic harmonica notes can drown endless baby squeals and constant talking. If uncomfortable moss-stuffed beds don't keep you awake, the snore choruses will. To think he left a full house to escape crowding, among other things, only to end up with less room. Only one week on this boat and Friedrich, more than ever, desires a place to call his own. Conceptualizing three more weeks voyage is beyond any human courtesy or ability to endure.

For now, Friedrich finds escape. To fill his mouth and nose with tobacco flavor before re-entry into the bowels of disgust.

"There you are!" Ludwig Hess' purposeful walk determined. Unmistakably all his. Wearing an Orthodox Mennonite beard, thick and perfectly trim. Friedrich is sure he is not a Mennonite. He earnestly approaches with a warm smile and dark eyes.

"Mister Hess," Friedrich welcomes with an outreached hand. "You are Elizabeth's father, right?"

"Yes, Bethie is one of mine. She has taken quite a shine to your wife, Eldora, right, that is her name, is it not?" Ludwig grabs Friedrich's hand and pulls him close.

Friedrich tips his hat and nods, "Ja." Ludwig smells like a man who has been up top all day. Wearing all the clothes he brought onboard. The man cannot possibly have any more clothes to wear. Enough to keep him warm on the North Pole. There are more layers than a rose has petals. His collar shirt has the top two buttons undone. Something Friedrich finds appalling and inappropriate, especially for a preacher man. He exposes a bright inner floral shirt. A design Friedrich remembers seeing Elizabeth wear. A worn-out sweater covers all but the gap about his neck. A vest guises neatness. To top it off, an overcoat unable to cover his wrappings and portly body. "It is brisk today!"

"Yes." Ludwig tugs his coat closer together and folds his arms around himself. "But every time

I go below, I find myself longing to return topside. It may be brisk, but it is the better of two evils."

"Agreed." Friedrich puts his cigarette between lips so as to tuck Martha's crocheted scarf into his drab brown woolen blazer. Working in a brewery you learn to adjust your body to temperature. There is no time to shed layers when you boil hops or put more on when you keg the beer. You wear what you wear and take what you get. "I find it hard to believe a man of your occupation prefers solitude." The cigarette bounces as he talks.

"Plenty of people to talk to up top without eavesdroppers," he says, leaning closer. "Don't you have anything warmer than that?"

"It is all I need." Friedrich takes a puff and says, "Elizabeth is such a comfort for my wife and I." Cupping his hand around the cigarette before a quick flick to toss dead ashes. "Elizabeth is one reason I can be up top."

"Yes. How is your wife doing?"

"Fine."

"One great blessing of a large family. There is always someone to be around when you need them. Or if someone else needs time to themselves. Do you come from a big family?"

"No." Friedrich is not sure how much truth he wishes to share, "Just Albert and I."

"Where are you from?"

"Odessa."

"Well, you didn't have far to go, then. My family is well traveled. My wife's family originated from Germany. Mine from Prussia. We have traveled in small groups. Villages to villages.

I remember an area up north of Odessa, where I met my beloved Lyna. A village by the name of Bessarabia. I was born there. When Lyna and I married it was a very large village. So, we moved with others to start another village, Jacobsonsthal, Romania. That is from where we traveled many river and land miles to get to Odessa and on this ship."

Friedrich takes the last puff and snuffs it out, saying, "I remember hearing something about Bessarabia. I think my grandparents are from there." He has no idea where Jacobsonthal is. All this matters not to Friedrich. He wants to forget his roots. To start fresh. He fixes another cigarette.

Ludwig points, saying, "Could you spare some tobacco?" He takes out a pipe in anticipation.

"Ja, sure." Presenting an almost full tobacco bag. "If you need more, don't hesitate to ask."

"Much appreciated." Ludwig taps tobacco into the pipe bowl. "I will have to wait until they open the store house tomorrow to obtain more tobacco. I find that an inconvenience every morning. Why must we wait?"

"I surmise so we don't run out. That would be a more unpleasant inconvenience."

"I suppose there is some truth in your words."

"I, for one, like the security. Wouldn't want to sit on guard watching my belongings during the whole voyage," Friedrich says.

"No, that would not be good," Ludwig says. He hands the bag back, saying, "I do remember a group of Bessarabia villagers going south. That might have been your family. Lyna and I left because the village was growing too fast. Too many ideas. Too many different religions. All in one place, causing much strife. Our family needed elbow space. Hmm, a small world we live in. Imagine our two families, originating from the same village." Ludwig wafts air through the pipe stem. "Now on the same boat."

"Ja."

"You and I are Bessarabia brothers." Ludwig gives Friedrich a friendly elbow, almost knocking Friedrich's cigarette free. Ludwig leans nonchalantly against the boat wood and quickly repels from it.

Friedrich can feel the cold wood without leaning on it. Much like the cold shoulder Father gives when there is a request for family information. Not one story can Friedrich conjure up about the Klucke family. The cigar case given is but one of very few items that indicate family beyond Father. The cold truth that family history has always ended with Father.

"My parents never left," Ludwig continues. "My brothers and sisters felt, as I did, still do, that if you're going to live in a big community, you could just as well be city folk." Ludwig closes the space between them. Getting uncomfortably close.

"Or be boat dwellers," Friedrich interjects, getting them both to smile. He rocks back and forth, inching away.

"Yes, with all the big city diversity. I wonder how we all get along."

"They escape to the cold."

Both men laugh.

"One can believe that there is a greater power that puts you and I together."

"What brings you on this journey?" Friedrich asks.

"Reverend Bonekemper."

The name is familiar to Friedrich. He combs his mustache with his thumb and first finger, thinking. *Bonekemper. Is that the man who preached in the background while Eldora and himself partook a picnic on the Potemkin steps near the town square?* Friedrich digs into his inside chest pocket and pulls out a handbill. "I believe the Reverend had a hand in our decision as well." The serendipity of it goes beyond understanding. Perhaps Ludwig is right. God may have a hand in their meeting.

"Yes, that is one of his handouts. I find his preaching to be refreshing. Like Romans 8:28 which says, 'And we know all things work together for good to them that love God, to them who are the called according to his purpose.' I feel so called."

"To preach in America. A noble cause."

"I like the community aspect of the Stundist faith. That is what it is, you know. It is much like how Bessarabia and Jacobsonsthal used to be. Where you have small meetings at homes and yards. More personable with no church building subsidy. More concentration on the Almighty God's word."

"Very devout."

"Yes, more one on one with God."

"Ja," Friedrich agrees. He never did understand why so much money and effort went into a building used once a week.

"Well, onto another subject. The meaning for searching you out," he says. "I have been wanting to chat about Albert."

"Ja."

"Albert, your brother, who is over there?" Ludwig doesn't point. Just raises his elbows and nods. Albert stands next to a pretty girl, not much older than thirteen, with pigtails poking out a knitted hat.

"That is my Rosie Albert talks to."

"I see."

"What do I need to know about Albert? Are his intentions honorable? Does he fear our God and creator? I mean, is he a religious man? Can I venture to guess that he is as gentle with women as you are with your wife?" Ludwig pokes his finger into Fricdrich's chest. "Can you give me a straight answer?"

Friedrich doesn't answer, being taken back a bit by Ludwig's questioning tone. He worries that Albert kindles trouble so early on the voyage.

"I do not want my Rosie to be spoiled by a womanizer, you know. I have seen him with other women."

"Albert is a social man, just as you are," Friedrich answers, knowing that Albert's aspirations sometimes get the best of him, but his heart is true. Friedrich can only hope Albert takes his example and that of their father's as to the treatment of women. Father may not appreciate his two biological sons, but he is a good example regarding women. "Albert likes to talk and involve himself with things he ought not. He is still young, impulsive, and spirited. But I assure you, Albert is respectable when it comes to women."

"Good to hear," Ludwig slaps Friedrich's shoulder repeatedly. "Good to hear. My Rosie is also very spirited. How old is Albert?"

"Twenty-one."

"Hmm," Ludwig leans back onto the ship and once again repels. He wraps his arms around himself tight. "Rosie is only fifteen."

They stand looking Albert's way. Soon Albert goes below, and another man swoops up next to Rosie. "Who is that?" Friedrich asks.

"That is Hildago. He came aboard at Port of Ponta Delgada. A robust Portuguese. He wishes to help me set up a church. We are going to Oregon City, but will not be setting up a church. Hildago pays no never mind to the fact there will be no building. But he is a very sincere man. I haven't got it in my heart to correct him."

"People put a lot of stock into buildings. And with such a large family there is always help." Friedrich reminds Ludwig as he strikes a lucifer match, bringing another cigarette to life.

"True," Ludwig crowds Friedrich as if the match will give some heat. "To tell you the truth, I think my Johannes, who is 17, is more suitable marriage partner for Albert and Hildago. She has a fiery heart. The kind that keeps a man on the straight and narrow."

That is the kind of woman Albert needs. Friedrich isn't sure about Hildago. Ludwig must want him to consult with Albert to consider Johannes's companionship instead of Rosie's. Not that Albert will listen to Friedrich. Besides, Friedrich recollects that Albert isn't looking for a female companion. Not just yet.

"I fear that Johannes' heart is swaying another direction. She is more into the Klingmann boy. I wish for her, and all my children, to find a hard worker and someone with a good heart."

"There goes your youngest," Friedrich says, "Henry, is it? I believe that's his eighth pair of boots this week."

"Yes, poor boy, I think he is going to be the first child to experience the evils of some people with their hearts focused wrongly."

Friedrich's eyes follow the boy who carries dirty boots towards the rear staircase. Henry disappears, going below. Leaving the boats furrows to flood Friedrich's view. Spellbound, and thinking on all the possibilities that await in America. The hope that this new journey will harbor such passion and opportunities. Like the kind Reverend Bonekemper, Reverend Hess and Henry have. And better conditions than the dismal place below.

Albert returns towing Elizabeth. "Looks like Albert has eyes on another one of your girls." Friedrich remarks. Perhaps Friedrich needs to have a talk with his little brother after all. To plant a seed on taking care to not look like a womanizer.

"Papa! Come! Some are starting to play music below."

Elizabeth turns to look at Friedrich with enthusiasm and states, "Missus Klucke requests your presence and for you to play violin. Come!"

"Yes, Friedrich! Come play." Albert twirls Elizabeth down the boat deck. Albert and Elizabeth's giddiness persuades others to join them below.

"I have to say, that Elizabeth is the proper age for your brother. Perhaps Albert can persuade my Bethie to refocus her aspirations. She wishes to stay single until she has seen the world. So unconventional." Ludwig shakes his head.

One long whistle blows.

"Well, ten o'clock curfew. All below. Shall we go make some joy, Ludwig?" Friedrich takes his hat off and bows for him to go first.

"Yes, it is right to make a joyful noise unto the Lord."

CHAPTER VIII

"He hath made every thing beautiful in his time: also hath set the world in their heart, so that no man can find out the work that God maketh from the beginning to the end."
(*King James Version*, Ecclesiastes 3:11)

Dick wraps the horse's reins around a fallen cottonwood tree limb and grabs a pocket handkerchief. Removing his hat, he wipes perspiration off the wide brim liner and forehead. The crisp fall breeze tussles his hair. It feels good. Deciding to tuck the sweat stained white hat between horse blanket and saddle an easy one. Autumn sun warms the small bald spot atop his head. Looking around, Dick surmises that the thick underbrush around the tree will provide adequate concealment for his white spotted horse, Sally.

    A big exhale allows Dick to slip the hatchet between belt and buckskin shirt. The belt is unusually tight, needing a new hole. A reminder that he eats well. Like the wild game feasted on a fortnight ago with George and the others. The night they all went to bed grinning like possums full on sweet corn. George's quick aim will provide another fine meal tonight. It guarantees indulgence and a repeat execution of overeating. Dick licks his lips and repositions the belt. Perhaps, later, he will need more than one hole punched into his belt.

In habit, Dick reaches for his gun. He makes a conscience choice to leave it behind. Besides, he has seen no bear, or bear sign, in these parts.

The back country always puts gladness into his heart. A place to let the breeze blow through his thin, curly hair. To observe virgin flat lands as far as the eyes can see in one direction. Distant mountains on the horizon in another. A tree bordered river before him. Thanking the good Lord for all this to wander through, worry free.

"There you go, Sally girl," he says, hunching over his six foot-six tall frame. Looking at Sally, eye to eye, he runs a hand through her white mane. "Be back in a jiffy."

Dick heads towards the riverbank. One lone prairie hen gets up at his feet, startling him. He watches it fly away. Then he looks at the grasses swaying against each other expecting more. The leaves rustle above and the trees creak and groan. Water trickles over rocks as the river burbles along. Again, thanking God. Praising him for all the enjoyment this land offers. For the great outdoors that replenishes Dick's soul. A tranquil concert that never replays itself. Dick hears a new edition to the concert as he approaches.

A beaver! Splashing about. Caught on the bank, right where Dick thought one might wander into a trap. Praising his good fortune in finding this spot on the North and South Platte River confluence. It is a little further North than Dick wishes to roam with winter coming. He thinks, *one must go where one must go to trap fur these days.*

The rambunctious critter's clamor soon overpowers the country's breeze symphony. It thrashes more and more the closer Dick gets, trying to escape. But the double spring trap holds the beaver firm. Hatchet in hand, Dick swings and thumps its head. Rendering the animal motionless. Its contribution to the concert is silenced.

Splashing continues.

Stricken with instant fear, Dick becomes motionless. Only his eyes move to assess the surroundings. Motion draws his eyes to a lone figure. A man silhouetted by the sun, Indian for sure. Wading the frigid water, knee deep, crossing the river. Dick mentally curses his preoccupation. His careless absorption into God's creation. It is, after all, uncivilized Indian country. Another reason not to venture this far north. *Why did he get so caught up in the moment? Why did he not notice him earlier? Hear him? The enormous concert!* Dick decides. That along with a hearing loss due to many years shooting guns, like the one he left behind. He left everything behind. Furs, supplies, and his trusty Azteca horse. A prize any thieving Indian would appreciate. Frozen, without a twitch, Dick surveys the riverbank up and down. Attentive to sounds like a branch snap. Anything out of the ordinary. Trying to hear more than the rustling leaves and a man's splashes. Determining whether this man travels alone.

Dick stands to make his presence known, broad shoulders back, chest out. To look formidable, like a huge bear. Praying this man is alone and peaceful. Knowing all too well how much ground is between him and Sally. His left hand covers the knife, right hand grips firm the hatchet. Ready. Poised to toss. Both, if need be. But no matter how proficient one is, there is only one chance the knife or hatchet makes the mark in troubled times. Then run like hell towards Sally just in case there are other troublemakers. Hoping Sally is still where he left her. Then jump on and ride like his life depends on it because it does. Ride hard knowing that you only have two shots loaded. Waiting to shoot until it is a life-or-death matter. Your life or theirs. That is a decision Dick wishes not to make, if he can help it.

The Indian stops. Stares right at Dick with an assessment look. Several shiny objects reflect the sun from on top the man's hair. Like what some Taos Texas girls wear. There are beads and metal things dangling from his buckskin. *Perhaps a Dakota tribes man, a bit south of his range*, Dick thinks. He has not seen many Dakotas. They have been, more or less, a peaceful tribe. It gives Dick some ease.

Taking a chance, he releases the beaver from the trap. Lifting it high and forward gesturing a gift. The Indian proceeds and walks within arm's length to accept.

"Je vous remercie," the Indian speaks.

Dick is quite sure that the man says thank you, but he still gives the man an inquisitive look encouraging any other language.

"Come, we feast in my small village in trade for honorable gift." The Indian speaks English.

"That is very kind." Dick motions towards his trap. "I must pull up my trap?" He does not want to re-set it in the Indian's sight giving away trade secrets. For sure, he cannot lose the trap or the fur it should catch to anyone. He can always find another spot to trap.

The Indian ties a beaver leg to his shoulder bag. A homemade bag made from a beaver pelt. It seems so appropriate to Dick. The haversack is more decorative than any Dick has ever seen. The thread work is interwoven with beads. Incorporated with animal fur, hair, bones and teeth to form designs resembling animals, like bear, moose, and beaver. Even birds like eagles are represented. Some stitches have depth detailing flower petals. Dick admires the intricate stitchery briefly before using his ax as leverage to release the trap from river muck. The man's treasures are strongly held in by a perimeter of bulging leather stitches. The patience and time one took to the details astonishes Dick.

There is nothing that alarms Dick about this man. This Indian seems harmless enough. He lacks weapons and carries an important bag. Possibly a peaceful medicine man. Dick feels safe. Loosening his buckskin shirt to let the breeze dry the sweat dripping down his chest and spine.

When they reach Sally, her calm disposition further relaxes Dick's trepidation. If Sally is comfortable walking near this strange man, so should he be. "My name is Dick," looking at the top of a small head with a long protruding nose, "what do they call you?"

"Mtegwagke Kno," he says, slapping chest proudly, then sweeping arms to the heavens. "It means Forest Eagle in Potawatomi." His chin becomes a prominent feature as he looks up.

Hesitating, unsure the pronunciation, "Glad to meet you, M-te-wa-ke Ko." Dick knows it was wrong. Especially since the man's face contorts.

"They call me Milwaukee," he offers politely, "outside our small band." He speaks soft and harmonious, brief and clear.

"Milwaukee. I can say. But Poe-tee-want-timi?" Again, Dick knows the pronunciation lacks. "I have never heard of that band." He specifically mentions band, not tribe. Dick recollects that only Indians who do not wish to associate themselves with the word tribe use words like band. The word tribe has thieving and savage connotations these days. Acts, Dick is certain, few Indians commit. Acts that tarnish them all. Milwaukee's choice word, band, eases any and all worries about this man and his people.

"Poh-tuh-WAH-toh-mee," Milwaukee sounds out. "Meaning people of the place of the fire. Some say fire keepers. We are part of the original peoples, way up north."

"How far north?"

"By the Gichigami," Milwaukee says.

"Yes, by the Big Lakes, I have heard of them, but I have never had the pleasure of seeing them." It becomes clear why they call him Milwaukee. About two years back George mentioned a new town up by one of those lakes. Dick cannot recall what they call the town, but it sounds similar to Milwaukee. *It must be nice to have a nickname that sounds similar,* thinks Dick. Not like Dick's nickname for his given name Richen. That has never made sense to him.

"The Big Seas," Milwaukee corrects, "they are most beautiful. Trees surround them."

"Poh-tuh-wah-toh-mee, you say?" Saying it slowly, trying hard to say it right.

"Yes. Poh-tuh-WAH-toh-mee."

"Please tell me more." Wishing to learn more about this band. Especially since Dick finds it hard to imagine going that far north. Way too cold, you know, for nether parts.

"We are the people who keep fire going. Culture alive. All teach our stories, our gifts to our youth." Repositioning his shoulder bag. "I am one who teaches good medicine to those worthy to learn."

One thing Dick likes about Indians, they proudly pass down their heritage and history from generation to generation. Keeping a trade like trapping alive. Not letting it die like so many of his companions. Each person claims a trade, learns all about it, and teaches it to their young. A passion that Dick respects.

They also incorporate things around them. Using nature. Using animal fur. Like beaver.

Making a useful bag. Each item carrying a story. He is confident Milwaukee's intricate, small, precise, and meticulous stitched bag holds many stories. "So much skill has been put into your bag," Dick expresses.

"My wife's sister, Sora, does great work." He taps his bag. "I have collected good medicine today."

"Like?"

Milwaukee cares not to share and silence hangs heavy, like the damp coolness of the treed valley they descend into. Dick buttons up his buckskin shirt.

"I am from Bineshiinh clan. The bird clan." Milwaukee gestures a spring grouse dance, imitating their dance precisely. Flaring out his arms like wings and rapidly stomping the ground while gyrating about.

Milwaukee's antics alarm Dick. He expects an ambush. Nothing else can explain the sudden ludicrous behavior. It must be a secret signal. Yet Sally is quite calm. As if enamored. Maybe bewitched. Dick doubts her credibility currently.

He stops flailing about, almost as fast as he started, and points ahead. "Can you see the village?"

"No." Dick squints. The setting sun's light cast no shadows, human or otherwise. He tries to see beyond and beside the trees that stretch along the Platte River's southern bank. Nothing. Nothing but trees and bushes.

"We live a quiet life. We take pride in staying unseen. This bend in the river keeps us hidden away from prying eyes."

"Hidden?" Dick's worst suspicions affirm Milwaukee's dance antics where to inform watchers.

"Yes, young men watch to keep us safe and hidden."

"From what?"

"Your people." He says it stern and painfully emotional. "Like when your people marched our band many miles away from our homeland, The Big Seas."

Dick's head hangs low, regarding the story. Yet, cautious. He takes time to look behind and glimpse peripherals. He remembers a northern tribe's relocation woe stories. Somewhere in The Unorganized Territory. But Dick thought it to be more southern than here. In any case, Milwaukee is right. Federal soldier's moved Indian's many miles away from The Big Seas. Dick's head bounces up and down. "I know of it."

"I remember it well. It was 1838. The year many lost family. Sora lost her husband. That is how she has come to be with my wife and myself. When her husband died during the march, Sora ran away."

Brave woman, Dick thinks.

"Sora found our camp, our place where we keep the old ways active. The one you cannot see."

A young man steps out behind a tree and makes himself known. Offering to take Sally's reins. Dick holds firm.

"It is fine. He will take good care of your horse and belongings," Milwaukee assures.

Dick takes his hat and gun. "Be a good girl, Sally," he says, rubbing her behind the ear.

"I see, you do not trust," Milwaukee says.

"It is more like taking temptation away from curious minds."

"Temptation?"

"Yes, wanting to know how this," Dick pushes the gun forward, "works." Resting the gun on his left forearm. "Wanting to know so bad they shoot their fool head off."

"Yes, you do not trust." Milwaukee waves the young lad off. "Come, we are almost there."

Where? Dick thinks. Trust is wavering as Dick follows close. They maneuver between bushes and around trees. Hard to see small dwellings tucked in here and there. Trying to remember passing these trees. Perhaps in the distance. *How long has this band been watching him?* He does remember! Thinking these trees and bushes were too dense to enter. Thicker than any prairie hen would like. Milwaukee's agile body weaves back and forth. Down a zig-zag path. One you would have to trip on and pay close attention to follow. A path leading past separate huts that support a thriving village.

"Are you coming?" Milwaukee looks back.

A grass hut encircles around a small tree behind him. One man sits at the opening. Cattails stacked beside and on top a rectangular wooden dwelling that two children run into. A complete village, hidden perfectly. Nestled with great care. Like the great stitching of Milwaukee's bag, which is all he can see at times. Dick must admit his tall frame is having trouble. It takes more than a slight bend to find his way through some places Milwaukee glides past. And stopping to admire the astounding network of incredible, meandering paths doesn't help Dick keep up. He can see how an admirer of this land, like himself, can get lost filling their eyes with God's wonders that they miss all this. Dick squeezes through one narrow and obstructed path after another. Milwaukee ducks under a big cottonwood that has been downed precisely to rest onto a nearby tree crotch and disappears. Milwaukee resurfaces under twigs and branches that create a canopy over buffalo capes. Leaf tufts camouflage his hut. Deceptive coverings a passerby, like Dick, would overlook. Milwaukee motions Dick to follow.

An excitable woman greets him just inside what looks like a beaver hut. Dick towers above the opening, questioning if he will fit. Bending over, peering in, he sees a roomy, cozy retreat. An unimaginable haven. He stands once again, looks around, then bends over, feeling like a grouse burrowing deep into the brush.

CHAPTER IX

"Say I pray thee, thou art my sister: that it may be well with me for thy sake; and my soul shall live because of thee."
(*King James Version*, Genesis 12:13)

Solace lies behind a quilt. The makeshift partition harbors Elizabeth's escape. A get away from ship life congestion. Intricate small, even stitches bind the quilt patches into an interconnecting double ring pattern. A symbolic assemblage that interlocks man and wife. The couple wrapped forever together, stitch by stitch. A similar quilt awaits Elizabeth's wedding day in Mama's cherished trunk.

Elizabeth shakes the thought away, whispering, "Mrs. Klucke?"

"Yes," a weak voice responds.

"It is Elizabeth. May I enter?"

"Why, yes!" Eldora's voice upsurges.

Unrestraint excitement provokes Elizabeth forward, quickly entering. "How are you today?"

Friedrich bolts upright.

"Excuse me," Elizabeth apologizes, retreating backwards towards the main common area.

"Please stay," Friedrich begs, clearing his throat.

"I didn't realize you were napping."

"Neither did I. It is fine," Eldora insists, adjusting posture. "You always brighten my day."

"Yes, please." Friedrich stands and props Eldora's pillow.

"Are you sure, Mister Klucke?"

"Friedrich, please," he requests. "Yes, I am sure. I welcome the change."

Elizabeth values the change as well to this pleasant respite. A tranquil space. Where Elizabeth can calmly debate things like proper English. Her day becomes more enjoyable every time she enters this space.

Friedrich kisses Eldora's forehead. "I will be top side if you need me."

Eldora puts a hand on his. They share a tender moment before he slips his hand away.

Elizabeth's cheeks feel warm embarrassment.

Friedrich maneuvers past, brushing against her arm. In an instant, matrimony allures. Mister and Missus Klucke's obvious love strikes her heart. It welcomes marriage and raises hope that there is a man like Friedrich out there for her. In America. It is the first time that she can remember marriage entering her heart as a possibility. The strong rose water aroma follows Friedrich's infective emotion down the corridor.

"I see you brought both bibles today."

"Yes." Holding up two bibles, Elizabeth asks, "English or German, today, Eldora?"

"Please, I must insist you call me Dora. May I call you Beth?"

"Yes." She likes it. It feels grown up without being pompous.

"Come, sit." Eldora invites.

The chair is still warm.

Eldora leans in, face to face and answers, "English, for the baby."

"I suspected you were with child! That is wonderful!"

"It has been hard to keep my strength up with this seasickness"

"You must let me tell Mama. She will have a tincture or a tea that will help you and your baby." Elizabeth offers, preparing to fetch Mama.

"Not just yet." Eldora grasps her arm. "It can wait. Disa put ginger in chamomile tea this morning. Please. Sit. Read."

"How was that?" Elizabeth asks, speculating uncomplimentary flavors.

"The tea? Most awful."

"Well, I am sure Mama will have a more pleasant option. She has many different recipes and ways to treat everything."

"Right now, besides being queasy, I wish to relax. Please, read."

"I am too excited to read." Elizabeth's eyes scrunch and her voice squeaks. "A baby!" *The one significant benefit to marriage,* Elizabeth thinks. "When will this bundle of joy arrive? On the boat? America? Having your first child be an American would be great! What will you name him? Or maybe it will be a girl! What will you name her?"

Eldora smiles. She gives endearment strokes across her small bulge. "If we have a boy, Patrick Albert."

"Patrick Albert sounds like an Irish name. I thought you were German." Elizabeth cannot believe a baby resides inside such a tiny, skinny body.

"True. Both of us have German ancestors. Friedrich and I were born in Odessa, Ukraine. None of this will matter to our child who will be American."

"Yes. That must be exciting. The first Klucke born on American soil. How soon after reaching America?"

"About a month."

"Mama says that the first baby a new mother has is always early. I hope, in this case, she is wrong."

"As do I. Don't you think that Patrick could be a fine American name? Like Patrick Henry."

"Yes!" Elizabeth's historical knowledge causes an outburst, "'Give me liberty or give me death!'" A fisted arm goes high, lifting her. Her butt leaves the chair. Elizabeth slinks back, thinking, *too dramatic*. "It would be a fine American name. Patrick Klucke!"

"Yes." Eldora smiles broadly. "After Patrick Henry, a gifted orator and influential man."

"If a girl?"

"Christina, after Fred's little sister." Eldora pulls covers over her shoulders.

"That sounds nice." Elizabeth tucks the coverings behind Eldora and adds another blanket. "I hope it is a girl."

"I hope so too, but a boy can be so helpful. Especially with farming chores and such."

"There are plenty of chores to go around. I have three sisters and five brothers, and we never run out of chores to do." She confirms.

"Even with the chickens? I hear Rosie lets them roam about freely," Eldora says. "Friedrich and I talked about letting our chickens roam."

"Rosie is good with chickens. We all do our best with what we can. Even when horsing around distracts us we get our work done. Even little Mags does a fair share."

"I have not had the pleasure meeting Mags. Is her name short for Magdalyna? Another nickname version so as not to cause confusion between her mother and herself?"

"Yes and no. Mama's name is Magdalyna," Elizabeth says, accent on the d. "Mags is Magthalena," enunciating the th. "Two different spellings."

Eldora raises her brows and smiles. "Your mother is Lyna, and your sister is Mags. Their given names sound similar to the ear, but not the names you call them. I have been giving nicknames great thought as of late. What will I or others call Patrick or Christina? Nicknames do arouse my curiosity. Don't they you?"

"Yes." Like her siblings. Jakey and Jo who are older and demand full names these days. Karl's has never changed. Rosie is short for Rosina. Fredric,

Fred. Ludwig, Wiggy. Mags. And baby Henry. Surely baby will be removed soon, and Henry will just be Henry. Being the oldest Hess child, Elizabeth has had more than her fair share. Her first one, breathy, because she used to breathe loudly in and out to calm Jakey and Jo in order to get them to sleep. Elly, Lizzy, Eliza, Betsie, and her current favorite, Beth. "Hmm," thinking on Patrick and Christina, she proposes, "Pat and Tina."

"Yes, Pat is the obvious choice to me. Tina." Tapping her stomach. "I like Tina."

"My middle name is Magdalyna, after Mama."

"Well, I am guessing there must be one great woman in your family who started that name."

"Three, actually. a Maggie Matteis, Grandma Dally Hess, and Mama."

"Interesting."

"There is no plan to name any of my children Magdalyna, Magthalena, or any variable. Simply because I believe we have run out of nicknames." Elizabeth smiles.

"I don't know," Eldora says, grinning. "You could start calling them by their middle names. I hear that is very popular among the men folk."

"Why not just name them the nickname and forget the long, hard to spell, names all together?"

"That would be easier. Not as much fun. That way I couldn't pick what I call Friedrich. Even though he prefers Friedrich, I call him Fred. Friedrich is so formal and stuffy, don't you think?"

"Like Elizabeth."

"So, you can name your girls Beth."

Elizabeth likes the connotation and smiles back, saying, "It is a good name, but, sadly, my great grandmother was called Beth first."

"Such a shame."

"Your name seems original. Are you the first Eldora in your family?"

"Eldora was my great grandmother's name."

"Well, originality seems to have flown out the window." Elizabeth opens the King James Bible. "Does Doctor Horace know about the baby?"

"Yes. Fred insisted."

"Good! It is best to have all the help you can get." Elizabeth is not sure the good Doctor will be helpful. The first time she saw Doctor Horace left an unwholesome impression. Him following the woman that distracted Shaun, the Captain's right-hand man, that first day. How a woman with stature and class allows that much intoxication baffles Elizabeth. A Doctor no less. The way Doctor Horace swaggers to and fro every day indicates no sobriety. None. Some excusing it as unsteadiness. The man seems incapable of his profession. "You are sure that the baby will not be born at sea? I would hate to depend on the Doctor's help and sobriety."

"Beth!" Eldora chastises.

"You could end up with an appendectomy." As soon as Elizabeth says the inappropriate words, she debates taking them back. Although, true words, they could insight concern and unnecessary worry. It is not her place to discredit the Doctor. Still, Elizabeth feels comfortable sharing her concern and improper humor.

"Didn't you just say it is best to get all the help you can?" A smile lifts Eldora's cheeks. "I am sure we will arrive before I need anyone's help. I hear that New York has the finest doctors."

"Well, that might change, upon arrival."

"Beth! I am sure Doctor Horace is a fine physician. He is just on holiday."

"I suppose you are right." Elizabeth removes the crochet cross marker and starts reading.

Eldora motions with one hand, covering her mouth with the other, looking a bit green around the gills. A phrase Elizabeth hears plenty these days. She places the spittoon just in time. Eldora expels what appears to have been her breakfast on the third heave, with chamomile flowers a float. All Elizabeth can do is hold Eldora's hair and pray.

#

Friedrich flicks out his time piece. Twelve days, seven hours and 22 minutes he recalls being confined. Henry shines another pair of boots. Missing daily brewing computations, he calculates Henry has shined about twenty-nine pairs. *Twelve days*. It seems longer to Friedrich, but it mustn't seem that long to a busy boy.

"Excuse me, Mister Klucke, you are Mister Klucke?"

A man grabs his hand shortly after Friedrich slides the watch into its pocket. The smell of livestock surrounds Friedrich. "Yes," admitting, hesitantly, "I am Mister Klucke, call me Friedrich."

"I hear that you might need an extra set of hands." The man pulls Friedrich closer to his permeating smell. Both hands clasp around

Friedrich's and shake vigorously. "The name is Hildago, at your service, if you please?"

Friedrich wonders who tries to pawn off this uncouth man. Perhaps Reverend Hess regards Hildago an unacceptable son-in-law. Friedrich remembers nothing being mentioned about needing a handyman or hired hand. Hildago's forwardness carries a forcefulness that means what he says. Perhaps it is best to hear the man out.

Hildago's strong hold keeps going, up and down. "I am a very good worker. I will work hard for you."

"I can feel that." Hildago's abrasive callouses are as harsh as his odor.

"So, sorry," Hidalgo says, releasing the stronghold. "I will work for a place to lay my head and any food scraps you can spare."

"I hear you are from Port Ponta Delgada."

"Yes, yes."

"It was cloudy on the day we arrived at that port of call. Is it true that they call it the Green Island?"

"I am not sure of what you speak. It is very green most of the year because of our tobacco fields. I have worked many years in these fields." Placing hand to heart proudly.

"So, it must also be true that some fruits of your labour are on board."

"Yes, yes. Some of the finest grown. I helped load it. It was too much to believe my luck to be offered to do so. Luckier still to be offered free passage to the Americas. All they asked was help tend to the ship's animals. I have also heard of many jobs available in Americas."

"Still, you ask me, a man of little means, for a job." Friedrich lifts his hat, drags a hand through short brown hair, and repositions the hat firmly.

"Yes."

"One should be careful who you ask. As my father would say, it is all a ruse to attract workers for a new country."

"Ruse?"

"Deception, trick."

"Yes, yes. That is why I must ask about, now, for any job possibilities."

"You are a wise man."

"I do hear you are a fair boss."

"From whom?" Friedrich wonders.

"Albert. He is very fond of you and never stops talking about you."

"Well, he is my brother."

#

The ships swaying and the full spittoon challenges Elizabeth. It takes everything she can muster to not spill the unpleasantness or, God forbid, fall backwards.

"Here, let me help you," a tall, rather lanky young man offers. In his haste, he spills some contents onto his already reeking attire.

"This is Hildago." Friedrich appears around the corner.

Friedrich's strong rose water fragrance cannot overcome Hidalgo's stench.

"Thank you, Hildago."

"My pleasure."

Elizabeth receives the empty pot and turns to escape a smell that is neither animal dung nor lack of hygiene. Definitely a smell all its own. A combination of both or something in-between.

"Is Eldora doing alright?"

Friedrich's question stops her. With a slight turn, Elizabeth says, "she is fine, Mama is with her."

"Thank you." His eyes sincere. "I should be along shortly."

"No hurry. I will fix Eldora some tea and read to her," she says, moving awkwardly down. The boat pitches and down she goes. Glad it wasn't earlier, she quickly stands. Elizabeth overhears Hildago say, "Mighty fine-looking woman."

"I see a fine young lady who will someday make a handsome wife," Friedrich replies.

Elizabeth welcomes the words as the boat tosses her back into its core.

#

"Here, Dora, I made you some carrot top tea," Elizabeth says upon returning.

"Thank you, Beth."

"How thoughtful, Bethie dear," Mama says. "Good choice. The tea will provide nutrition for both mother and baby. It should settle nausea as well." Mama stands. "I am very proud of your initiative, Bethie. I couldn't have done better." She kisses Elizabeth's forehead. "I will leave you in Elizabeth's good hands."

"Thank you Lyna."

"Where did I leave off?" Elizabeth asks, handing Eldora tea.

"I don't remember starting," Eldora remarks. "Sorry about the interruption."

"I feel sorry that you can't keep anything down."

"May I suggest closing the book, opening it, point somewhere on the page and read where your finger falls?"

"Impromptu!"

"More like spontaneous."

"Unmethodical," Elizabeth adds, finding this vocabulary exchange delightful. Closing the Bible, she fans the pages with her index finger. Once. Twice. The third pass, she slips the finger in, closes her eyes, and taps a spot. The words above her finger read, "Thou art my sister."

Wonderment unites their eyes.

"Is that the whole passage?" Eldora wonders.

"It is Proverbs 7:4. It says, 'Say unto wisdom, thou art my sister; and call understanding thy kinswoman.'"

"I like 'Thou art my sister' better."

"Me, too!" Elizabeth agrees.

CHAPTER X

"Art thou bound unto a wife? Seek not to be loosed. Art thou loosed from a wife? Seek not a wife."
(*King James Version*, I Corinthians 7:27)

"This is my wife Nanoke, meaning hummingbird," Milwaukee says to Dick.

The woman gives a quick nod. She places a woven grass mat on the ground.

Dick's eyes widen. The space is much bigger than the outside portrays.

"And this is her sister Sora, meaning chirping songbird. Be careful, she will talk from the rising sun to the setting sun.

"And beyond," Nanoke adds.

"Now sister of mine, that is not so, I spend several hours sewing, not talking at all." Sora pats the mat, encouraging Dick to sit.

"Unless someone sits next to you," Nanoke warns.

Dick's extremely tall brawny body awkwardly maneuvers around baskets hung below his height.

Bumping his head on some and pushing others aside. One falls, outpouring rose hips.

"Never mind that," Nanoke says. Her hand sweeps up the buds.

Milwaukee squats down beside the abode's opening. A spot all his own. "This is Dick." He lifts both hands. "Please, sit."

Dick admires the mats intricate weave pattern. Sitting, his eyes follow the mats design to Sora's hand, arm, buckskin dress with simple but beautiful metal ornaments. To her shoulder, to the braid that drapes her breast. Sora's posture, straight and true. He finds it hard to resist looking into her persuasive dark chocolate drop like eyes. They melt away any distrust. Still, out of habit, he places the unloaded gun barrel facing the only opening.

"What do you think of my pukwi lodge? You like?"

"Yes, very much," Dick says, "What does pukwi mean?"

"My lodge of sun. This is my living on the sunny side lodge," Milwaukee pauses, "it is like the happy side. Like I said before, we try to live a quiet, happy life. There is too much unhappiness," Milwaukee adds. "And mistrust." His eyes study Dick.

Dick yields to his stare and looks down. Milwaukee's straight forward words were meant for him. It is true that Dick still has some misgivings. "I thank you for your hospitality."

"Yes." He detaches the beaver and presents it. "A gift from Dick."

"Merci," Nanoke thanks.

"Very kind of you," Sora mentions. "I can make another bag. This time I will put the story of how you two met. That is if you two will tell me the story. Maybe now. Or after we eat. I am very interested," she says, her breast heaving excitement.

"So, Sora is talkative, much like you, Milwaukee," Dick remarks.

They all smile confirmation.

"I believe we have had a long, comfortable talk."

The walking and talking was comfortable, agrees Dick. Much like the treatment he has received. It illustrates Milwaukee's importance. They trust Milwaukee, explicitly. Giving these women ease to treat strangers like family. Dick wishes that there was more comfort in his own home.

Milwaukee opens his bag. Both women look curious to see what treasures lie within, like children awaiting Christmas packages. Just like his little girl, Aliza, will do when he gets home. Assuming that his wife, Dolores, has softened her resolve.

A floral hanky wraps the first gift. He presents it like a bouquet. Nanoke's eyes light up as if it contained something truly desirable.

"Merci," Nanoke says, taking her time opening it.

"What is it?" Sora leans in.

Very precise and carefully Nanoke reveals a fine conch shell assortment. She Flashes a delighted smile before holding one up for display.

"Let me see," Sora requests.

"Later. I love them." Clutching them close.

It has been a long time since Dick has seen such joy in a man's woman. It has been even longer since Dick has seen the likes of such beautiful seashells.

"There was a strange man at Fort Laramie trading these shells with everyone but Indians. I did not understand."

"That is strange. I have never heard anyone refuse a trade," Dick says.

"I have never been turned away before. I knew not what to do. I wanted them so much for you, Nanoke. So, I sat, and I watched. It was true he traded only with white men."

In all of Dick's trading days, he has never seen such a thing. How odd. The man must have been unfamiliar with Indians. Regardless, a trade is a trade.

"I spy a man needing help with his wagon and no one helps. I do. I notice why no one offers to help. One side of his face is covered with a horrible rash. I am sure you know the kind."

"I do." Sora offers. "He must have laid down his head on some bad itchy weed. Did you have some wasa'shiak?"

"Yes, gave him a good portion of it. I have very little left."

"I will pick some tomorrow." Sora repositions herself. Her knees and upper thighs protrude from her dress. The leggings that wrap them tight do not hide their shapely form.

"What is wasa'shiak?" Dick tries to pay no mind to the beautiful woman that sits close.

"It is what some call touch-me-not. Others call it jewelweed," Sora explains. "An ointment is made from it that soothes poison ivy rash."

Milwaukee continues, "I tell the man that I can make itch go away and soon look better. He is so grateful. He wants to pay. I ask for favor instead. After three days his rash is much improved. So, he makes my trade for me. I get shells, for you." He lovingly smiles at Nanoke. "It shows what time and patience can provide."

"Also, that there are good people in this world." Sora leans forward, turning her head, saying, "Like you, Dick. You honor Mtegwagke Kno with your gift."

The look she sends, the curvaceous figure, warms Dick's nether region. Fearing a show of desire, Dick covers his crotch. It is not right to want another woman. He reminds himself that he is a married man.

Milwaukee digs out another gift, "And for you, Sora," presenting porcupine quills with autumn color pond reeds binding them.

"For me! Very much thank you, Mtegwagke Kno." receiving them with closed eyes and a reverent nod before bouncing excitement.

Milwaukee takes more bundles, one by one, setting each item between himself and the hut's animal skinned wall. Taking great care. Announcing each treasure. "White bark from up north. Michigan moss. River stones, this one has stripes."

"It is very pretty." Nanoke's shells clink into an empty clay bowl.

Sora explains that white bark is for baby's poop.

He could listen to Sora all night. But he must avert his ears and eyes. He distracts himself by admiring the organization of Milwaukee's space. Full and bursting like his bag. Many weaved baskets have grasses, vines and leaves peeking over the edge. Some bundles at Milwaukee's side have various animal parts intertwined within reeds. "What does that bladder hold?"

"That?" Sora points.

Dick confirms.

"That is White Oak Bark juice. It is powerful medicine, cures everything."

"Must walk many miles to get the bark," Milwaukee makes known.

"Have to boil long time to get its extract to make this juice," Nanoke adds.

Milwaukee picks it up and wiggles it. "This will have to last until the next time I go North."

"Yes. There is very little white oak in these parts," Dick agrees. "You have a very full puckwee. Did I say that right?"

"Pook-wee," Milwaukee annunciates.

"Pook-wee," Dick repeats. A weaved mat similar to the one he sits upon hangs close to the wall beside him. It has more tans and browns arrayed in a simulated, circular motion. Looking like it was moving. It accommodates lustrous beads, large shells, metal pieces, feathers, animal fur, and leather stripes and string.

"That is my work rug. I can roll it up and carry outside to work." Sora crawls in front of Dick and points out a thimble. "I traveled with Milwaukee once and took my work mat with. A woman approached and gave me that. She said it helps push the needle through. It is better than a rock."

Clearing his throat, saying, "It is a very handy workplace. I suspect it will display porcupine quills soon."

"Yes! Soon." She twists and reaches. "This here, is one of the friendship bands I make." Sora plucks it free. "Is this your favorite arm?" Breasts brush his forearm.

"Yes."

"For you!" The knotted band matches the color of her dark, warm, friendly eyes. "Here, you must have." Sora wraps it around and ties a knot that guarantees it can never be undone. Not that he wishes to ever remove it.

"Merci," is all he can say as she leaves no room for even a sharp blade to separate the band from him. Not without shedding blood.

"My pleasure."

Milwaukee puffs a long pipe to life. "Join me, my friend." handing the pipe over.

"Thank you," Dick cradles it. "Peace Pipe?"

"I do not understand why white man has to make names for everything. Smoke travels ahead of requests, prayers and friendships. It signifies honesty. Trust." Milwaukee accents trust. "Smoke travels before words. It is an action."

"Yes, an action to promote peace, a peace pipe!"

Milwaukee just shakes his head.

"Merci. It is kind to consider me, a stranger, your friend. For trusting me." Dick reaches across Sora's lap to receive the pipe again. He cannot stop noticing her fine figure accentuated by the belt around her waist. The fine, handy embroidery work on her leggings. Designs displaying animals similar to Milwaukee's haversack with the addition of many flowers. It is not the leggings, the stitchery or any one thing that attracts him. It is her. Her overall beauty surrounds and consumes him like the smoke in the air.

#

"You missed dinner three nights now. I was beginning to worry," George leans close to his face, whispering, "Where have you been?"

"Might as well explore all this big country while I am up North," Dick replies. He half believes George's voice carries some concern. "You never know when I will be back up this way. Besides, you need not worry about me, old man." He fills a plate full of venison stew, adding, "Looks like someone shot himself a deer." Dick places a couple biscuits on top.

George grabs his wrist. "What's that?" Not waiting for an answer, "You find yourself a fine Indian squaw to dip your wick in?"

"No!" Dick pulls away, "I'm a married man."

"Even married men have needs when their woman wants none of it."

"I assure you there was no dipping of my wick." *The desire to, yes,* Dick admits to himself. One thought remains constant on his mind, Sora.

Thinking his time with Milwaukee's family was most pleasurable and sends warmth through his veins.

Johann asks, "What?" Overhearing the conversation. "What's this I hear? You've been dipping your wick?"

"No, I have not!"

"Explain the Indian jewelry, then." George let the men know what they were talking about.

"I will not." Dick refuses.

"Well, I will say that it is pretty clear you have been," Simpson adds.

Dick's cottonwood chair welcomes him without questions.

"Do tell?" August begs for details.

"Can't a man eat in peace?"

"Not when he has missed three fine meals, one of which he was supposed to supply!" George dishes himself a plate.

"Sorry about that," Dick apologizes, shoveling food as fast as he can, ensuring the inability to speak. How can he get so lost spending time with Milwaukee and Sora, especially Sora, that he forgets his obligation?

"That's fine. We prefer old George's meals to yours anyway," Johann says. "Besides, see," he bites into a biscuit. "You can actually eat the biscuits without dipping them." His muffled chuckle is followed by, "So, you going to tell us why you missed your turn or what?"

Dick just stares straight into the fire, chewing, eating, chewing, like a hungry animal.

"Looks like he doesn't want to talk about it, pretty clear, I say," Simpson repeats. He sets an empty plate down.

Dick swallows and says, "Okay, you want the long or short of it?"

"No matter," George comments, "you're going to tell it the long way anyway."

This time, however, Dick keeps it brief. He wishes to keep his two days and three nights all to himself. A bliss he wishes not to share.

CHAPTER XI

"O give thanks unto the Lord, for he is good: for his mercy endureth for ever."
(*King James Version*, Psalm 107:1)

"Front and stern," Henry whispers to Elizabeth, standing straighter than the mast.

"Isn't it also called front and center?"

"Yes, Ma'am!" He clasps hands behind, looking more like a man than a little boy. "Some passengers call it midship," he says, eyes forward. "Mister Drake says midship is below. Between this deck and the ship's bottom."

Henry's grown-up mannerisms pacify Elizabeth's urge to correct proper usage of ma'am. A word used to address married women or an important person like a Queen. She prefers to ignore and prod the immediate conversation, "So, we face the front?"

"Yes, the bow."

"Not the back which is called the stern."

"Yes." Henry keeps eyes forward.

"Why then is it called front and stern?"

Henry dips his head and shakes it, saying, "Because we are on the deck between the front and stern."

"I see. Yes, that makes sense." Elizabeth is quite aware. Two weeks since Henry and Shaun shook hands. Henry's stance, polite manners and bestowed knowledge compensates for Shaun's unscrupulous arrangement. Elizabeth tussles his hair and says, "We, also, stand on Port side."

"Yes." Henry flashes a quick grin her way.

"We, also, stand on the quarterdeck." Elizabeth knows the quarterdeck is behind them. Where a man stands, day and night, at a big wheel.

Henry doesn't flinch. Just stands, serious, forward bearing. "No, Ma'am."

Papa and Captain Harrison ascend to the upper most forward deck. They both place hands behind like the ten-year-old brother beside her. The Captain and Papa stand unbending, aligned, ready.

The assembly awaits.

"Last Sunday, Reverend Martin preached," the captain announces. "Today, Reverend Hess will grace us with a sermon, Reverend." The captain steps back.

Henry stands taller. His replication stance is simultaneously honorable and sad. Soon there will come a day, like Mama says, when Henry will go his own way.

"Welcome, fellow believers." Papa sends salutations. "Good morning!"

"Good morning," the group mumbles like in a children's song sung in a round.

"It is a much better morning than that. God's sun shines, illuminating our ways and warming our bodies. God's wind fills the sails that propels us closer to our dreams. It is a grand day! So, again, I say, "GOOD MORNING!" His voice ringing strong and exuberant, clutching the authorized version of the bible, waiting.

They echo a heartier, "Good Morning!" Now more responsive and awake to receive Papa's message.

"I, Reverend Ludwig Hess, have spent many hours walking the very deck you stand on. Many of you have as well. We pause and gather today to respect our holy Sabbath day." Papa twitches his head Friedrich's way.

Friedrich acknowledges the signal. Shoulders his violin. Wedges it tightly under his noble jaw. He breathes in and out and relaxes both shoulders. The bow beside his leg sways. His wrist loosely moves a three four beat. Elizabeth embraces the rhythm. One and two and three and, one and two and three and.

"We will begin with 'Grace! 'Tis a Charming Sound.' Sing as you are able." Papa states and starts singing the hymn.

> *"Grace! 'Tis a charming sound,*
> *harmonious to the ear;"*

Harmony is not what Elizabeth hears and struggles to not match her intonation with the off-key voices around her.

*"Heav'n with the echo shall resound,
and all the earth shall hear."
"Saved by grace alone!
This is all my plea:
Jesus died for all mankind,
and Jesus died for me."*

"ME!" Henry and the children shout out making Elizabeth smile. She hasn't lost baby Henry yet.

*"Grace first contriv'd away
to save rebellious man;
And all the steps that grace display,
which drew the wondrous plan.*

Elizabeth abandons the crowd all together. Instead, she sings loud and strong with the violin notes. Accompanying the true tones resonated by Friedrich. Elizabeth's voice soon overpowers, singing a solo. All other voices fade.

*"Grace taught my wandering feet
to tread the heavenly road.
And new supplies each hour I meet,
while pressing on to God."*

Papa ceases singing. He opens the Bible and prepares.

Elizabeth continues to perform.

*"Grace taught my soul to pray
and made mine eyes o'er flow;*

*'Twas grace which kept me to this day,
and will not let me go."*

The final chorus ends with the children's staccato, "ME!"

Violin music continues. Eldora hums the melody and Elizabeth joins. They exchange smiles before Friedrich concludes.

Papa begins, "Today I read from Psalm 106:6-12, which states:

> *We have sinned with our fathers, we have committed iniquity, we have done wickedly. Our fathers understood not thy wonders in Egypt; they remembered not the multitude of thy mercies; but provoked him at the sea, even, at the Red Sea. Nevertheless, he saved them for his name's sake, that he might make his mighty power to be known. He rebuked the Red Sea also, and it was dried up: so he led them through the depths, as through the wilderness. And he saved them from the hand of him that hated them and redeemed them from the hand of the enemy.*
> *And the waters covered their enemies: there was not one of them left. Then believed they his words; they sang his praise.*

Amen. Let us pray the Lord's Prayer together."

Methodical and precise, they all repeat the words. Elizabeth hears the words like a chant. Their voices together rise rhythmically, similar to waves hitting the boat. Words intensify to a peak, then dwindle. Like every wave slaps more sound until the loudest seventh wave crashes and a repeat begins. Many voices rise and dwindle the memorized words until a resonating, "Amen."

Papa looks over the crowd and clears his throat. "The sin spoken in the passage is rebellion. God's people rebelled by the Red Sea. Holding onto disbelief and doubt. Questioning God. Why would their God lead them to a place with no obvious escape?" Papa closes the King James Bible and clutches it close, leaning forward. Stern and confident. "They hardened their hearts. Darkened their minds. Refusing to believe that God would provide. So often, we see people of faith sing God's praise until some difficult trial hits. Then grumble. I have heard grumblings aboard this very ship. Some, I must confess, I have done myself."

A soft consensus murmur arises among those gathered.

"It reminds me of Jesus's parable, the sower. The one where the seed is sown on rocky ground. It quickly springs up but cannot establish roots. Exposed and vulnerable, it soon withers and dies. Similarly, a person can receive the gospel, hear its words, but fall away when exposed to difficulties. But when difficulties arise, when persecution comes about, or when you are surrounded with no way out like the Israelites." Papa readjusts the Bible, tucking it between his upper arm and side.

"And God shows you the way. Believe and sing his praise. For there is no education like adversity. But don't soon forget like the Israelites did. They believed God's promise when they saw it fulfilled, but not until then. Those who do not believe our God's word till they see it performed are doomed to repeat their grumblings. To fall into sin again and again."

The wind catches ribbons sticking out from his Bible's gold edge pages. They flit about like Elizabeth's mind.

"God sometimes grants our selfish requests, along with consequences, so that we learn not to crave evil things!"

Elizabeth's pride stands out. *Pride,* she confesses, is her sin. It grasped her tight. It overcame her to sing the opening song fervently above others. Singing solo. It took away everyone's desire to sing praises to God. It doesn't matter they fumble words or are discordant every stanza. Elizabeth's selfish self-worship while praising God weighs on her as reprehensible.

"Moses was not prepared in the palace. He was prepared on the back side of the Median Desert. Prepared to respond to the Israelites deprivation. He tried to calm their desires and fears. Yet, their immediate struggles, demands and cries to God persisted. God knew these things. He wasn't surprised. He feels and hears them. Knows all they go through and knows them."

Elizabeth bows her head and asks forgiveness for domineering the music. Yet, she thanks the good Lord that she is able to sing.

"But one must remember God's salvation and the many kindnesses God bestows on us. The ability to have faith, genuine life-saving faith that endures and bears fruit unto eternal life. To pray fervently and believe we will obtain it." Papa points a finger to the heavens, "This day belongs to God!"

Elizabeth agrees, finishing her prayer with a whisper, "Amen."

"Every day belongs to God. Everyday day holds uncertainties and offers no promise of tomorrow. Where every day the unfit sinner does not, nor ever will, diminish God's care over his creatures. Big and small, from anywhere, from nowhere." He looks about. "God cares for you all. German like mine self, Russian, Prussian, Polish, Romanian, Ukrainian," pausing briefly with each, "God cares for you!"

"Italian," someone shouts.

"Portuguese," Hildago calls out.

"Hungarian."

Does it matter anymore? Elizabeth wonders. Less than two weeks and they will all be Americans.

Papa grabs his Bible, shaking it towards the audience. "It matters little if you are Roman Catholic. Anglican. Presbyterian. Methodist. Mennonite. Eastern Orthodox. Mormon. Baptist. Protestant. God cares for you! Even for the Pietists, Calvinists and Stundists."

Papa's pauses allow each individual religious society time to confirm. They nod to one-another and cement belief that God does care.

"A few denominations I have had the privilege to learn more about. Thank you all for sharing your faith. I have hopes that in the next few weeks of our journey together there will be more sharing. I look forward to that privilege." Papa puts the Bible behind him, clasping with both hands.

Henry's pose. Elizabeth names it. After all, Henry is the cutest presently holding it rigidly at attention.

"I do not stand up here to preach religion. I merely want to point out that we as believers have religion. So, as we work together with God in our mist, I must implore that we do not receive the grace of God in vain. Because, beyond our sins, our unbelief, our trials and grumbles. Beyond nationality and convention. God, like the last stanza sung, will not let you go." Papa stands solemn. "Unlike the Israelites, we travel with differences. Differences our God cares about. Like the Israelites we travel with strife. Strife God cares about. He cares for everything and everyone. The power of God, who can split the Red Sea, make the ground dry instantaneously, and save believers from peril. This God. Our God deserves our full gratitude and devotion."

An exuberant porpoise fleet, as if sent by God, playfully leap the green brine waves, both sides of the ship. Elizabeth notes, *Mostly the port side!*

CHAPTER XII

"Therefore are my loins filled with pain: pangs have taken hold upon me, as the pangs of a women that travaileth: I was bowed down at the hearing of it; I was dismayed at the seeing of it. My heart panted, fearfulness affrighted me: the night of my pleasure hath he turned into fear unto me."
(*King James Version*, Isaiah 21:3,4)

"My stomach feels funny."

"Is there something I can do, Dora, dear?"

"It is as if something, or someone is squeezing my stomach. Like how Martha describes the night Christina was born." Eldora's face changes. She groans and forcibly wrenches Friedrich's hand and places it on her belly. "Feel."

"It is so hard," Friedrich stops himself from saying more. Fear that something is wrong enters his mind.

"There it goes again."

"I will go get Disa."

"No need." Disa appears. "I heard you moan way down at the other end." Disa points as if the fact escapes them that her berth is that direction. Disa, also, waves her hand as if beckoning someone to come. "Come, Lyna. I think the baby is coming," she shouts down the alleyway.

Friedrich approaches Disa and whispers, "Is it not too early?"

"I can hear you!" Eldora makes known and contorts into another contraction.

Friedrich is not sure what to do.

"One cannot tell a baby when to be born." Disa shoos Friedrich, saying, "You go now."

Friedrich's wish for this baby, his baby, to be born on American soil evaporate. He kneels at Eldora's side, secretly begging God to repress the child's coming into the world. *The child mustn't be born on this filthy ship.*

In the background Disa asks someone to retrieve the Doctor. Lyna tells Elizabeth to boil water and throw an onion into it. Disa asks why an onion.

Friedrich curiously awaits an answer.

"To ward off diseases," Elizabeth expounds.

Eldora clamps his hand tight between ever shortening intervals.

"You must go," Disa insists. "This is woman's work."

Friedrich leans in close, putting his forehead on Eldora's. He internally pleas again with God, *not now!* He kisses Dora's forehead, just above her furrowed brow that signals another spasm occurrence. "I love you. You know this." He gives her another kiss when the pain subsides.

"Promise me, Friedrich." She looks at him with pleading eyes. "If we do not meet again, that you will take good care of our child." Eldora pulls down on his arm.

He did not like her mind withdrawing to such a dark, unmentionable thought. Now he too, worries. "I will," Friedrich promises, adding, "We will." The possibility of losing his sweet Dora is a heavy burden. Like raising a child on his own. Something unthinkable and frightful.

"You must promise me, no matter what." Pulling him close.

Eldora's stern tone accentuates Friedrich's worries. Bringing back the painful memory of mother's final words after Albert was born. His mother's request to look after Albert. A request that he tries to fulfill even though Albert is a grown man. To abide Eldora's request, make such a promise, wells up fear that she too will die as Mother did. "Everything will be fine," Friedrich says, trying to assure Eldora as well as himself.

"And let the chickens roam free," Eldora says, forcing a smile.

"What?"

"Remember when we talked about letting the chickens roam free in America like the people get to."

Ja," Friedrich says, kissing her hand, "we will let the chickens run free," and he looks into her eyes and says, "I a-Dora you."

Ludwig interrupts, "Come, let us go up top. We will do some heavy praying. The women folk know this business. The Doctor will be along shortly."

Deep down he is glad a doctor is aboard, but Friedrich puts more faith in the women at his wife's side. Dora kisses her fingers and place them on Friedrich's lips before another contraction takes her attention away.

"She is in good hands," Ludwig asserts.

Friedrich memorizes Dora's face as he backs out. He can't shake the depressed feeling and hopelessness. Or the anger. *How can God allow their child to be born now?*

"My Lyna is not new to childbirth. She has seen many children enter the world." Ludwig comforts as they climb the stairs.

Still, Friedrich leaves cursing this god damn vessel full of stench and unsavoriness. It is an unfit habitation. Even more so for a newly born child. His child!

The ropes creak, loosen and tighten with the uncertain wind. The sea breeze fills the sails as Friedrich gasps air and expels, "This damn ship!" His hands slam the gunwale. The upper edge of the vessel's side doesn't waver, unharmed by his brute force. His hands sting. It seems that nothing comes to a halt. There is no stopping things set in motion. Not a child being born. Not this voyage.

"What will be, will be, my friend," Ludwig conveys.

"That is no comfort." Friedrich stares into the endless horizon as the sea absorbs the sun. He reaches into a side pocket. Past the tea tin Martha gave, holding substantial funds. On the bottom lies a silver cigar case. The smell upon opening it sends him back to better times. Times when Eldora felt fine. One long sniff takes him back, back to many nights smoking alongside Father. Surrounded by Father's illusive comfort. Much like tonight, comfort is an illusion. "I am to celebrate the birth of my first child with this." Friedrich finds his heart less than celebratory. "Actually, my first-born son." Friedrich soulfully considers a life of servitude under Father's stepson is better than losing a precious child, or worse, his weakened wife. Friedrich wants off this ship. To stop this voyage. To have some control. The cigar tin goes back, way deep into his pocket, hidden away.

"Let us pray," Ludwig coaxes.

"Ja."

Ludwig's words flood over Friedrich. His mind tries to grasp them all. The usual prayer tranquility lacks. It just isn't there. An uncontrollable, uneasy doom submerges him, followed by a flashback vision. When Albert's life began and Mother's ended. "Amen." Ludwig pats Friedrich's back, "It is in God's hands."

Friedrich lights a cigarette. The moon rises to bring light into the imminent night.

#

Ludwig's eldest son, Jakob, interrupts mindless, superficial conversation. "Excuse me, Papa, Mister Klucke," he says, ascending, unsteady, clutching both stair rails. A tall wave splashes over. He balks. The jostling boat challenges Jakob's balance.

Friedrich finds some humor watching Jakob maneuver towards them like an acrobatic tight rope walker.

"You have a boy, Mister Klucke." Jakob's tall, lanky body lurches towards Ludwig.

"Congratulations! You have a boy!" Ludwig says. He steadies Jakob and adds, "I believe you have a cigar to smoke."

"Ja." The young lad's earnest face gives Friedrich trepidation. *Is there more that needs to be told?*

"Doctor Horace wants you," Jakob announces. He seems hesitant to speak more.

One long whistle sound and then complete silence. Scary silence.

CHAPTER XIII

"If I beheld the sun when it shined, or the moon walking in brightness; And my heart hath been secretly enticed..."
(*King James Version*, Job 26, 27)

The full moon slowly peeks over the eastern trees. The shimmering leaves shine like a starry night sky. A stark reminder that it doesn't get any better than this.

Dick chinks river mud mixture between logs. He is grateful the job is almost done. There are far better things to do. Like leaning a chair against a wall to enjoy a pipe and watch the moon rise.

"The spring air is upon us." Sora stands, arching her back. The moonlight silhouettes Sora's petite frame and pregnancy. She looks more radiant than the first day he saw her. More and more, Dick finds Sora's encouragement and suggestions beneficial. Her recommendation to dig half the house into a side hill should keep them cool all summer long and warm during winter. Besides, he prefers to dig and carve out a living space than drag logs. "Did you hear me?" She says, a little louder, looking up at Dick. "Besides you cannot see the mess you make."

"Yes, I hear you?" Dick knew her first statement indicates it is getting too chilly to be outdoors. Her last a needless concern in his opinion. "Does it matter if I make a mess?"

"I reckon not to most."

"You reckon, do you." Sora's companionship has grown so much these seven moons now. Since parting ways with crusty old George and the others. Even to the point of picking up on some of his southern words.

"Yes, I reckon it doesn't matter to those that never see it."

Dick appreciates her new southern speech and drawl. Not so much that she thinks it doesn't matter while she evokes that it does. What matters to Dick is that the job will soon be done.

Dick cherishes these moments since he must divide time between his southern family and his Sora. He finds time with Sora most pleasurable.

"I'm a fixin' to clean up your sloppiness after this baby is born."

"You can stay away from my handiwork." Dick pushes the remaining mud in. Dick must admit that this is not his expertise. Nor is having two wives. The two past Texas bound trips have been more than he can bear. The tension, the strife, the unreasonable responsibilities and demands weigh him down. Sora may be fussy when it comes to chinking and such, but she uplifts his broken spirit. Every time he returns to this paradise slightly south of the Platte River. She is the only one these days who can give him joy. She inspires him to settle down. "Almost done."

A wolf's cry brings him delight. Sora looks at the moon and listens as more wolves join in song. Dick climbs down the rickety ladder remembering to step over the rung that needs reinforcement. *Such bliss,* he thinks. Their enchanting songs echo through the valley as he approaches Sora.

"Good, you are done for the night. I love the wolves' cry, but it gives me an eerie chill," she says, picking up her craft basket. On top is his beaver haversack she works on.

"After you," Dick says, taking off his wide brim hat and directing.

"So gentlemanly, you must teach our sons, someday."

Ducking under the threshold he throws the white hat at deer antlers above the fireplace. His aim remains true. It lands perfectly on the right topside antler point. The hat's off-center white color splash against the stone fireplace helps claim this place his home.

"You never miss. Another thing that you must teach our children." Sora places wood into her arm crook.

"No, you don't." Dick takes them from her and adds them to the glowing embers. They smolder and flare. Then he glides Sora to the rocking chair. "I will tend the fire and make rabbit stew." He insists. "Sit!"

"No!" She pushes against him, refusing. "I have been sitting for hours because you would not let me help. I need to help. Some movement is good for baby. Besides, you make poor stew."

"Now, now you just sit and let me try to make better stew. My Aunt always told me 'Practice makes perfect.'"

"You cannot live that long." Sora smiles.

Dick chuckles. "Sit Sora, please," adding, "you must finish my travel bag and the doll for my niece?" Dick hates lying about the doll. But Sora can't know the doll is for his daughter, Aliza Jane.

"Very well." Sora gingerly sits.

He places her basket close by. "I will need my bag soon. I must travel again."

"Again. You tell me to rest then tell me you go again. Why?" Sora persists, "Why must you leave?"

"Hunting." He lies again.

"Hunting? Without me? I want to go with. I can ride. That way you can still force me to rest."

He kneels and rubs her abdomen, saying, "I do not want our baby bouncing about on a horse right now. I will be back before the next full moon."

"I don't trust you."

"I promise."

"No, I accept you will return by next moon, I don't trust you will be hunting the whole time. You go to Taos."

"Yes, to see my niece."

"I want to see niece."

"It is too long a journey."

"I want to go."

"You need to take care of the garden and rest."

"The garden can tend for itself."

Dick stands and firmly states, "It isn't safe. If you wish to not be alone, I can take you to visit Milwaukee and Nanoke."

"No. I will stay home and worry. But soon," she looks down, "after the baby is born. We will travel together to see your family. I wish to see this niece of yours."

"Someday," he answers so as not to raise contrary suspicions. Knowing full well it can never happen.

"Good! But I do not like your watery stew. I would rather have Welsh Rabbit. Wouldn't you little one? Yes! The little one wants Welsh Rabbit. We both know you can make that very well."

He laughs. "We are out of cheese, too. I will pick up more this next trip."

"No, you are wrong, we have cheese."

"Not the right kind for a good Welsh Rabbit."

"How do you know? You never try my cheese."

"It is too soft." Like his heart when it comes to Sora.

He prepares a meal that he will eat little of. Not because it is true that he makes poor stew, but that the guilt he carries juggling two families is heavy on his heart. Delores and Sora deserve the truth. The real reason he is away so long. Dick fears neither will understand. The one thing he knows is the undue heartache it will cause unleashing the fact. Similar to the heartache he feels thinking about it. There isn't anybody that can accept his indiscretion, even less his unfaithfulness.

Chopping carrots and slicing venison soon diverts those thoughts.

#

"Goodnight!" Sora rises and wraps her shawl over Dick's shoulders.

"Thanks, goodnight dear." Dick touches her soft hand.

She kisses his temple. "Don't be long."

Gently, he grabs several buckskin fringes, pulling her close. Her soft lips meet his. For a moment all is right in the world. "I will be along shortly," he says, looking into those deep chocolate drop eyes. "And you," gently tapping her belly, "don't give your mother any grief tonight little squirrel."

"Don't be calling our baby that."

"What, you don't think this one is squirrelly?"

"Well, maybe a little." Sora gives him another quick kiss.

"Goodnight you two," he says after them. Dick is happy. The cabin is done. One wife is happy. One child coming to fill the house with happiness and laughter, and so much more. This he knows because Aliza supplies that. He stirs the coals into a pile and places two more logs. Enough heat to last the night. Above the crackle, Sora snores.

He removes a brick from the fireplace wall. Inside lies his nightly libation. The glass flask feels good in his hand as he swallows a good portion. *Better than dinner,* he thinks. He leans back against the wall, licks the pipe stem before taking two puffs and watches the smoke go separate directions.

Disgruntled Delores' demands brought him here. They keep him hopping to and fro, like a rabbit, between Taos and the Unorganized Territory. Between adobe civilization and the open prairie where men have no roots. But, here, Dick settles. *A rabbit indeed,* he thinks, *one that wants to burrow right here forever.*

CHAPTER XIV

"Have mercy upon me, O Lord, for I am in trouble: mine eye is consumed with grief, yea, my soul and my belly."
(*King James Version*, Psalm 31:9)

The calm sea reflects the morning sunlight. Elizabeth squints against the brightness. The last few stormy days were dark, harsh, and unbearable. The hatches battened down. Everyone a prisoner. Elizabeth's olfactory nerves, ears and very being basks in liberation.

People crowd the upper deck, much like the first day, shoulder to shoulder. Pungent vinegar replaces the previous days stench and unpleasantness. Elizabeth welcomes this above the misery, confusion, cries, screams, sorrows, and smells endured. A memory nothing can extinguish. She closes eyes, looks up and lets the sun drench her soul. The brilliant sun provides respite.

Friedrich's faint rose scent, hardly noticeable, escorts her back. It sends Elizabeth back to the first time they met. When his strong arms saved her. Before the powerful sadness that grows more each day since the storms beginning. Before today. The strong voice of the appointed priest brings her back to the present.

"We commend this body in the name of the Father, Son, and Holy Ghost," the priest says and makes the sign of the cross. Moments later, a splash is heard.

A family intently watches over the ships side, concentrating on the place where their grandson, eldest son, and brother now resides. Their memory is all they have left as the encircled water ridges get bigger, wider and disappear. Their hearts forever fractured more than the sea's surface.

Disa leans into Phillip, barely able to stand. Friedrich stands solid and makes sure she doesn't fall backwards. He shows no visible emotion. Disa's loss combines and intermingles with the grieving family. It is all incomprehensible. They weep. She weeps.

Why? Elizabeth doesn't understand. *Why did the boy have to die? Why did her new friend have to die? Why doesn't Friedrich show care?*

"You should cover his head more," Doctor Horace says.

His breath reeks strong drink. The Doctor tugs the blanket covering over the baby's head. A baby without a mother lies in Elizabeth's arms. The Doctor's unsteadiness pushes her towards Friedrich's bicep, that is surprisingly flexed, rigid and unmoving like his emotion. Unlike the wavering Doctor.

Perhaps, it is Doctor Horace's fault. She readjusts Patrick Henry's swaddling. So many questions fill her mind. Some have answers, like why she holds Patrick. The only woman in Patrick's family, Disa, is clinging on two men. Phillip and Friedrich. Albert is obviously as drunk as the hovering Doctor Horace. Elizabeth was the first to hold Patrick when he was born. Everyone else too busy trying to save Eldora. All Elizabeth could do, as she does today, is stand holding Patrick and watch things unfold. And surmise that the Doctor's concern is either because he cares about Patrick, feels responsible or both.

Doctor Horace leans in and says, "It is truly sad that our dear Lord took back to him this lad's mother into his eternal realm of joy."

Elizabeth pulls Patrick close while tears threaten to escape her eyes. Patrick will never feel his mother's bosom. Eldora's kindness, comfort and joy are vacant forever, never to be felt again by Friedrich, Patrick or Elizabeth. An unfillable void. Elizabeth's chest painstakingly tightens. "Leaving no joy behind as I see it," she responds.

"Surely this child has a special call from God. The Devil tried to kill him, but Christ has rescued him from the grave," Doctor Horace's wife utters as she looks around her drunken husband at Elizabeth.

Tears well up. Elizabeth blinks them back, numbly staring at the shimmering horizon.

#

"Klucke's!" Bellows Mister Shaun Drake. One arm sweeps direction, then slams against a set of keys on his waist. The keys clink together and continue to make a sound as he helps two men place Eldora's lifeless body on a plank.

Friedrich's despondent heart hesitates to step forward. Their wedding quilt wraps around the one person who gave him joy. *Immeasurable joy,* he reminds himself, looking towards the previous family standing and staring over the side memorizing the location that they can never return to. Friedrich does not look forward to doing the same. He never wants to say goodbye. His feet move regardless.

The captain clears his throat. "Let us have a moment of silence for the deceased, Eldora May Klucke."

Friedrich holds the family Bible, embossed with Eldora's maiden name, Lutz. Her genealogy written inside. Patrick Henry's name recently inscribed. Historically recorded like Eldora's death date. Soon, Friedrich's quiet and solemn voice asks, "May I speak a few words on behalf of my wife?"

"If you must, be brief. This calm weather will not hold out forever."

The captain's callousness ignites emotion. Friedrich angers, thinking, *the day can't get any worse than this. Even the previous confinement cannot compare.* He doesn't care that the captain wants to get it over with. Somewhere, down deep, Friedrich wishes there was no need for ceremony. To hold Eldora again. He quelches anger and an unnecessary outburst. Eldora deserves more. A suitable farewell. Not a few uncaring, rehearsed words from a man who doesn't know Eldora or care. Friedrich rubs the German Bible pages open to Ecclesiastes 3:1. Looking to the horizon, he recites from memory:

> *"Zu jeder Sache gibt es eine Jahrezeit und eine zeit zu jedem Zweck unter dem Himmel: eine zeit getragen zu werden und eine zeit zu sterben."*

His thick and unfailing German accent carry the words. Voicing the verse that says there is a time for everything. *There can't be a time without Eldora!* He feels his heart shout. Closing the Bible, Friedrich whispers, "Rest in peace, dear Dora." Not succumbing to tears, he clears his throat and adds, "I will do my best to take care of our son." Friedrich's hand lands where the rings on the quilt intersect. Remembering Eldora's last words and request, he says, "And let the chickens roam free." The vow given, what seems a lifetime ago, doesn't give him purpose. He is lost, without direction. Time stands still and lingers foul. Even the quoted biblical words cannot comfort or calm his storm inside.

#

How proud Eldora would be to see her husband's fine care to her eulogy, thinks Elizabeth. Moisture pools around Friedrich's eyes. Elizabeth thinks on how Eldora's spirit must have smiled down from heaven at his promise to let the chickens roam free. The unspoken symbolism in Friedrich's gentle touch. The interlocking rings broken by his hand. It releases a tear that runs down Elizabeth's cheek and neck. Unable to blow her nose, Elizabeth sniffles. Loud enough to gain attention. For people to see the precious bundle she holds. Disa sobs and wails. The young boy's family increase their sobbing.

"Very well," the captain affirms the finality, "Reverend."

"We commend this body and soul into your hands, dear Lord God." The sacramental sign of the cross concludes the service. Two men slowly, slowly incline the board. Eldora and the wedding quilt slip off.

Splash!

Ripples become bigger and bigger circles until they are no longer seen.

CHAPTER XV

"Trouble and anguish have taken hold on me:"
(*King James Version*, Psalms 119:143)

"Here you go lad," Shaun says, handing Henry the promised telescope, "You have earned it."

And then some, thinks Elizabeth.

"Now, skedaddle and go play with your new toy."

Henry dashes off. "Thank you!" He shouts back.

Shaun puts his arm around Elizabeth. "May I talk with you for a moment?"

Elizabeth pushes his arm off, "I suppose."

"Let's walk."

They walk. Shaun utters no words. He appears pondering. Suddenly, without warning, Shaun shoves her. Mean and harsh. His quick, forceful push traps her inside a swab closet. The small space confines movement. Shaun blocks her only escape. Fear renders her mute like a bad dream. The door is pulled closed. Shaun clasps a latch. *Why a latch on the inside,* thinks Elizabeth, afraid the answer is not acceptable. He faces her briefly before rotating her body to face the wall. Her cheek pushed between the wood and Shaun's head. His warm breath rushes past her ear and cheek, right into her nostrils. Vinegar mingled with chewing tobacco assaults her senses. Nothing else can she smell. Just masticated tobacco as he presses her tight against the wall. "What?" Elizabeth manages a word, a mere question, before Shaun's hand muffles silence. Elizabeth's mind freezes. Staring at a hooked latch. That one detail. That oddity inside a closet. A latch holding her in. She is motionless as Shaun violates. Elizabeth's mind generates nothing as time evaporates.

#

"What have you there, young man?"

"A pirate scope."

"Well, that is a mighty fine one. May I take a look?"

"As you wish, sir."

As Friedrich lifts the glass. There is a background noise like jangling keys. A rhythmic clink. Like keys swaying about. "Thank you, little man," he says, handing it back. "Enjoy the fruits of your labour."

Henry gives him a befuddled expression, saying, "How do you know I earned this."

"There are no secrets on this boat." Friedrich pats Henry's head.

Friedrich walks towards the sound. Trying to determine the source. The noise gets louder and more distinct. The rhythm faster. Then stops altogether.

A door swings open, slamming into Friedrich. His shock meets Elizabeth's frantic look. She bolts. Friedrich is stricken instantaneous fear that an unthinkable act against a responsible, caring young lady crosses his mind. Anger comes to the surface. *Who could do such a thing?*

"We were just having a little chat." Shaun states while buttoning his pants, emerging from the small space.

Without hesitation, Friedrich pulls Shaun's collar and positions a sound punch squarely to his jaw. Anger blisters and pops inside Friedrich. He releases a deep dark contained anger in another punch. And another. Shaun avoids the power behind another and Friedrich whirls about into a solid hit into Shaun's gut. It scrunches him over. Friedrich's rage is kindled, and repetitive punches ensue, giving Shaun no relief or time to defend himself.

"What is going on down there? Stop that at once!" Captain Harrison shouts.

Friedrich swings another hard punch before two shipmates restrain him.

"Bring those two disruptors to my quarters at once."

#

Elizabeth huddles, knees to chest. *Why?* She screams internally. A question without an obvious answer. She wraps arms tight around and tucks into a ball. There is no comfort. Nothing will ever soothe her feelings.

"Here, drink," Mama says, pushing a hot beverage in her view.

Elizabeth takes the mug. Mama's presence cannot alleviate nor diminish the empty, shallow thoughts that interchange with profound emotion. Mama sits and rubs Elizabeth's back. It gives little comfort. Her bottom lip touches the mugs rim. A gently blow delivers a warm mist and painful memories. Her face contorts. Closing her eyes and changing focus towards the expectant chamomile flower bouquet. A tea Mama always gives to calm her children. Elizabeth slowly inhales. An unexpectant carrot tea smell. Her first sip leaves an oily residue she licks off. Her eyes pop open. The flavor is something Elizabeth has never experienced before. "What is this?"

"Queen Anne's Lace."

"It smells, tastes and looks similar to carrot top tea?"

"Yes, they are similar, but the effects are different." Mama turns and looks serious. "You are old enough to know." Placing her hands flat on her lap. She peers directly at Elizabeth. "It is used to stop pregnancy."

"Women drink this tea to not have babies!" Elizabeth states not as a question but more as disbelief. It is horrific enough that a man has stolen her virginity. But, to stop a child's entrance into this world is preposterous. She has no mixed feelings about that and sets the cup down.

"Yes. It also is used to provoke a woman's monthly and encourage childbirth."

An unimaginable thought makes Elizabeth suddenly queasy.

"Drink up," Mama insists, handing her back the tea. She gets up and leaves Elizabeth alone.

Elizabeth thinks the unimaginable. *Is it possible? Did she mistake Queen Anne's Lace for carrot top tea?* Elizabeth sets the tea aside. Sure that of the possibility, she tucks into a tight sphere and hides her face. *How could she make such a horrible mistake?* She grabs and pulls her hair. Feeling the roots protest. She lifts her head, eyes wide, wondering, *how many cups did she give Eldora?* Plenty. *How much is too much?* Anguish fills her being. Elizabeth's realization makes her heart ache. Doctor Horace is not to blame. She is! Elizabeth rests folded arms on knees. Her mind bounces between enormous guilt and the unspeakable violation. She slams her head down and weeps.

#

Rubbing his sore, bleeding hands, Friedrich feels no remorse. Deep down he wishes to inflict more pain on Shaun who stands smug and wisely not looking at him. But, for Patrick, he must take care and control his anger. Set a future goal as a good example. Yet, right now, Patrick doesn't know. He flashes a loathing look at Shaun.

"Explain yourself, Shaun. How is it you are in such sore shape?" The captain folds arms across his chest and sits on his huge Davenport desk edge.

"I was talking to a girl and this man came up and started pulverizing me," Shaun states. The dorsal side of his hand swipes blood off his nose. He gives Friedrich a menacing side glance.

Friedrich tilts his head at Shaun and sternly states, "Talking? In a closet? Buttoning up your pants while Elizabeth dashes away?"

"Elizabeth? Hess?" The captain assumes and doesn't wait affirmation saying, "is a handsome young lady." The captain rises up like the desk lit him a fire. "Shaun, you know the rules. No fraternizing with passengers. "Perhaps, I need to remind you what that means." He tugs on his vest and approaches Shaun. "No talking or making bargains and deals with passengers. Yes, I know about the boy who shines your boots, and the boots of your shipmates. All for your financial gain."

"But... um... sir," Shaun stutters. "Honest, Captain, I meant no harm to the boy. He was happy to do it."

"Perhaps," the captain states, staring him down. "And this incident with Elizabeth?"

Shaun does not retreat, but his voice trembles, "We were just talking."

"Talking. Well," looking at Friedrich, then back at Shaun, he sputters, "I don't believe you."

"You believe a passenger over me. I have been by your side for years, sir."

"I am much more inclined to believe a normally peaceful man who has, out of the blue, become violent. His anger must be justified to do so. Without a doubt, you have defiled a young woman," the captain shouts in Shaun's face. After finishing his words and without warning, punches the air out of Shaun.

Friedrich has a fiendish inclination to smirk as Shaun struggles to gain air back into his lungs.

"Elizabeth now is a rose that has lost her bloom," the captain states. "Take him out of my sight." Exhibiting disgust, waving one hand and turning his back on Shaun.

"I will make it right," Shaun sputters, gaining a firm stance.

The captain pivots about and delivers raw power in the question, "How?" Placing hands behind him, looking dubious.

"I will make an honest woman of her."

"NO!" Friedrich shouts. "Captain, sir, this scum, took advantage!"

Shaun juts out his chest, stands tall and states, "I will treat her right, sir."

"I doubt that!" Friedrich emphasizes. "I quote Jeremiah 13:23, 'Can the Ethiopian change his skin, or the leopard his spots? Then may ye also do good, that are accustomed to do evil.'"

Captain Harrison smiles. "A man familiar with the Bible, I see."

"I will change. I promise." Shaun pleas. "Elizabeth is worth it."

"You are not worthy of her!" Friedrich wants to punch him silent. "The likes of you deserves to have his manhood removed."

"You should mind your own business." Shaun antagonizes.

Friedrich is ready to unleash more pent-up anger.

"Enough! Get this pernicious bastard out of my sight." The captain decides. "Shackle him to the main sail. Have each and every shipmate give him a lash or two."

"No. Sir. We were just talking, sir. I swear, sir." Shaun's verbal distressful plea betrays him.

"Really Shaun, you just asked to make an honest woman of her." Captain Harrison's head shakes. "You disgust me."

Two shipmates practically drag Shaun away.

"As for you," Captain Harrison points, "I hope you won't make this a habit."

"Only giving what that scum deserves," Friedrich boldly says.

"That is my job. Hear me?"

Friedrich nods and hangs his head.

The captain walks slowly towards his desk chair and sits. Moves a few things about. "This is not good, not good at all. There will be unwelcomed rumors tossed about. An onslaught of murmurs. Later, if Shaun's abuse produces a baby, those rumors and murmurs will follow Elizabeth abroad and all the days of her life."

Friedrich stands still.

"I will be happy to perform a marriage ceremony before we reach shore to quench any gossip. It is in Elizabeth's best interest. Perhaps yours as well."

Shock jolts Friedrich. *The gall!* The inappropriate suggestion stings like Friedrich's sore knuckles.

"Your dismissed."

#

Ludwig is waiting outside the captain's quarters.

Friedrich approaches Ludwig and says, "Sorry."

"You have nothing to be sorry for." Ludwig puts both hands down on Friedrich's shoulders. "Thank you! Let us walk. We need to distance ourselves from those who wish to overhear."

"Ja."

Friedrich ponders the captain's words. What makes the captain believe he can take on any more responsibility. Patrick is more than enough.

"I need to know if that son of a," Ludwig swallows hard, "if Shaun will get a just punishment? More than what you already allocated."

Sailors clamor about the main mast.

"Ja." Friedrich nods towards the commotion.

Leather hits flesh. Shaun caterwauls.

"I do fear Elizabeth may never recover. Her spirit may be forever broken. Unlike that foul man getting his licks." Ludwig's angry eyes glisten moisture.

"Ja." Friedrich agrees, looking down at dried blood and feeling the throbbing pain. Knowing it was worth it. Not only for Elizabeth's honor, but for his own venting of anger.

"The captain is a good, God fearing, man, it must have been difficult to command violence for violence."

"He does what needs to be done to run a decent ship." Friedrich glances up. The captain stands overseeing the floggers and his ship. Their eyes meet. Captain Harrison nods. Friedrich doesn't want to ask for Elizabeth's hand. He cannot imagine having another wife. There must be someone else. "Captain feels that Elizabeth should marry before we reach America."

Ludwig stops and rubs his beard. "I suppose, it would be for the best. I hate the thought of it. Especially since it is another thing that goes against her will."

"Ja."

"But, who? Who will take care of Elizabeth and still let her be Elizabeth? More importantly, who will Elizabeth want? Who could possibly make her happy?" Ludwig nervously states.

Silence prevails as they both stare at the crowd gathering. *Who indeed?* thinks Friedrich.

CHAPTER XVI

"You shall not mistreat any widow or fatherless child."
(*King James Version*, Exodus 22:22)

Whispers congest the quarters below. It provokes Elizabeth's bravery. Emerging onto the deck brings back painful memories. The funeral. The closet, the latch, and Shaun's transgression. Elizabeth feels a chill run up her spine, even though the day is sunny and inviting.

She cautiously searches for a lone, welcoming spot. Somewhere to allow numb daydreaming. There has been too much thinking. So many thoughts waver inside her brain, like the undulating waves. She is unsure if her thoughts will ever land anywhere safe again. She didn't ask for what happened. She didn't slip into, run into, fall into, or clumsily fall prey. The plot to get a man's attention was never on her mind. Shaun, all by himself, plotted, not by accident, but by intention. But, still, Elizabeth resolves to be surreptitious.

Eldora's cousin, Disa, sits on a chair shaping a crocheted doily into a basket. Elizabeth cannot go that way.

"May I talk with you for a moment?" A voice from behind surprises her.

Hildago's smell reaches her before the words. The exact words Shaun said. They fill her with a painful emotion, bordering panic. It has only been days since Elizabeth heard those similar words. Her chest tightens and her breathing quickens. She walks opposing Disa's direction and away from Hildago.

"Elizabeth?" Hildago moves around, faces her, and walks backwards. The strong smell emitting begs he uses something, rose water, vinegar, a bath, anything to destroy odor.

"What?" She harshly snaps. Elizabeth stops and suppresses a desire to retreat. Back to her berth. Under a blanket.

A woman redirects her two daughters, shielding their eyes from viewing Hildago and Elizabeth. Before turning away herself, she gives a judgmental, disapproving glare. Staying far away like Elizabeth was contagious. Elizabeth's urge is to tell those little girls the truth, that being raped isn't contagious. That Shaun should receive the glare. Everyone's glares. Lack of compassion boggles Elizabeth's mind. No one desires the company of a girl who allows herself to be defiled. *Make room, defiled girl on your left,* is what she assumes the woman and others say in their minds as they walk by. Hoping and praying, every day, her endurance holds up. *Soon, just a few more days*, she tells herself. *Land will bring an end to cruel whispers and actions.*

"If you please," Hidalgo pleas as he grabs her hands and bends a knee. "Will you be my wife? I will take good care of you, this I promise."

"Get up," she says, lifting encouragement upward. She discerns all eyes are on them.

"I am sincere," Hildago continues, "I will work very hard to be a good husband."

"I don't know you very well, Hildago."

"My intentions are pure. I will treat you right. Ask anyone. Ask your father."

That she will. This is the third offer since Shaun had his way. Elizabeth can't help but wonder if Papa isn't behind all these pushy marriage proposals. Since Elizabeth strongly refuses to drink Mama's abortion tea. The same tea given to Eldora. A sad truth she cannot share. Ever! Elizabeth longs for port. To see land. For all this nonsense to end. This pressure to do things she wishes not to must stop!

"Please, consider it and know I will do everything to make you a happy wife."

"I will give it some thought," is all she can say. Just like the time before and the time before that. She mustn't give up on her dream. Not just yet.

"Please," Hildago requests, and like a nervous animal, he retreats back to the makeshift stables beneath the jolly boat where this voyage started hopeful.

Elizabeth leans over, unladylike, forearms resting on the ships edge. *Being seized by Shaun was not her fault. Why does everyone judge and demand compliance to their ways? To marry. Does she not matter? Does she not have a say? If only they knew all that she struggles with.* There is no control over her present or future life. One small thought, for a minute, creeps into her mind. *Overboard!* Elizabeth rises and clutches the edge. Resisting the urge. Telling herself it is just an urge. It solves nothing. Deep inside, no matter how dismal life is, she cherishes life. Still, the word clings to Elizabeth's mind. *Overboard!* It clings as tight as she does to the ship. Tighter and tighter as she watches the waves blur into one.

"Excuse me."

The familiar voice. A rose water aroma. A gentle touch, "Friedrich!" Elizabeth welcomes. A pleasant interruption from her dismal state.

"You should not be out alone. Come," Friedrich motivates movement. "The sea air can be therapeutic just as much as walking."

His friendship makes her feel comfortable despite the secret she bears about his wife's death. "Is therapeutic another word for healthy?"

"More like good for the mind, body and soul."

"That covers everything." Elizabeth's anxiety melts walking beside Friedrich. The motion brings life back into her numb mind. Breathing deeply, "Therapeutic," she exhales. "Yes! That is what it is."

"I think Patrick misses you."

Taking another breath. "How is Patrick?"

"Patrick is fine. He makes me think of the future and not so much the past."

"That is good, I suppose."

"When my mother died, I was very young."

Elizabeth stops him and looks intently and says, "I am so sorry, Friedrich."

"It was Albert's birthday. It is a memory I will never forget. Much like the loss of Eldora."

Thinking of her part in Eldora's death makes Elizabeth look down, intensely sorrowful. "Those are painful memories."

"My mother's death has helped make me the man I am."

He holds her hands gently and messages warmth into them.

"I do not wish my son to feel as Albert does. To carry guilt and responsibility for his mother's death."

"It isn't his fault." A tear runs down Elizabeth's cheek.

"He needs a mother." Friedrich gently caresses along her jaw, catching the tear. He lifts her chin and says, "I have given it great thought."

No! He isn't. Not another proposal. His intense blue eyes look right at her.

"Will you marry me and help me raise Patrick?" Standing resolute and unfaltering.

He is serious, Elizabeth thinks, releasing his hold. Turning away towards the never-ending waves that are like the never-ending requests.

Friedrich faces the waves too, placing one hand next to Elizabeth's. They stand beside each other. No words exchange between them. He doesn't beg an answer. Elizabeth's mind actively thinks about one reason not to say yes. Eldora's death! It will loom in the air like a bad smell. It will permeate their relationship. She understands the request. Patrick does need a mother. Friedrich's caring approach endears her heart. It gives Elizabeth no hesitation. Her secret does. Still, she cannot give her standard answer.

"I know you are fond of Patrick." He turns, placing left elbow and forearm down, looking up at her. "Elizabeth, I will help make your dreams of travel and teaching possible."

Her forehead tightens. "How can you promise that?"

"I can't promise."

True honesty is rare, thinks Elizabeth. It only endears her further.

"No one knows where the future goes. But God," he adds. "I can only do my best to make it possible."

Elizabeth's emotions arise. They teeter between the words spoken and what she now knows of most men. "How do I know your intentions are good and not carnal?"

Friedrich stands straight and looks at the horizon. His voice changes to a low, sad tone, he slowly says, "You, of all people, are aware of my deep love for Eldora. Nothing can compare to it. All I am asking is to provide for you and a potential child. In exchange, you can provide for Patrick. In addition, I will, gladly, help you achieve your dreams and your goals. I will not stand in your way. All I am asking, is that Patrick has someone to call mother. My desires died with Eldora."

Silence fills up time and space. They both stand holding the edge of a ship that has given them both heart ache.

Elizabeth finds Friedrich's proposal more than inviting. Especially knowing Friedrich's care for Eldora. She believes him and wants to say yes. The part she played in Eldora's death dissuades her to say, "Let me have some time to consider." Not her standard reply, but close. This time replying truthfully.

He grabs her hands again, "That is all I ask." Softly he kisses them both while looking up at her with those deep ocean blue eyes.

Can she marry for convenience? So many women have throughout history. Like Catherine the Great, who accomplished so much for Russia. Elizabeth, indelibly, owes Friedrich a wife.

CHAPTER XVII

"If a man have two wives, one beloved, and another hated, and they have born him children, both the beloved and the hated; and if the first born son be hers that is hated: then is shall be, when he maketh his sons to inherit that which he hath, that he may not make the son of the beloved firstborn before the son of the hated, which is indeed the firstborn."
(*King James Version*, Deuteronomy 21:15)

The night is dark. Clouds obstruct any hopes the full moon will guide him into town. It is later than Dick wishes to arrive. "Whoa, Sally," like a lone stranger, he hesitates. Surveying the town Dick still calls home, not knowing why. Taos glows, a warm invitation. More light, more adobe houses. Dick doesn't receive its welcome. A sad hatred fills his heart every time he crests this hill. The once small town has grown too large for his liking. Makes him long for another place. Only three days ride away. The doll Sora made rests under buckskin, next to his chest. Aliza Jane's enthusiastic welcome tomorrow morning will make the journey worthy. As for tonight, he suspects, Dolores will be colder than the night air and nowhere near as warm as the glow below.

"Let's go Sally," he encourages, onward towards brief captivity.

#

Everywhere Dick turns Aliza is there. He sits, she comes to sit. He stands, she begs for him to pick her up. As if she knows their time is brief and wants all she can get. It warms his heart. A pleasant pause from his constant focus on time. The slow agonizing tick of passing time. Aliza is the only joy that brightens the day.

Dick carries Aliza outside and places her down.

"Icky," she complains, brushing dirt debris off her hands.

Right then and there he looks up to the sky and wishes his future children to be boys.

Aliza raises arms, grunting insistently. Dick cannot refuse and hardily obliges. Aliza cuddles close, turning his heart wholeheartedly into not minding, one bit, that she is a girl who doesn't like the dirt. Dick sits and leans the chair back. The adobe wall gives off warmth. Dick's heart softens and melts as Aliza finds restful slumber on his chest.

Looking up at the expansive blue sky, Dick adds to his mental diary, *March 25th, 1850, A fine day to be a father. It doesn't matter if offspring are male or female.* Kissing Aliza's cheek ever so gently. *Doesn't matter at all.* He whispers, "I love you, Aliza Jane." Dick's last thoughts before dozing off is he must keep his secret. All the way to the grave. And cherish all the joy he can.

#

"Out!" Dolores' aunt shoos Dick.

It is, was, his bedroom once he wants to say. "I know how birthing goes," Dick states, refusal. He advances forward. "I want to be with Delores. She is having my baby."

"Woman's business." The bedroom door shuts him out.

Dick barely knows the women, for that matter the men, who now occupy his house, hovering about. If he were not a gentleman, there would be no compliance. Furthermore, these people would have to wait outside. The house is way too small. But then he would have to be indoors. If he can't be by Dolores' side, he much rather be outdoors. Impropriety intensifies his urge to escape. He feels like a stranger in his own house. But what can he expect? He only visits once a month or so. He just recently learned Delores was pregnant. *She kept that a secret far longer than she should of*, thinks Dick. Standing on the porch he wishes that his wife's family wouldn't have whisked Aliza away. Without her, his thoughts turn sour on this place. He sits wide legged readying his pipe. Far from where he wants to be. Exiled from his house, wife and child by unfamiliar people invading his space.

#

"Come see! You have a boy!" The same impertinent woman who, many hours ago, shoved him aside requests he re-enter.

Dick moves quickly to Dolores' side. Through the gathering swarm of people around the door, wondering if they got first glance at his boy. The crowd closes behind, still gawking. Dolores looks plum worn out.

"Our son," Dolores says, unveiling, "Your namesake."

Dick cannot contain a smile as he gingerly brings the child up close. He kisses Richen Lacy Junior's dark curly hair. Knowing full well that his life has become ever more complex, he says, "So many things I have to tell you. So many things I need to teach you."

"All in due time," Dolores says.

That day and those that follow pass slowly. Aliza splits her admiration between the new baby and Dick. There is little to no contact with his newborn son. So, he conjures up a lie that allows him to flee city life and return to Sora.

#

Dick swings his long leg over Sally's neck and jumps off sprinting towards Sora. Her outstretched arms invite him into a lingering hug. He kneels to greet her stomach, "I hope you haven't been giving your mother any trouble." He rises and embraces Sora again.

Sora grabs his new whisker growth. Both sides and shakes while looking at him eye to eye. "Not much trouble. Good to see you, husband. Have you been staying out of trouble?" Rubbing noses together. "Did your niece like the doll? Did you remember the cheese?"

"Answers will come in due time, my dear," he says, picking her up. Carrying her indoors, he repeats, "In due time."

CHAPTER XVIII

"And if some of the branches be broken off, and thou, being a wild olive tree, wert grafted in among them, and with them partakest of the root and fatness of the olive tree;"
(*King James Version*, Romans 11:17)

The seagulls disperse, squawking. Elizabeth pretends they are snow white doves. Doves have positive connotations. Like the biblical story where Noah sends a dove out. It comes back with an olive branch in its beak conveying new life. They represent peace, love, faith, purity and eternal life. Since dove's mate for life, they signify a long and happy marriage. *A more appropriate bird for the day*, she thinks. Yet, she will accept any flock of birds, even those who may poop on her head. They announce prosperity, progress and abundance will come.

The Klucke's, Rauser's and all the Hess' gather on the pier. Ever since their joyous arrival, many days ago, they have formed a family bond. Together they keep New York's formidable alures at bay. What one wants another can talk them out of. Saving money for their travels west. Like sharing one lower east side apartment. Only three rooms, a small water closet, and a kitchen to share. Living together inside a huge tenement building where you can reach out and touch your neighbor. And hear every conversation. Absolutely no privacy. Mama, Papa, Jakob, Johannes, Karl, Rosie, Freddie, Wiggy, Mags, Henry, Friedrich, Patrick, Albert, Disa, Phillip, Hidalgo and herself all contribute towards a common goal. Preparing for an exodus. So far, Elizabeth finds them an agreeable flock.

"I will ask for these when it's time." Mama hands Elizabeth two white tapered candles.

"Yes, Mama."

They all congregate around Mama's extravagant candle lantern justified by necessity. The vertical glass still pristine. The top perforated vent holes, Mama says, keep her hands warm. The ornamental tin leaves on top, Papa says, have no value. Mama disagreed, telling Papa that it fits a person who believes and understands herbs and leaves can heal, saying it is well worth the money.

In some cases, herbs can harm, Elizabeth remembers. She doesn't want to think on that today.

Mama's lantern glow becomes less distinct as the sun rises. Its rays give vibrancy to their drab church attire. The city comes alive as more and more people emerge onto the pier.

A desire also emerges deep inside Elizabeth. *Where are these people going on a Sunday? What is their story? Their occupation?* She typically watches from their third story window and guesses. Longing to ask. Always enjoying impromptu conversations that confirm her conjectures on these fascinating travelers and city dwellers.

There is no time to speculate today. Even though the groom is late.

Elizabeth bides her time watching the sun kiss magnificent church steeples. Elizabeth personally appreciates spectacular archways that welcome events like this. Churches adorned with colorful stained glass, elaborate chandeliers and comfortable sleek wooden backed pews. *That is where they should be. Inside a church.* Elizabeth doesn't believe it truly matters, since marriage is all about a commitment between two people. It is just an agreement. But it would be nice. Unfortunately, not one Church deemed acceptable or affordable. Some churches were so hostile and rude about regulations, stipulations, and demands. So, here they stand. Among the vocal birds this beautiful spring day.

"Sorry I am late!" Mister Klucke's new dark blue cravat is a stark contrast to his plain gray suit. The tie makes his blue eyes sparkle bright against the early morning sun. "Had to wash off the night soil stench. I didn't want to smell on my wedding day!"

"That is quite alright," Papa says, "We couldn't start without you."

Mama wraps a kerchief around Rosie's neck. "Something old to tie you to your past. It was your grandmother's."

"Thank you, Mama." Rosie wraps the ends into a bow.

"Something new for your new beginning." Johannes displays a delicate, lace trimmed handkerchief. She leans in and says, "Don't tell anyone, but I made it at the shop. Those new machines are so fast. And the stitching is perfect." Lifting it up, "Look how tiny and precise these stitches are. Hope you like it."

"Thank you! It is perfect!" Rosie hugs Johannes.

Elizabeth marvels at how much her sisters and siblings have matured. She is even a bit jealous. Johannes gets to leave the apartment every day. To pedal her foot on some machine that does the stitching for you. Since Mama has a job weaving, Elizabeth does Mama's household chores, oversees younger siblings, and takes care of Phillip. She also helps with Mama's second job. They all do. Every spare moment during the day and into the late-night hours Elizabeth hand stitches. Hemming pants and mending clothes. Every day Mama brings more and more home from the nearby cleaners. The more Karl, Rosie, Freddie, Wiggy, Mags, and Henry help, the better off they all will be traveling west. At least that is what Mama and Elizabeth tell them when they complain about the constant sewing. Far harder work than Johannes' in Elizabeth's humble opinion. Nonetheless, they all are becoming sensible, hardworking grown-ups.

"Something borrowed, for luck." Elizabeth hands the bride a crocheted basket. "And something blue to represent purity and fidelity."

Pointing inside. A brilliant blue ribbon woven in and out pronounces a crocheted cross Elizabeth made. "You can use it as a page marker."

"Thank you, Beth, I shall." Rosie gives her a hug and a quick kiss on the cheek.

Albert welcomes Rosie to his side.

"Thank you all for coming to our wedding," Rosie says. The Hess family's way of announce the ceremony to begin.

Simultaneous they all respond, "The Lord bless thee and keep thee."

"Let's begin." Papa stands back-lit.

Friedrich whispers, "Isn't that the basket Disa made for us?"

"Yes," Elizabeth whispers back. She remembers the day Disa crocheted it. The day Friedrich proposed. Then the beautiful day, similar to today, Disa gave something new.

Friedrich's breath smells like strong drink. He probably has been drinking all night again. Elizabeth can't begrudge him, though. Friedrich, Albert and Hidalgo have the nastiest job. Cleaning out outhouses between nine at night until five in the morning. Night soil cartmen earn three American dollars a shift. Each! Removing fecal sludge. A job no one wants to do, not even Friedrich. Elizabeth assumes nipping on whiskey must make it more bearable.

"We are gathered together this fine Sunday morning on the 14th day of April to join this man and woman in holy matrimony. Let us begin with Psalm 128:1-3."

Soon, all Friedrich's efforts and their combined labors will pay off. They'll be on their way to Independence, Missouri without delay. Not by stagecoach, which is the fastest. They are far too expensive and have little luggage space. Definitely not on another boat. *God forbid!* Steamboat city ports have unpredictable departure times, and they take months. Elizabeth doesn't think she can wait that long to see the countryside again. If the promised countryside even exists. Maybe America is just one invigorating city after another. Elizabeth's excitement cannot await four more days, when they will load their belongings into a wagon and ride out beyond the city and ascertain what lies beyond the city.

"Thy wife shall be as a fruitful vine by the sides of thine house: Thy children like olive plants round about thy table," Papa finishes. "I will now read from Ephesians, chapter 5, verse 20 through 33."

Friedrich gently caresses his hand across Elizabeth's back and rests it on her hip. *Is Friedrich trying to insinuate fruitfulness?* Papa hardly ever deviates from his wedding sermon. Surely Friedrich has heard this part before. On their wedding day. Words back then didn't mean anything to Beth. It was just a formality. *Does he want more than what they have agreed upon?*

Elizabeth distracts herself from overthinking the reason and surveys the city. Thin little smoke squiggles fill the skyline. Originating from various elegant brownstone buildings, wood or scrap metal houses. Most have water coming out of the wall.

By turning a simple knob. Water that flows right into a basin attached to the very same wall. Just thinking about it makes her giggle with glee inside. A city full of wonderful fascination. Even the walk towards the pier allures. The cobblestone streets meticulously lined with enticing shop window displays. No one can possibly afford all the luxury this city has to offer. Nor have the necessary time to explore.

"However, let each one of you love his wife as himself, and let the wife see that she respects her husband." Papa closes the Bible. "Do you Rosina Jacobina Hess wish to enter the state of matrimony with this man? Do you love him? Do you take this step of your own free will and under no compulsion, not even that of your parents?"

"Yes, I do."

Rosina slips a plain wedding band on Albert's right ring finger, as it is customary in Romania.

Elizabeth looks at her plain and simple wedding band.

"Do you Albert Johann Klucke wish to enter the state of matrimony with my daughter?" Papa repeats similar questions to Albert.

"Yes, I do."

Albert places a petite, embellished ring on Rosina's finger. "I hope you like the design." He looks up at her and kisses the ring.

"I do!" Rosina smiles.

"You have given each other golden rings. This most precious of metals symbolizes that love is the most precious element in your life together. The ring has no beginning and no ending, which symbolizes that the love between you will never cease."

Elizabeth fidgets the wedding band Friedrich gave her. Making it reflect the sun. It represents a never-ending debt. Owing Friedrich and the previous owner, Eldora, forever. A vivid reminder of her blunder.

"Bless, O Lord, the giving of these rings that they who wear them may live in your peace and continue in your favor all the days of their lives, through Jesus Christ our Savior. Amen."

Mama nudges Elizabeth. "It is time." She opens the lantern's glass door, waiting.

Elizabeth ignites the two wicks with Mama's candle.

"These candles symbolize your willingness to follow the light of truth."

Elizabeth can never share truth. The truth about the harmful tea she gave Eldora.

Rosina receives a candle first.

"Share the light!" Papa reminds the couple.

Their flames meld into one.

"This is a glowing reminder that in a true marriage, your lives are both individual and together as one."

Mostly individual, Elizabeth expects in her case.

"May its light shine bright and steady upon your path together," Papa says. "John 2:1-11 states, 'And the third day there was a marriage in Cana of Galilee, and the mother of Jesus was there....'"

A young couple and small child stop near and become a distraction to Papa's words. The mother breaks bread and hands a piece to her daughter. Barely old enough to walk, the girl toddles and tosses it at the gulls and giggles. The gulls fight and squawk. Papa intensifies his words. Elizabeth smiles at the joyful display. Longing to be sure she is pregnant. It is too soon to know, her monthly is only three days late. Elizabeth considers how great it would be to have a little girl of her own.

"This, the first of his signs, Jesus did at Cana in Galilee, and manifested his glory. And his disciples believed in him." Papa finishes. He pours sweet wine into one cup and raises it high, saying, "Blessed are You, Eternal One our God, Ruler of the Universe, Creator of the fruit of the vine." Presenting it forward, he says, "This cup of wine is symbolic of the cup of life. As you share this cup of wine, you undertake to share all the future may bring. May you find life's joy doubly gladdened. Its bitterness sweetened, and all things hallowed by true companionship and love."

Rosina takes a sip. Albert tips it back and gives the empty cup to Friedrich.

Papa reaches towards Rosie, palms up. Rosie hands welcome Papa's marriage blessing. "Missus Klucke," leaning forward, "Rosina dear, I wish you great joy, prosperity and happiness." Papa places Rosie's hands into Albert's. "I give you Mister and Missus Klucke. From this day onward, may they bask in the beauty of the light of their love, may its light shine bright and steady upon their path together." Papa releases and encourages, arms open wide. "Seal your love."

They embrace affectionately.

Elizabeth blows out the candles signaling the ceremony's end.

Albert and Rosie raise clasped hands and flash a happy smile.

Elizabeth congratulates Rosie by saying, "Its official, we are now both Missus Klucke."

"Did you see my ring, Bethie, it has birds on it. Look!"

"It's exquisite! They look like bluebirds. A symbol of joy, contentedness and hope," Elizabeth comments.

"They do look like bluebirds!"

"Yes!" Elizabeth tells Rosina, "The birds foretell happy occurrences in the coming times."

CHAPTER XIX

"For by me thy days shall be multiplied, and the years of thy life shall be increased."
(*King James Version*, Proverbs 9:11)

"Whoa!" Hildago stops the horses beside the congratulating wedding party. Sitting high aloft a green wagon. So green that it stands out against the city's browns and grays. "All aboard for a Sunday ride about town."

"Bride and groom first!" Friedrich conveys. He helps Albert lift Rosie up into the box.

"You are going to like the route we picked out," Albert says to his bride.

"Don't forget to stop and pick up our picnic lunch. There is jellied chicken, bread and butter sandwiches, among other things," Lyna commands.

"Yes!" Disa adds, "and some sweet pickle relish."

"Jakob," Hildago says, "come take the reins."

Jakob looks at Ludwig. Ludwig looks at Friedrich. "He needs the practice. We will need him on the long haul to Independence. Plus, he deserves the honor. He has made some fine additions to our ride. Take a look." Friedrich says, assisting Lyna.

Disa hoists up Patrick, saying, "Go to grandma."

Phillip helps his wife and refuses Friedrich's assistance when he struggles to boost himself up.

"Very well, then, Jakob." Ludwig tugs his lapels and adds, "But listen intently to Hildago's instructions."

"Thank you, Papa!" Jakob proudly says, "I made extra sturdy benches."

Ludwig clambers up. He bravely tests them, standing and plopping, twice. "Very sturdy, my son. I believe you have found your calling."

Phillip runs his hand down the wood and agrees, "mighty fine work."

Friedrich helps Ludwig's younger children and adds, "I think you need to add a step back here, Jakob."

"Will do," Jakob responds. He quickly scampers up next to Hildago.

"This is so exciting!" Elizabeth kisses Friedrich's cheek. "Thank you!" She accepts his hand and springs up into the wagon bed like a little girl.

Friedrich closes the back end. He secures a foothold on the wide wooden rim wheel and scales over into place beside Elizabeth. "All in," he announces, and hooks his fingers with Elizabeth's.

"First stop," Hildago instructs Jakob as well as informs, "Our humble abode." Nodding to Jakob, "Straight ahead, nice and gentle."

Jakob snaps the reins and the team lurches forward.

"Then off to the Custom House," Friedrich proclaims.

The steady clip clop is mute against everyone's excitement.

"Will I get to see that church?" Mags asks. She points out the white steeple in the distance.

"Ja. We will be going right by St. Paul's Church," Friedrich confirms.

"I want to see the hospital," Karl requests. "I'll bet it is huge."

"How about the evening post?" Phillip is always interested in the current happenings.

Friedrich finds very little interest in worldly happenings as long as it doesn't affect him.

"I would like to see the Historical Society Museum on 77th and central," Elizabeth says precisely. She squeezes Friedrich's fingers tight. "I hear they have all of John James Audubon's life size prints with names and descriptions. In watercolor!"

"Ja." Friedrich's heart gladdens with her enthusiasm. "I wish to see it as well. Unfortunately, they are closed on Sundays." Elizabeth's excitement vanishes. Seeing her disappointment, he adds, "Let's plan on going on Wednesday between my shoveling poo and slinging booze."

"How poetic. But I can't leave the children alone. There is no one to care for them during that time. Besides, that is the only time you can rest."

Elizabeth's caring nature is what Friedrich cherishes most. "I can rest when I'm dead."

"Don't say that!" Elizabeth immediately snaps.

"You know what I mean. I can rest up another day. This is an opportunity of a lifetime. We can take them with us."

"Really!" Elizabeth's face brightens more radiant than the sun. Her eyes sparkle delight.

Several excitable cheers ring out. The most prominent being, "Yay! no sewing!"

"It will be an educational outing," Lyna instructs. "You will make sure of that Elizabeth."

"It will be my pleasure, Mama."

"And the sewing will get done. Even if you have to stay up later to do it." Lyna looks sternly at Elizabeth.

Friedrich suspects Elizabeth will have more than her share of work to do.

"Whoa!" Jakob halts movement.

"Here we are ladies," Hildago says. "What shall I grab?" He jumps down ready to retrieve.

"I will help," Friedrich offers. He must grab a picnic blanket. In his pocket a unique gift awaits Elizabeth. They need some alone time so he can present it. He hopes she likes it.

"Please let me out and I can point to what we need."

After many trips back and forth, Friedrich realizes the preparational magnitude it takes for a large picnic. A much more elaborate affair than the small picnic Eldora and himself had one hundred and fifty days ago. Plus, twenty-four days, nine hours, and fifteen minutes without her. The memory glimmer brings a tear to his eye and tugs his heart.

"Yaw!" Jakob commands. The horses lumber forward.

Architecture passes by similar to Odessa's grandeur. It is like Friedrich is seeing it for the first time. Impressive buildings with ornamental fixtures. The identical columns on Saint Paul's Church and the Custom House stand large and formidable.

"Isn't this city full of contrasts?" Elizabeth adjusts her position. "There stands a church. And there, across the street, is a bier haus." Using the German word. "What do they call them here? Taverns? Pubs? What do they call the one you work at?"

"I bartend in a pub. Back home," Friedrich pauses. Back home is where he and Eldora lived. In a house that was not their own. The small room shared with Eldora and his brew room were the only comfortable refuges in an uncomfortable, stuffy environment. Not some place to call home. "Back home, we called them Jerrys and Malthouse's."

"We just left a cobblestone street and now ride on a bumpy, muddy, manure smelly road." Elizabeth continues, "Crowded buildings over there. A park full of trees over there."

"Expansive shops on one corner and men selling wares off makeshift box crate tables on the next." Friedrich adds.

"Yes! And things like that!" She points out an umbrella store front. "When would you have a free hand to hold one of those?"

"Never noticed them much or gave it any thought." And why would he? Those sticks with cloth on top are hideous and impractical.

They turn another corner and Hildago announces, "Here we are, our picnic spot!"

"I have a surprise for you," Friedrich informs Elizabeth, gliding her down. He introduces one of the horses, "This is Daisy, Daisy, this is Elizabeth, your new owner."

"Really?"

Friedrich gives a confirming nod.

"She is beautiful!" Elizabeth strokes Daisy's mane. "Yes, yes you are." She cuddles in. "You know I love horses. I always had to share and never had time to ride."

"Well, you will still have to share and probably have little riding time. But we needed our own horse. Later we will have to trade our horses for oxen. All except Daisy. She is yours to keep."

Elizabeth wraps arms around Friedrich's neck and says, "Thank you so very much."

"I have another surprise after lunch."

"I don't know if I can handle more. Daisy is already more than I could ever want."

It is the longest picnic Friedrich can ever remember. He whispers into Elizabeth's ear, "Let's take a blanket and sit by ourselves awhile."

"Should we take Patrick?"

"I got him," Disa overhears and offers.

Hand and hand they find a tree to sit under. Friedrich spreads the blanket down. Assists Elizabeth and sits next to her. "You know that I don't want you to be unhappy." He fondles the box in his pocket. "Or feel that you are a replacement." He presents a velvet box. "Here, open it."

Elizabeth's brows scrunch together. "What am I looking at?"

"An astronomical necklace. It can also be a ring. Here, let me show you." A little twist and the small global mass falls into a ring. "I wanted you to have your own ring." He places it in her palm.

"It looks a lot like Rosie's except engraved with roses." Elizabeth presents it back. "I can't accept this. We can't afford this," she prattles practicability.

"A sailor who lost the woman he loved offered me a reasonable price. I had it inscribe. Go ahead, read it."

"Consensus?" Her lips pucker. Friedrich can see her ponder. "Consensus! That seems appropriate. That is what we have. An amicable agreement."

"Ja!" It is the perfect word to convey their relationship. "And since it is inscribed on the inner circle, it cannot be returned."

"No, of course not. But you shouldn't have. What will we ever do with Eldora's?"

"Well, I thought," he grabs the ring and twists it back into a globe. He strings it onto a gold chain necklace and says, "you could wear this one around your neck." He clasps it on her. "An astronomical reminder of our agreement."

"Yes." Elizabeth centers it. "Then, one day, if I may be so bold to suggest, Patrick can give Eldora's to his bride."

"Ja. That would be nice." The very reason Friedrich believes Elizabeth deserves her own ring. Her intuitiveness that is uniquely Elizabeth's. He kisses her forehead and says, "You will always be a valued addition to my family."

"That may be larger soon. I am late on my monthly visitor." Elizabeth informs him.

"You're pregnant?"

"Maybe." Elizabeth shrugs her shoulders. "Most likely."

"I look forward to meeting your little one."

"Our consensus was that you would be their father. So, our little one."

"Ja." Friedrich is extremely content in this moment.

CHAPTER XX

"What time I am afraid, I will trust in thee. In God I will praise his word, in God I have put my trust; I will not fear what flesh can do unto me."
(*King James Version*, Psalm 56:3, 4)

"Finally!" Elizabeth is glad when her feet hit the solid ground once again. Except for the short interim in New York, her feet have had brief contact with land. The men wasted no time. Pushing the work horses onto the next, then the next, stagecoach and cargo wagon stops. Cities like Baltimore, Cumberland, and Wheeling. Elizabeth lost track and didn't much care after the city of Wheeling. City life and travel is wearisome and nauseous. She feels much better standing than jostling about.

"So, this is Independence, the Queen City of the Trails," an elderly man says exiting a stagecoach. "I am not impressed." Pounding dust from his suit.

Elizabeth must agree with the man. Independence is not impressive. New York, after all the repetitive paperwork, bustled with excitement. Independence looks confused. It makes her long to go back to New York. Or better yet, skip forward to quiet, endless prairies. The statement stuck between a rock and a hard place comes to mind. Elizabeth hopes it is not as bad as it looks. An odd smell fills the air, strong and pungent. Elizabeth wants to cover her nose. It smells like a dung pile ready to fertilize the garden and a stomachache gone seriously wrong. It provokes Elizabeth to vomit.

"Are you alright?" Disa's handkerchief appears.

"Yes, much better." she swipes the cloth across her lips.

The unsightly, chaotic, disorderly dwellings remind her of childhood stick houses. There is no rhyme or reason. *How can people live like this? Will we have to live like this?* Elizabeth wonders. Makeshift tents jumbled up so close together you cannot tell them apart. Haphazard and close. So close it causes worry that a strong wind may falter one, toppling all the rest. It makes her cringe.

"Fred!" That is what Elizabeth calls him now. Just as Eldora had. Their respect for one another grows daily. Fred is a good father and a man true to his word. "Fred!" She shouts, walking almost to a run after him.

Not stopping, he replies, "We have to procure more wagons, Beth," walking backwards.

"I am coming with," she says.

"No! You stay."

"No! I am coming with. Papa," Elizabeth shouts. "Make him stop."

"We have to hurry, Beth," Papa answers. "We don't want to get on the bottom of a long list."

"I must insist, Beth. You stay put." Fred turns away.

Elizabeth understands the rush. The need to hurry. The prime time to travel west is upon them. Upon everyone. But her need to be involved is strong. "Wait for me." She pleads. "I will follow you," she threatens.

"No, you won't," Fred shouts back.

"Don't go without me," she warns, trying to catch up.

Mama grabs her arm, stopping Elizabeth's momentum.

"No. I want to go." Elizabeth yanks free. The urge to run after Fred dies as a gaudy umbrella, similar to those in New York shop windows, blocks her view. It forces compliance. Having no control brings up unpleasant memories. It fuels her stubborn nature with no purging outlet.

All the challenging adaption that has been needed since disembarking the ship fill Elizabeth's mind. The daunting paperwork giving rise to nicknames and abbreviations. Many people changed their names! Some families, like Johannes's favorite Klingmann boy, dropped the last letter. Beth suspects it is due to signing so many times that the n's become one. Many hours standing, watching names change. Becoming so short they no longer resemble themselves. Like Bottilier becoming Butler. It still baffles her. Like why Mister John Johnson from Norway puts Johnsdaughter as a surname for his little girl. Endless paperwork for health, country of origin, naturalization, belongings and money. Keeping your name intact took endurance. Struggling with a new name herself! *Elizabeth Klucke*. Still hard to believe! A name that cultivates her acceptance more and more every day. Especially the way people give voice to it. With respect. And the new abbreviation, Beth, fits. A new name for a new beginning.

#

The first crossing at the Kansas River gives a taste of what comes. The cold rushing water, fast and deep. Fred worries if he has what it takes to cross this intimidating river. Weeks learning along with the four oxen team. Now they must perform. Yet, he feels there is no preparing for this. You must experience it. Like a good brew, the practicing leads to success or failure. Fred is uneasy.

Fred looks at the task at hand awaiting his turn. Mister Jack Lamme, a man not unfamiliar with water crossings, reaches the other side, jumps on a readied horse and instructs several other wagons across. Phillip and Disa succeed as do the Hess family. Jack rides alongside them. It looks easy enough to Fred.

Watching Jack approach, Fred thinks it is now or never, knowing that never is not an option now.

"You're up!" Jack encourages, "You can do it Fred, nice and easy."

Fred is comfortable with his team but handling them while crossing a river is new. Jack trained all the "greenhorns." Now everyone gets to do what Jack calls the most challenging task. Beth pats Fred's upper thigh and holds tight to Patrick. Taking the reins firmly, Fred cracks the whip beside Bobby's ear. "Get," he encourages the six-hundred-pound beast into the perturbing river.

Slowly the animal enters the water and hesitates. Bobby's partner Ingrid flares.

"Snap the whip again," Jack instructs.

"Get," Fred commands with a quick snap of the wrist the whip crackles once more.

Bobby lumbers cautiously forward. He gains a confident stride, calming Ingrid's fear and giving Fred relief. Bobby's sure footing and leadership carries the team and wagon safely across.

"Ho!" A sense of pride overwhelms Fred as the wagon wheels leave the water behind. Fred jumps down from the buckboard, grateful. Rubbing Bobby's nose in gratitude and watching others cross. He is ecstatic to have the riverbank behind him.

"Don't get cocky," the wagon master, Mister John Holander, shouts out after all have crossed. "This is one of the tamer crossings, mount up!"

Fred welcomes the satisfying feeling. It is better than working inside a brick building under someone else's rule. He likes this new independence.

#

The air is crisp and the fire warm. Beth's tired body melts into the chair, becoming one with it. *Sixteen miles!* She marvels. *Sixteen miles of walking tall grass.* Beth never imagined walking this much would be so exhausting. Of all the walks in her life, this day has been the hardest and longest.

"Let me," Fred says, reaching for Patrick.

A happy glow illuminates Fred's face as he jostles to the ground beside her. Beth smiles as Patrick still slumbers through the movement and rough rocking to and fro embrace of his father.

The crossing today lifts everyone's spirit, dismissing any worries ahead. All the fresh air, and Fred's swaying relaxes Beth. The songs and laughter cannot generate any interest in keeping awake.

"I don't know what all the big fuss is about crossing rivers. It is a piece of cake," Mr. Klingman bloviates.

"Y'all ha-ven't seen anything ya-et,." Jack says confidently. "Try not to gaum up." Jack's southern dialect and drawl pinpoints his Ozark Mountain heritage to some. To Beth, it is interesting. It is a unique addition to the melding or mixing of people. Like a one pot stew.

Beth whispers to Fred, "Guam up? That's a new one." Fred and herself have had many discussions on the different and similar cultures, religions, and language.

"I suspect, he means not to get too confident."

"You suspect!" Beth commends his usage. *Another interesting thing about differences,* Beth thinks, *they influence.* Beth smiles.

It feels good to be able to share the love of words and usages with someone as able as Fred. To share his apprehension over crossing the river. Then see his joy. Beth's hand touches his shoulder and rubs up to the back of his neck. Spreading her fingers to comb through his short hair to the top. Giving a gentle pull on his ends. It feels good to be able to share with such a fine man.

"I have a story. Shall I tell it?" Jack announces, raising up his full eyebrows.

His girls, Laura and Alcis nearby, enthralling voices chime, "Please, Papa, please!"

The littlest Lamme, Francis Ann, sleeps. The cute girl, older than Patrick, makes Beth rub her belly. Beth looks forward to holding her very own child someday.

"How long?" Their mother, Amanda, asks.

"Oh," Beth cannot recollect telling Missus Lamme about being pregnant, "eight weeks." *Oh, no!* Thinks Beth. That is about Patrick's age. Beth hopes that exhaustion keeps Amanda from questioning. The realization that the truth can cause the past to resurface bothers Beth. Changing her answer to, "About eight," lacking confidence of how soon a mother can conceive after giving birth.

"Not wasting any time starting a family," Amanda says.

"No sense waiting," Beth states.

"All, right, then," Jack begins the story. "One Sunday afternoon. Midday, mind you. A hot July day in 1776…"

"that's a long time ago," Henry says.

"Oh, I like this one," Laura says looking at her younger sister Alcis.

"Me too," says Alcis, wrapping a corn silk husk baby doll up, nice and cozy.

Jemima and two friends, Bitsy and Franny, took a canoe in search of wildflowers along the shores of the Kentucky…"

"River! Right, Papa." Alcis, obviously, knows the story.

"Yes! The Kentucky River."

"Will we get to see the Kentucky?" Jakob asks.

"No, that is further East. Now, the girls, Jemima, Bitsy, and Franny, being almost full-grown women with prospective husbands, should have known better than to wander off without an escort." Jack looks stern at his girls. "But they wanted to gather flowers and wild grapes."

"And prairie poppies," Laura adds.

Beth loves flowers and the interchange happening with Jack's girls brings the story alive. It awakens her. A distraction from thinking about what others may think or say and fosters good memories. When she was that small, young and innocent and without worries or secrets. Plain and simple, like a flower.

"Much to their surprise, an Indian came out of the cane break and began pushing them toward land. They soon realized he was a foe when four others appeared." Jack holds up four fingers and with an evil look leans into his audience. "A blood curdling scream came out of Jemima's mouth, waking her napping father, Captain Boone."

Jakob whispers to Karl, "This is a story about Captain Boone."

"Bitsy tried to jump into the water," Laura says.

"Franny hit him with a paddle." Alcis giggles as she animates the motion, hitting Laura.

"Ouch," Laura responds. She gives Alcis a cross look.

"Now, now, you two," Jack says, firmly. "It was all in vain. The girls became prisoners and were told to be quiet or they, the Indians, would cut their throats." Jack mocks the action with a finger swipe lengthwise along his own throat. "Thus, the scream. Jemima wanted her father's attention."

More pioneers gather around the fire, drawn in by the animated drama. Jack Lamme pauses, as some get up and move over to give more space. Jack's charismatic nature awakens their interest as well. Or maybe it is the mentioning of the famous Daniel Boone. The name definitely piques her brother's interest, and a similar interest shows on other anticipating faces.

"Captain Boone quickly learned that it was his daughter, Jemima, who was in danger. He gathered some men and started pursuit. Unfortunately, they had to go several miles downstream to cross the river. This allowed the captors to get a head start. The girls knew that Captain Boone and others would come, so they tried everything in the book to leave a trail and slow down their captors. Jemima limped and complained about her sore foot. An injury from jumping out of a tree days prior. Jemima claimed a corn stalk attacked her. Such a tomboy, you know, so much like you, top daughter." Jack touches the top of Laura's head.

At that correct moment, Laura claims, "Bitsy broke twigs and Fanny left torn undergarment pieces."

"They almost got caught," Alcis says, coughing.

"Cover your shoulders, Alcis, dear, with your blanket," Amanda instructs.

Beth can tell the two girls knew the story well enough. Able to give an account all by themselves.

"You are so right." Jack continues, "They even went so far as to tickle a horse. Yes," Jack looks about, "horses are ticklish, believe it or not. They would tickle the horse and he would rear up." Jack gets off his chair and lifts his hands high to the sky. "And the girls would fall off. Soon, the Indians chose to abandon the horse rather than put up with the constant interruptions."

"That seems unwise," Henry says.

Beth agrees. Walking is very tiring.

"Even with all the girls' efforts, especially Jemima's exaggerated limping, the kidnap party stayed ahead of the rescuers."

The interaction between father and daughters is delightful. The collaboration together leaves all of the onlookers, including her own siblings, waiting for more. All eyes watch Jack, even Fred's. Looking at Fred, she wonders if he, too, will be a good storyteller. A smile crosses her face. Certainly, there will be opportunities. Stories to tell Patrick and the little one she grows inside. About this trip. Someday, soon, they will sit by their warm hearth telling stories to their young. Enjoying small moments like this. Looking down at her belly, then at Patrick. Being a mother is gratifying.

"Well, despite the girls' efforts, the trail was hard to follow. So, Captain Boone…"

"Humph, Boone," Mister Olson says walking by. "That opportunistic land monger."

"Mind your words, he is my relation and there are children present," Jack voices sternly, staring down the man.

Beth's tries not to let her face show the disappointing enlightenment and acknowledgement of Captain Boone being anything more than the stories she had read. A look she sees brother Jakob, Karl, Freddie, and Wiggy surely match.

"Our Great-Great-Grandfather," says Alcis, strong and proud.

"Yes! Your Great-Great-Grandfather," Jack repeats, turning back to the story. "Knowledgeable of the Indian ways." Sending a side glare at Mister Olson, who now stands listening. "Grandpa Boone decides that they must take a straighter course. In doing so, they soon spied a buffalo carcass recently butchered with blood still flowing."

"Disgusting. I don't like this part." Alcis gets Beth's little sister, Mags, to agree. "I don't think this part is necessary, Papa."

"Oh, yes, oozing blood from its veins." Jack accents scraping his fingernails from the crook of his arm all the way to his wrist. Flinging his hand towards the audience and Mister Olson.

Mister Olson leaves.

"I would have sliced off a piece for later," Karl says.

"I would have too. I would have been so hungry after all that searching," Wiggy says.

"Me too!" Henry agrees.

"They caught up to the butchers in no time at all. According to the story Jemima told, it was just as the girls were losing hope and experiencing great despair."

Beth believes that, given the same circumstances, despair would have been much sooner for her.

"Captain Boone's group crawled up, and with one shot, chased the Indians away. The girls all rejoiced with joyful tears. Everyone feasted on buffalo. The girls went home to become wives, mothers, grandmas, and great grandmas. Jemima herself had ten little ones."

"Grandma Francis is one of them," Laura points out. She looks over at her mother and her sleeping sister. "Little sis is named after grandma."

Beth feels warmth in being part of a family history lesson. Leaning over towards Amanda, she says, "I believe your husband is just as adventurous and loyal to family as his Great Grandfather Boone." Beth knows the legend of Daniel Boone, though a legend is all she thought it to be. The Lamme's family is turning out to be a very interesting. Beth craves more family stories. "Perhaps, we can walk together sometime?" Even more, Beth craves to create her own family history.

"That would be nice," Amanda responds. "Time for bed, Laura, Alcis," she says, accompanying them towards their wagon.

Jack picks up his flute. The soothing notes encourage Mama to gather up her brood to roost.

"Shall we?" Phillip stands and offers Disa a hand up.

Albert and Rosina slowly walk away into the darkness.

Beth curls up next to Fred. He lays down beside her, Patrick between them.

CHAPTER XXI

"He brought streams also out of the rock, and caused waters to run down like rivers."
(*King James Version*, Psalms 78:16)

Alcove Springs is the prettiest sight Fred has ever seen. Cold, pure freshwater flows over rock. Yellow roses bloom colorful against the green trees and shrubs lining the edges. Prairie roses display themselves above the grasses that haven't been trampled. Spring at its peak.

Beth places a tub down and gracefully sits at the edge. The stream glistens before her as she makes her feet bare and dips them in. Ripples form around her legs. Then Beth lifts Patrick gently out of the laundry tub. Patrick clamors towards the water. Beth allows him to splash until his interest wanes, which doesn't take long.

Fred cuts free a fully bloomed rose. He carefully removes the thorns. Finding this beautiful place is a perfect rejuvenation after fourteen days on the Oregon trail.

"I see you found a spot," Fred says, displaying the yellow rose, "for you." Gliding it towards her with both hands. "Harison's rose, I am told." He finds Beth a quintessential companion.

Beth's eyes light up as she smells its aroma and places it in her hair. "Thank you!"

Fred kneels beside the two people he cares for most. Without them, there would be no reason to carry on. It would be better to return home to continue laborious worker bee trudge for an ungrateful patriarch. "May I?" Reaching for Patrick.

"Yes."

"You want me to wash or rinse," he offers.

"You don't have to help."

"It won't take long if we both do it. Then we can sit and enjoy the day. Perhaps have a picnic."

Hildago marches into the water, clothing and all and shouts, "Mise well clean everything all at once." He rubs soap all over his clothes, leaving suds floating downstream.

"Now that is one way of doing it," Fred says, laughing.

Elizabeth says, "A cold way." She chuckles, shaking her head.

"At least he will smell better."

"There is truth in that."

"Eldora used to love days like this," Fred says, setting Patrick down. His son's attention immediately transfixes on the swaying grass. Patrick swishes his hands back and forth.

Beth dumps the clothes out. Fred watches her shapely body bent over to fill the tub. Sadness consumes him again. Beth will never know the true comforts a man can give. Only the unjust treatment of one man. He longs to be the man who shows her proper treatment. But that day will never come. She is unreceptive to it. Friedrich understands why.

"If you really want to help," Beth says, holding trousers. "Rinse these."

"Ja."

"It would be a wonderful day for a picnic," Beth says.

"Ja. I agree." Friedrich hands Patrick Christina's goodbye gift. Patrick isn't sure what it is. "You think it is alright for Patrick to play with that."

"I think it is fine. All my siblings played with rocks. That one is pretty."

"Albert used to eat dirt. What I can see, it didn't do Albert or your siblings any harm," Fred says, wringing out trousers.

"Yes. They have grown up and changed. I remember my first encounter with Albert. He seemed so arrogant."

Fred smiles. "I assume Rosie has something to do with that change."

"Partly, I am sure. Keeping busy helps."

"Ja. What is up with his helping nature lately? Yesterday he was helping that loudmouth, Mister Olson, hitch up oxen."

"You know what they say, idle hands are the devil's workshop." Beth hands Fred a soapy dress.

"Albert seems to really enjoy readying the oxen. And is very proficient on fixing harnesses, greasing axles, and calming the herd. I think he has found his calling." Fred is not sure how much twisting is allowable on a dress.

"Yes. He has a way with animals. Daisy seems to like him better than myself."

"I don't think Daisy will forget she is your horse."

Patrick gurgles, alarming his guardians. The large rock doesn't fit inside his tiny mouth.

"No!" Fred removes it from Patrick's clutches. He picks Patrick up. Rinsing a shirt with one hand proves challenging. Fred isn't sure which is more rinsed, Patrick or himself. Surely not the shirt.

"That is the last." Beth rings out another shirt instead of handing it over.

"Shall we find some shade while they dry?" Fred offers Beth his free hand.

"Yes!"

Accepting his hand, they both exert too much effort towards each other. Their bodies smash into one. Fred holds her tight like their first day onboard ship. Her eyes lock into his.

"The rose brings out the green in your eyes," Fred says.

"I have green in my eyes?"

"Ja. Light emerald." He comes in close and kisses her. An impromptu kiss that lingers.

Several people start to heckle their closeness.

"Sorry," Fred apologizes.

"No need for apology," she says. Beth looks down, wiping hands dry on her apron. "Shall we find some shade?"

"Ja. Over there. I have a few things already waiting."

"You anticipated?"

"Ja. Who can refuse a picnic?"

"Not me." Beth pulls the yellow rose from her auburn hair and inhales. "I have never seen a prettier rose. Or smelled one so divine," she says, twirling it between her petite fingers.

"Eldora was very fond of roses. She knew all about them. Yellow roses convey friendship and caring and sunny feelings." Fred assists Beth onto the blanket.

"Interesting, Tell me more."

"Did you know there is a flower that looks like a rose called Ranunculus?"

"No. That is a ridiculous name."

"Ja. I think so too." Fred smiles. "As most know, red roses convey deep emotions like love. White roses signify peace."

"Pink conveys admiration, joy and gratitude." Elizabeth divulges.

Fred walks towards the taller grass and picks a pink prairie rose for Patrick knowing there is no harm in him eating it. He then picks one for Beth and sits down close. He leans in and softly says, "This Rosa Setigera is for you," using the Latin name for prairie rose. Fred has hopes she gets the demonstrative meaning in the giving of a pink flower.

#

It may be the way Fred says it or the way he looks at her, or both, that makes her believe Fred is trying to tell her something. Beth is confident he is.

"We should grow a variety," Fred says. "Once we settle."

"That is a wonderful idea!"

"Besides the beauty they provide, rose hips add a fine essence to beer."

"Oh, I see how it is." Beth prods him, "you are thinking of yourself."

"What? No," Fred stammers, "n-not at all."

"I thought, maybe, in a unique way, you were conveying something special to me. A complement perhaps."

"Well," Fred admits, "I am." Looking at her sideways he says, "I love our friendship, and I am grateful for all you do. I think we work well together."

"I agree we work well together. I, too, enjoy our friendship. But I am not a beer drinker."

"I am aware of that," Fred says seriously. "We can make rose hip tea for you."

"That would be nice." Tea briefly reminds her of that one mistake. Guilt clouds her mind. She turns her attention back to the flower. Looking at how the flower comes to life when she twirls it. Beth feels her secret will always keep them separate and distant.

"What I like about roses is that once they have lost their bloom, they can still be beneficial," Fred says.

Beth ponders his words. Remembering people saying that she had lost her bloom after Shaun's assault. Surely Fred doesn't mean what he is saying. Or does he? "Yes, like rose water." Remembering all the times she smelled it. The smell when she tripped into his arms. The smell when Papa gave his sermon. When she sang loud and strong along with Fred's violin. The aroma when Eldora's body drifted away under the waves. The strongest memory being their wedding day. How it smells right now intermingled with the surrounding roses. That is what she wants to believe he means. Roses do benefit throughout all stages. Growing, blooming, preparing seeds to grow flowers once again.

"You are the rose of my life, Beth." He says, kissing her cheek.

#

Later that evening, Fred takes a walk. Carrying a jug of water. Carefully, he cuts off several yellow rose bush stems. He puts one end of each into the jug. He takes an empty tobacco bag and fills it with rose hips. *This will be a beautiful start to our rose garden*, Fred thinks.

CHAPTER XXII

"He delivereth and rescueth, and he worketh signs and wonders in heaven and on earth, who hath delivered Daniel from the power of the lions."
(*King James Version*, Daniel 6:27)

A small dark cloud billows, snatching Fred's attention. He stops grooming Daisy's backside. Daisy lets out a nervous whinny and prances about. Something about Daisy's mannerisms and the cloud approaching unnerves Fred. There is no wind. There is no cause to worry about the weather changing. Yet the cloud seems to grow. Toppling over and over like a beers thick head of foam when you pour too fast. Rolling dust can only mean one thing. *Surely, someone is aware.* John, Jack, Hildago and Albert huddle. John mounts his horse and shouts, "Stampede! Man your posts! All others take cover."

Hildago runs towards Fred. "May I use your Lancaster?"

"Ja," Fred goes to the rear of the wagon. Among all the men, Hildago is the best shot. It is more than wise to let him use the rifle now. Fred hopes that Hildago can make the rifle worthy of the money Fred is sure Martha forced Father to give.

Beth struggles to get Henry and Patrick up into the wagon. Fred tries to help her.

"I can do it." Beth shoos him away.

All the shouting and vociferating about encourages Fred to let her be and make haste. He glides the rifle out from the wagons inside edge and turns to catch Hildago lustily look at Beth. Fred shoves the rifle at Hildago. "None of that!" Making an emphasis on inappropriateness. He hands him ammo just as roughly.

Hildago disappears.

He is left standing, alone, with the imminent view of the dark shadowing clouds getting closer.

"Henry! Where are you?" Lyna hollers.

"He is in our wagon," Fred assures.

Fred then reaches and glides his double-barreled percussion shotgun out. He is careful so as not to disturb the burlap sack holding the yellow Harison rose cuttings, a fresh reminder of the Alcove Springs kiss. Thinking how Eldora taught him how to love. How to care for flowers. Beth teaches him more about love, caring, and friendship. *He lost Eldora, he will not lose Beth or Patrick*, he vows. *Not if he can help it.*

"Use Rifles," Jack instructs, raising his rifle high on top a horse. Approaching, he adds, "Thanks for letting Hildago use your rifle. He is the best shot amongst these greenhorns. Besides me, of course." He boasts and rides off yelling instructions, "Use buckshot if you don't have a rifle. Don't shoot until you see the whites of their eyes."

The thundering pounding hoofs makes Fred's chest vibrate. He rushes to use the buck board as a gun rest. Loading the double barrel with buckshot, thinking. *There is no way to see the whites of their eyes in the cloud they produce. Not until they are well upon you.*

Fred grabs his loaded Colt pistol from under the buck board. He spins the cylinder to check that it is full of shells. Laying it down beside his resting shotgun, Fred knows that the two buck shots and his six-shooter will not do much damage. It can only scare such big animals. Hopefully away from his family. *Yes, his family,* he smiles. Firmly shouldering the shotgun, resting it on top of the wagon seat. Steady and looking down the barrel.

"Stay inside the wagon, no matter what. It is your best protection," Fred cautions. Peripherally seeing Beth clutching Patrick tight. "You will be safe. Just stay with the wagon." Henry curiously lifts the canvas. Peering out. Fred wonders if they will be safe. Steering his whole attention to the dust cloud, conviction envelopes him like the dust that will soon encircle them. *Not until you see the whites of their eyes,* he tells himself. The docile creatures of the prairies turned into a ferocious act of nature against the caravan shakes the ground beneath him. Fred waits, ready, as the animals close the gap.

Hoofs hit the ground soundly, drowning out Fred's heartbeat in his throbbing ears. Dark buffalo shapes appear out front.

"Boom!"

"Boom!"

Two shots ring out.

Two Buffalo fall.

Fred is steady, waiting, ready for his chance. A chance that never comes. The precise downing of those two animals split the approaching herd, right down the middle. Splitting into two directions, around the encircled wagons. Fred still waits, ready for a stray. Choking dust fills the air. He does not flinch. Suppressing the urge to cough. Not blinking. Afraid his eyes will blur. Methodically, Fred searches the dust for any movement towards his wagon. His family. Movement that never comes. Not until the dust clears does Fred release the grip and feel his arm muscles ache. Tension he finds hard to release.

Only when it is obvious that Beth and Patrick are clear of danger does Fred relax.

Quickly everyone, including Fred, realizes who made the great shots. Hildago and Jack! A crowd hurrahed around them. *Money well spent,* thinks Fred. Fred turns and sees that even Beth admires. Looking through him. Unaware of Fred's concern and relief that she is safe. Her frozen gaze haunts him, thinking, *is Hildago a better man in her eyes?* Hildago can certainly handle a gun. Fred's gun. Luck, Fred suspects, is how those shots diverge a charging herd. Fred suppresses his jealousy, telling himself, *it matters not. The danger is gone.* Despite Beth's obvious admiration, she is safe.

"Wow! Did you see that?" Henry jumps out running, not waiting an answer.

Fred removes the percussion cap, disabling the gun and carefully slides the barrel beside the cherished rose cuttings. He fears that the roses will die and never reach their intended destination. What he fears more is that Beth will never see him as a suitable husband and will flee into another's arms. Leaving him unneeded like the gun he stores away.

#

Beth refuses to sit still and accept whatever fate this day holds. She moves to the back of the Conestoga wagon and unties the canvas enough to allow Henry and herself to see the impending disaster. The wagon shakes. She remembers seeing buffalo many times before, noticing them being calm and thinking they were just like cows. She's even once slapped a buffalo calf's buttocks to move it along. How can such docile creatures now appear so threatening?

Beth glances to see Fred. Furrows crease his forehead.

Beth holds tight to Patrick, who sleeps uncaring in her arms. Looking about the wagon, Beth assesses any danger that might befall them if the wagon gets overturned. Seeing none, she looks out at the approaching dust. Two shots ring out. Two huge objects fall. All the rest veer around. The commotion of the moment makes it hard for Beth to determine whose marksmanship downed the creatures.

When the dust clears, a cheering crowd admires Hildago, Albert, and Jack. Hildago looking proud and strong. A rejected man who proves himself worthy. A man one can respect. She prys her eyes off Hildago and notices Fred looking cold and distant. His eyes look sad and angry at the same time. *He must have misunderstood her admiration*, Beth thinks. *Or was there something else?* Beth isn't sure why the look. But she doesn't like it.

CHAPTER XXIII

"Then I will give you rain in due season, and the land shall yield her increase, and the trees of the field shall yield their fruit."
(*King James Version*, Leviticus 26:4)

Dick kneels beside Sora, wiping her forehead, refreshing the damp cloth when needed. Dipping it in cool water and wringing it out.
 "I should not have eaten so much Welsh Rabbit," she says. Leaning her chest against a smooth anchored pole on supporting notched posts. Sora expels the meal.
 Dick hands her the cloth to wipe her mouth.
 "That is great waste."
 "Not if you enjoyed it going in."
 "I did."
 "Then let's concentrate on the task at hand." Dick pours water over the rag. Leaving it dripping, he places it on the nape of her neck.
 "That feels good," Sora says. "I am ready, little one, if you are," she says. Laying her head down on the pole and looking at her stomach.

Remembering that it took several women to deliver his son, Dick worries that he will not be enough help. The memory of Dolores' screams during the birth of Aliza Jane and Dick Junior still haunt him. Dick is not sure he is up for what is about to take place. Not sure at all. Yet, there is no other place he wants to be than by Sora's side.

Sora leans hard onto the pole. Relaxing after the contraction, she says, "A child born when the sun is below the horizon and west will be a confident leader." Another contraction hits. The pain crinkles Sora's face. The look tugs Dick's emotions. There is really nothing he can do but wait. Sora's strong composure, especially after releasing what she consumed, amazes him. Through each labor pain there is not one scream. Sora just hums and chirps, like a small bird.

Dick busies himself with rewetting the rag, wiping Sora's brow, and rubbing her back.

"It is soon." Sora tightens her whole body. A bloody, naked child eases into the world between her legs. Sora guides the child forward onto the reed mat. She tightens again.

Dick watches Sora squeeze out what appears to be her liver. His heart skips a beat.

Sora quickly ties a knot between the liver thing and their child. "It is all good. We have a girl." She announces.

"What is that?" He had to ask, seeing the loss has no effect on Sora.

"Afterbirth." She does a humming chant and says, "cut."

Dick maintains confusion.

"Cut!"

Sora's sharp tone awakens Dick to separate the liver looking thing from the knot tied umbilical cord.

Sora picks up the baby. Placing her mouth on the baby's, sucking then spitting, again, and again. The baby cries.

Dick now knows more about childbirth. Nothing like animals giving birth! He admires Sora's handling of the birth. Precise and knowing. Washing the small creature in the prepared cedar bath. He couldn't love her more.

"It is custom to bury the afterbirth under a tree."

"I know just the tree," Dick offers.

"No, you do not understand. It must be new tree. We must plant tree over it. It will represent her life, her growth." Sora wraps their girl tight. "Our girl." She presents.

Dick's arms receive the girl. His heart enlarges.

CHAPTER XXIV

"My bowels boiled, and rested not: the days of affliction prevented me. I went mourning without the sun; I stood up, and I cried in the congregation. I am a brother to dragons, and a companion to owls. My skin is black upon me, and my bones are burned with heat. My harp also is turned to mourning, and my organ into the voice of them that weep."
(*King James Version*, Job 30:27-31)

Beth turns her face towards the wind. Tucking escaping hair strands under the new bonnet proves impossible. Her wise purchase, from a soldier's wife at Fort Kearney, keeps the sun at bay. The hand sewn head covering is not effective at keeping hair tickles under control like a kerchief does. But it does keep the sun off her face. She pivots and walks backwards giving her forward moving legs a rest. The convenient wind direction blows the caravan's kicked up dirt aside, allowing a more pleasant walk on trampled ground.

Beth relishes that Romanian day, so many months ago, when the wind took her breath away. When Henry proclaimed, "we go!" When worries and uncertainties were small. When a warm hearth was a place to sit, read, braid a rug, or embroider. Those days seem distant. The anticipated future, also, seems distant.

Travel chores consume every waking moment. Rise before the sunlight. Build a buffalo poo fire. Blow smoking poo chips in one breath, coughing the next. Wait until the smolder becomes hot enough. Boil water. Prepare the same scrambled egg breakfast. Grind coffee beans. Throw coffee grounds into boiled water, wait. Sprinkle cold water on top, forcing grounds to the bottom. Yet, Beth still chews a few grounds each day. The taste lingers. Looking up, shielding her eyes, the time of day disappoints. Nooning at least an hour away. Then the cold, leftover lunch flavors will fill her mouth. Sustenance lasting until nightfall. When building a fire and preparing the meal will disgust her again. Beans, potatoes, bacon and fried cakes usually. The past, simple farm life structure finds yearning appeal.

Clouds glide quicker than moving wagons. They taunt temporary relief just to move along, allowing exposure to the sun once again.

Beth swirls to make Patrick laugh. "You like that? How about this." Beth skips. Patrick giggles. She skips slower, tires, walks.

Patrick squirms and fusses. Beth readjusts him further into the sling hideaway, moving the top knot off her collar bone. She puts a bounce into her walk and a gentle, rhythmic tap on his behind. Patrick whimpers refusal.

A meadowlark trills. Beth mimics with, "two plus two is four." Just like Amanda warbles to all her children. Patrick listens for more. Beth hums the notes and leads into another song Amanda introduced. A song about a man longing for his beloved. "*Oh, Susanna.*" Since Alcove Springs, Beth thinks about Fred. Her proclivity towards pleasing him. Longing to be the wife he deserves. The wife he lost. The meadowlark's fluty song continues in the background.

> *"Oh, Susanna,*
> *(Two plus two is four)*
> *Oh, don't you cry for me.*
> *(Two plus two is four)*
> *I come from Alabama,*
> *(Two plus two is four)*
> *With my banjo on my knee.*
> *(Two plus two is four).*

Trees bend with the wind towards her as if bowing reverence to her thoughts. Perhaps a god given approval. Long prairie grasses flow like ocean waves carrying cares away.

Amanda collects flowers and plants down by the Platte River. Her head bobbing up and down like a robin digging worms. Soon Amanda will join her behind the wagons. Then they will talk about her collection. Beth will learn more about this country's provisions. Beth cannot see the North Platte River behind Amanda, but knows it is there.

She painfully becomes aware of the dehydrating wind. It has made her thirsty.

She breaks off a tall grass stem and snaps the top off, using it to suck fresh cool air into her mouth. Her hums become irregular, creating a new song. Thoughts turn back to Alcove Springs. The memory of Fred's passionate kiss. She licks her lips.

Amanda walks up, "My little angel is asleep, how about yours?"

"I think Patrick has a little fight in him still," Beth vocalizes the new tune. Bouncing, tapping, humming mindlessly to her melodious creation.

"Don't mind me while I show you my finds," Amanda states. She slips her hatchet tool into a belt around her waist.

Beth adds words between hums, "I have to get one of them," drawing out them as a note that never ends. It is a horseshoe forged onto a rod. A two-prong hand rake. Simple enough to make. "It would be a very handy gardening tool," Beth sings. "Allowing you to dig and scrape."

"Let me assure you, it is." Amanda pulls out a plant with little white flowers attached to a huge root. The root bigger than the flower. Amanda pinches a flower off and hands it to Beth. "For you."

Beth nods appreciation, giving up the song, speaking softly, "What will you use the root for?" It is obvious to Beth that the huge root is the real prize.

"Ah, yes, this is bloodroot. So exciting to find it this far west. I plan to mix it with dried beef gall, molasses, mayapple resin, and a touch of colocynth. Make some pills to ease dysentery."

"How do you make the pills?" Beth knows how Mama does them. Curiosity begs Amanda's expertise.

"My recipe is to thicken beef gall with molasses. Add the herbs. Roll out with flour and cut into small bits. You don't need much herb, though. But I have been running out. Glad I found some."

Beth thinks, *Mama never runs out of anything. Not even Queen Anne's lace.* Beth will never forgive herself. The anguish of keeping the secret rips at her heart daily.

"I found some mint too."

"For Alcis cough."

"Yes, Alcis has that horrid cough. Had it since we started this journey. I am afraid Francis has picked it up. Hope this mint will help."

"I am sure it will. Anything is better than doing nothing." Beth listens to the words coming from her mouth. She once believed that. Her belief, now, is as fickle as the wind.

#

"Beth, come here," Amanda beckons.

Laura and Alcis giggle. Their hands squish a wet, off white, cake batter substance.

"That looks fun." Beth kneels down next to the bowl.

"It's a mixture my mother swears reduces mosquito bite swelling and itch." Amanda dabs a little onto Alcis' nose. "There's one," then Beth's forehead, "and there's another. It is also great to play with. Try it!" Amanda encourages Beth to be playful. A playfulness Beth misses more and more these days.

Beth finds the mixture more like a watery bread dough. Memories working with bread dough under Mama's tutelage floods her mind. Hearing Mama chastise that she was kneading the spring out and that it would not rise properly. Everyone ate it anyway. Much like they do the hard tack bought at the forts. They soak it in any liquid available. The memory is warm and pleasant, just like the mixture between her fingers.

Beth squishes away adult weights. Marriage, chores, promises and responsibility. "So, what is this?"

"Oh, some flour, some baking soda, some salt and water."

"Very basic."

"Yes."

"Seems like a waste of precious flour." Beth wrings her hands over and over. Thinking. The Hess family never have time for fun. The Klucke family never have time for fun. She doesn't have time for fun. It is all work and no play. Work she must get back to and stop squandering time.

"Well, it can be if you don't plan to make a watery stew for dinner and turn this mixture into a biscuit topper. It makes hard biscuits, but with the right amount of soaking they are still quite good. One should never waste, you know. I remember a time when I was young and wasteful."

Beth rubs hands together. Dried crumbs land on her lap.

"One hot summer day our mother wanted to get some baking done. Bread and cakes occupied her mind, not us, yet we were horribly underfoot. She made some of this, calling it play dough, and sent us out to play. Telling us to make some animal shapes and set them out to dry. She would appreciate them later. Well, that was too boring, especially the drying part." Amanda pauses. She helps remove excess dough off Alcis' hands. "I was about Laura's age."

"Can we go wash our hands now, Mama?" Laura stands.

"Yes."

They take off with a handful each, looking devious.

"Just your hands, ya hear! And keep that handful off of each other," Amanda hollers after them.

"Yes, Mama," they both reply, giggling all the way.

Amanda continues, "We lost interest in making creatures and watching them dry. I, brilliantly, suggested we stick things to the exterior of the cabin. I started with my handkerchief." Amanda adds more flour to the dough and works it in.

"So, I secretly went inside and got some of our mother's quilting squares."

"Oh, no! You didn't," Beth says. Holding her hands, still staring at Amanda.

"We watered down the mixture so it would spread nice and plastered those squares all over the front of our home. With no rhyme or reason. Just having fun."

"What a mess! Your mother must have been livid?"

"Not really. Well, anyway, the house, we thought, had much improved looks. It sure set us apart from any other houses we had ever seen."

"It sure would."

"All my siblings, my brother John being the loudest, told our mother it was my idea. The very next day, I learned how to do the wash. My mother said, 'if you can make a mess, you can learn to clean up a mess.'"

Beth pictures quilt squares. Wedding circle quilt squares. Beth stares at her hands.

"From that day forward, laundry became my job when our mother baked."

Beth's mind dwells. Earlier she welcomed being a wife and mother, seeing it as her duty. But the cost of endless burdens given her is too much. Beth's travel hope is just a day in and day out humdrum grind.

Hearing Laura and Alcis play in the distance reminds Beth she can never leave Fred or Patrick. Beth is trapped. Forever a slave to ordinary life. She tries to refocus thoughts. Patrick sits on Mama's lap as she stirs a pot of beans. Beth stares at her hands. Her life is not hers. Her pregnancy was not her idea. It was her decision not to abort, but not her idea. Yet, she is not alone. So many women are forced to marry and have children right away. Unsure of how she feels about this revelation of being like other women, Beth goes somber.

"What's wrong?" Amanda's elbow nudges.

Amanda's questioning look is all the encouragement Beth needs. Beth divulges truths. All the truths weighing her down. The desire to tell spills out. More words than she wishes to share or let be known. Even the mistake only God knows. And now Amanda. Amanda's compassionate eyes beg release. And it spills forward.

"Oh my, sweetie, you mustn't blame yourself," Amanda assures. "Queen Anne's Lace affects the baby more than the mother and Patrick is fine. The mother must have been too weak to give birth."

"Because of the tea I gave her. I am to blame!" Beth condemns herself.

"Trust me, you cannot blame yourself for the course life takes or when death must come."

"Thank you, Amanda, for listening to me blabber."

"It's all fine, my dear."

Is it all fine? Beth wonders.

"My mother always said, 'Home is where the heart is.' I believe it to be true. I don't want to preach to you, sweetie, but put the past in the past. Then put your heart into what you got."

There is comfort, beyond relief, in her words. Perhaps more in the sharing of a secret that weighed done her heart and mind.

Familiar violin music fills the air. It seems like a lifetime ago that strings vibrated joyful notes. Not since that night in the belly of a ship. A pleasant time before her secret, before being molested.

Beth goes to enjoy Fred's performance and hopefully add vocals while she does her nightly chores.

#

Fred's fingers move up and down the violin's neck, pressing notes for the bow to resonate. Sending joy throughout the night air. It feels good to do so. It uplifts his spirits.

All the while he plays, he remembers past times. Of Eldora and her soft skin. Her smile. Her willingness to accompany him despite possible hardship. Not knowing what might be in the future. Even if she could have foreseen the outcome, she would have still taken the journey. His Eldora would have followed him to the ends of the earth. The memory of Eldora's devotion floods his mind.

But it is time! To let her go and rest. He must pull the reins on self-pity. Move forward. Leave the past in the past. Not forget Eldora but cherish her memory. It is time to give his new family, his new life, space to flourish and grow.

The new song Jack taught him easily expresses his loss and springs forth a new outlook. "The girl I left behind." A fine tribute to his lost love. *Things will be different.* This he vows. A joyful jubilation pours fourth from his violin. One that has never been heard of from such a sad song.

When he finishes the song, he feels a release of pain. A final tug on his heart to move towards a new future. To hold on to what he is given.

CHAPTER XXV

"That day is a day of wrath, a day of trouble and distress, a day of wasteness and desolation, a day of darkness and gloominess, a day of clouds and thick darkness,"
(*King James Version*, Zephaniah 1:15)

"May I join you?" Beth asks Fred, poking out past the front wagon bow.

"Ja, if you please." Fred welcomes the company. "The ground a little muddy today?" Fred slows the team allowing easier transition.

"Yes." she crawls out and sits close.

"Patrick asleep?"

"Yes. The gentle wagon sway helps calm him. I hope our travels continue having the same kind of gentleness."

"I don't think we will be that lucky." Fred points towards the distance. "I believe that is Courthouse rock. It looks rugged to me, no matter what they say."

"They say that the ground around it is as flat as a pancake."

"Don't they also say that about all the rocks around here? A priest inscribed on Chimney Rock the words, 'Remember one day you will die, your days are numbered.' I take that as a warning." Fred snaps the reins and narrows the gap between wagons.

Beth leans forward and looks at Fred. "How would the priest know what is to come?"

"Hmm, never thought about that." Fred must confess he likes Beth's inquisitiveness. "Premonition?" Beth always lights up when he uses big words. He thinks about Charlotte and her persistence in teaching. Fred never imagined needing such word knowledge. The women in his life, past and present, have had much influence. Beth's benefit on his life goes beyond all others.

"Maybe." Beth sits up and adds, "Perhaps he was sending a message like James 4:14, 'Whereas you know not what shall be on the morrow. For what is your life? It is even a vapor, that appeareth for a little time, and then vanishes away.'"

"That would seem more likely." Fred accepts the bible verse challenge and adds, "I think a more well-known verse like Psalm 23 should have been used."

"With the way people describe Chimney Rock the verse should have more reverence like Psalm 95:6, 'O come, let us worship and bow down: let us kneel before the Lord our maker.'" Beth clasps hands together and lies them down on her lap.

Fred smiles. "Ja. They say it is flat for many miles around. So why not call it Steeple Rock?"

"Amanda says that the Indians call it Elk Penis."

"Beth!" Her blatant indecency surprises him. "I like Chimney Rock better."

"I can see the top of it now. I will have to agree with its original name so far."

"I doubt you have ever seen an elk penis."

"I have seen my share of penises," Beth informs.

"Being the eldest in your family I am sure you have. But an elk penis is different."

"Is that Amanda running out towards the tall grasses?" Beth changes the subject.

"Ja. She has been going all morning."

"Are you all right, Amanda?" Beth hollers.

Amanda gives a weak nod that neither confirms nor reputes.

Concern crosses Beth's face. Fred worries that Beth or Patrick will get whatever is going around. That they will be taken from him. Fred cannot bear the thought.

#

"Beth you mustn't."

Beth climbs into Amanda's wagon box way before the request.

"Keep your distance." Amanda does not try to sit up.

"Where are your girls?"

Amanda looks more decrepit than the last time she saw her grandma. On her Death bed!

"They are with my mother," Amanda answers, weakly. Only her lips move.

"You think that this is contagious?"

"Not taking chances. That is why you should go. Go take care of your family."

Beth understands. A person must take care of the family given to them. A family that has become hers. "I will, after I take care of you." Beth wants to help, but not like she wrongfully did with Eldora. "Tell me what I can do."

"Please, go." Amanda says. Her voice vibrating concern.

"No. Please tell me what to do. Have you taken the pills you made?"

"I never got around to it. Please, dear, leave me," Amanda insists.

"I am not leaving you." Beth balks.

Pain wrinkles Amanda's forehead. "If you must do something then make Missus Klingman's tea." Amanda turns painfully to her side and curls up. Beth can hardly hear what Amanda says next, "She claims that equal parts sage, and the herb thoroughwort steeped in hot brandy saved her child." Amanda takes a moment to catch her breath. "It can't hurt to try."

"I will make you some."

"I feel it is too late for me. I meant for you to make for your family."

"I don't accept that." Having something to do, anything, that might help bring the spring back in Amanda's step fuels Beth's determination. "Perhaps it will help, even if it is a little. It is never too late to try and pray. I shall do both."

Amanda gives in to Beth's dogged stoicism. "Okay. I pray that the merciful be with me."

#

"Death! It will soon surround us all, this 'Vibrio Cholera.'" Doctor Ferdinand Hayden announces as he dismounts Amanda and Jack's wagon. Brushing hands against lapels as if to disperse the disease away.

Beth barely remembers a doctor being among the travelers. Fresh out of schooling, she hears. Having a medical doctorate from some eastern college. Beth does not like his stoic composure or his apathetic disposition.

"Dehydration, that is how it claims victims," Doctor Hayden states, then he is gone. Retreating swiftly between wagons before the echo of his words and their meaning absorbs into the audience.

Beth wants to speak with him. So, she intently tracks him through the caravan. The doctor walks some distance away. He crouches out of sight in a buffalo wallow. Beth follows, surprising him when she steps into the depression.

"What on earth!" He says, "Are you following me?"

"Yes, I want to know. Will Missus Lamme die?" Beth is afraid she knows the answer.

"Nice to meet you too, I am being a gentleman and Doctor should get up, but I just sat down." He digs out a notebook and pen. "But this you already know. Most certainly."

"Sir, you are most rude."

"As are you." Doctor Hayden opens his journal and starts writing. His letters are sharp and spike across the page. Beth can see fountain pinpricks press and scratch through the paper.

"Amanda is my friend. Will she die?" Beth asks, her tenacity demanding an answer.

"I have already answered you."

"No, you have not!"

"When I said, 'most certainly,' I was answering you." Not bothering to stop writing or look up at her.

"You uncaring..." Beth continues into unladylike words, so upset that the bad words seem to repeat and never stop.

Ferdinand reluctantly stops writing and calmly looks up at her. "Missus Lamme is very dehydrated and will surely die."

He doesn't mention Beth's language. All he can say is 'most certainly' and 'surely die.' Beth wants to run and hide. She tumbles down like a tree trunk being chopped, falling to the ground. Beside the doctor, knees to her chest. The wet ground dampens her dress. "I cannot take any more sadness," Beth says, hands to face. Losing Amanda to a dreadful disease hits her hard. "Not another friend," she whispers. She cannot cry. Mainly because Ferdinand continues to write. Like ignoring her is some sort of doctoring strategy. Perhaps a technique begging emotion. She will not give him the satisfaction. The doctor's actions infuriate Beth. Causing her sadness to stand aside for anger. Just as she is about to unleash this anger…

"Take a look at this," Dr. Hayden digs into his bag. He unwraps a large tooth from a handkerchief. "It is a fossilized tooth of a mammoth, I believe."

"People are dying! And you are showing me a tooth!"

"Yes. It is a prehistoric animal that roamed the earth a long time ago. These bluffs and rocks bear evidence of animate beings once living. You see, animals, like people, die. But their memory of existence continues."

"I don't want a memory. I want my friend to live."

"I understand." The doctor wraps up the tooth and hides it back away. Looking miffed saying, "but, there is nothing I can do." He jots down more words while saying, "I plan to leave the wagon train and head out searching for a colleague of mine. To show him what I have found. I hear he is up north in Yellowstone country."

"What kind of doctor are you? That you find some mythical dead creature more important than people in need of a doctor?"

"There is nothing I can do." Dr. Hayden doesn't look at her when he says the words that hit Beth like a rock. "It is out of my hands and expertise."

"From what I can see, you have no expertise, or care."

"You're incorrect, both accounts." He finally looks at her. "But if I show expertise I don't have, I will look like I can help when I can't. Cholera takes away life without any mind to care. I will be leaving to go do something that I can do for the betterment of mankind: to search for answers the past holds with the hope to find future answers.

The fossils may hold the answers as to why this area bears so much death."

"It is the past." Beth stands. "Go then! You coward! Go help no one." Tears heat up the corners of her eyes. Time to flee. Time to find refuge to shed tears that will not stop once they start.

"What was all that about, you and the doctor?" Fred asks helping her climb up into the wagon.

"Nothing," Beth replies, throaty. Holding back tears until inside.

#

In the dark, starless night, Albert's voice asks, "Do you think Father ever loved us?" Albert sits down and leans his back on the same spot Beth emerged from, distraught.

"In some way, perhaps." Fred joins him. "I plan on letting Patrick know without a doubt."

"Good plan, brother. I plan to let my children know as well." He turns towards Fred. "We haven't told anyone yet. Because we aren't sure. Rosie thinks she is with child!"

"Congratulations, brother!" Fred squeezes Albert's shoulder. "Is that why you requested stockade duty tonight for me?"

"That, and the night-watch gets lonely."

Gazing into the darkness, Fred understands.

"Besides, it is your turn."

"Ja. I was due."

"Try not to fall asleep."

Little chance of that, thinks Fred. Picket guard duty gives several hours to think. Beth's actions today play out in his mind. Seeing her talk emotionally to another man conjures doubt, anger, and jealousy. Beth's earlier emotional display and intensity makes him wonder if their squabble was more than concern for Amanda. Perhaps a lover's quarrel. Angry at himself for not paying closer attention to Beth's comings and goings. But her freedom is what she requests. Maybe his jealousy is unfounded. Still, he feels it in his very being. Fred wants to hold Beth tight in his arms. Close. Claim her forever as his own. Let her know there is no other man who could love her more. Fred doesn't know what to think or do. He only knows there is an agreement stopping any physical affection. The kind he wishes to give. The kind he thinks about more and more these days and nights.

"I wish you would change your mind and come to California with us."

"Ja. Nein. I am more a country boy."

"They have country in California." Albert insists.

"I am sure they do. But I fear that road is a hard one to travel."

"You're not talking about the physical road are you. You're talking about a road full of hornswoggling, flimflam, and chicanery." Albert smiles.

Fred smiles. "You should flourish in such an environment," he says, giving a slap on Albert's back like the one Conrad placed with that same statement months ago. "We have come a long way." He puts his arm around Albert and then quickly pushes him away.

"Without seeing any footpads or muggers."

Fred chortles. "There is still time."

"Not if I can help it."

Not if Fred can help it either. He lights a cigarette and folds his arms across his chest. "Do you think Beth loves me?"

"Of course. In some way," Albert says with a smile.

#

Patrick stirs early, just as the sun rises. Beth sleeps. Quietly, Fred picks up his son and takes him outside. Patrick, as usual, happily kicks the whole time Fred tries to change his soiled diaper. He makes it difficult to replace a diaper that is snug. So, it is unable to stay on. Especially with Patrick's exuberance. Fred searches for help. Finding Disa he says, "This boy of mine is losing his diaper."

"Here, here, let me see." Taking him. "I have him now. Why don't you go see what that is all about?" She nods her head towards a commotion surrounding Jack and Amanda's wagon. "It can't be good." A little adjusting and Disa fastens the diaper snug and tight.

Jack breaks away from the crowd and approaches. "Excuse me Missus Rauser, Fred." He takes off his hat and looks down. He moves his finger across the hats stitched brim. "Amanda didn't make it to the morning."

"So sorry to hear that." Disa reacts solemnly.

"Sorry, Jack," Fred says. He is sorry that another family must deal without a mother. "It is a sad day." Remembering his losses, the day he lost his mother and the day Patrick and himself lost Eldora.

"There are too many of them as of late," Jack adds. "Be sure to tell Beth before the others do, will you?" He positions his hat where it belongs on is head.

"Ja. Anything I can do?"

"No. Thank you. Amanda's father and I will be going up to that small knoll yonder to…," he chokes up, swallows hard. "To bury her."

"You sure you don't need another set of hands?"

"I appreciate it. But this is a family matter."

"I understand."

"I know there is no need to tell you that there will be a delayed start today," Jack states.

Fred does not look forward to telling Beth the sad news. Patrick keeps Disa focused away from sadness. Children tend to do that. Fred hopes that Jack's three girls will help him manage. Like Patrick has been for him. Hopefully Patrick will be for Beth. But Fred is afraid that nothing will help Beth. Amanda's death may overwhelm her.

"Beth, dear, time to get up."

"No."

Fred climbs into the wagon and lies beside her. "Then we will both stay in bed today. It is just too sad a day." Beth turns to face him. He can see she understands.

"Amanda is gone," she says to confirm as tears, like a spring, start to flow.

Fred invites her to come close. Without hesitation, she tucks herself into his chest. Like she belongs right there. She does. As long as she likes.

#

"I won't," Jack shouts at the wagon master. "Amanda needs a proper marker. She deserves that much."

"You have responsibilities to the wagon train," John sputters.

"I am going back to Fort Kearney to get my wife a headstone."

"You can order one at Fort Laramie," John informs. "There I can obtain your replacement."

"You know that they are slower than molasses in January when it comes to unusual requests," Jack says. "Can't imagine how long a gravestone will take."

Fred adjusts Bobby's bottom harness chain and loudly says to Albert with hopes to be overheard, "I cannot believe it is such a bother to let a man do what he feels he must do."

Albert tightens Ingrid's leather strap. "Yes. I see no harm in that," he says, as loud as Fred did.

"Mind your own business," John snaps.

"I am going, and you cannot stop me." Jack stomps off.

"I can do Jack's Job," Albert offers.

"I don't want a replacement. I want Jack to stay on."

"Really, I can. He has taught me everything he knows." Albert continues his request.

"I believe he can do the job," Fred says. Albert's bold initiative sparks deep pride.

"Very well then, I will give you until we reach Fort Laramie to prove yourself. You start now. Go help that incompetent Mister Olsen out."

"I am off." Albert points out Ingrid's other leather strap. "You got this?"

"Ja."

"Line them up!" John's words reverberate through the humid summer air.

Fred cinches the harness. "There you go, Ingrid," he says, rubbing her nose and watching Albert work. *Albert will do just fine*, thinks Fred. Just as he will.

CHAPTER XXVI

"Her ways are ways of pleasantness, and all her paths are peace."
(*King James Version*, Proverbs 3:17)

Dick watches carefully, not truly understanding. "Why don't we use the crib I made? I can take it outside so we can keep an eye on her."

"It is the way," Sora says, laying soft buckskin down on top of the cradleboard. The leather overshadows the two-foot-long piece of wood cut to Sora's specifications. The hard wood hoop he softened with leather to protect the girl. He can see now that it doesn't matter since the child will be far from the hoop. That the hoop is just to protect their child if, God forbid, is accidentally dropped. "Husband, I have told you, this is so the baby grows straight and strong." She places a square blanket down on top. Cattywampus. Corners pointing north, south, east and west. Folding the top, northern corner down a bit. "It will keep her from kicking the covers off like she does at night."

"She has always been a kicker. Way before she was born. Why restrict her now?" He is afraid that such a device will hinder his girl from loving the land. But then again, Aliza had no such device.

"Now, watch," Sora instructs, placing a piece of white bark down the middle.

"Where did you get the bark?" Dick knows there is no aspen or birch trees available for miles in any direction. The Platte River harbors none. Nor the Pumpkin River bottoms.

"Milwaukee supplies," Sora answers, putting some cattail fluff down onto the bark. "Come here little one," she says, placing the baby's bottom on the fibers. "You fold in this corner, tuck tight."

The baby struggles against the bondage.

"And the other side tucks around her back."

The girl cries.

"That's too tight. She doesn't like it." Dick intervenes.

Sora swats him away like a fly. "Give her time. She will get used to it. You watch me finish, so when you get a chance, you will know how to free her." Sora smiles at Dick. "Maybe, you don't need to watch. You go again. Leaving baby and I alone."

"I am only going to Fort Kearney for supplies."

"It is long way. Almost as long as Taos."

"I will do my best to make it a quick trip."

Sora resumes instruction. "Slip this strap through these straps attached to the board. Like this," Sora informs, showing. She weaves the one-inch strap back and forth like a shoelace. Careful to exhibit the embroidered, decorative floral design.

"What if our child would have been a boy?" Dick asks pointing to the flowers.

"I made bird straps for him. Someday we may have a boy."

The closer Sora gets to the baby's feet, the more she kicks rebellion. Cries turn into screams.

Dick softly rubs the baby's face, talking baby talk. "I think she likes birds better. You do, don't you, little squirrel?" *Better still, not to be restrained*, thinks Dick.

"Are you paying attention?"

"Yes, but I don't understand. I don't think she does either."

Sora gives Dick a stern look and continues, "Bring up the bottom end and tuck before you do the last few." The kicking minimizes.

The cries stop, a huge breath, and then screams. Ear piercing screams.

"There, finished." Sora picks up the contraption. Bounces a gentle rhythm and adds soothing hums. Screams become cries, whimpers and stops. The baby smiles. "We are ready to plant her tree."

"You may be able to lull her by your sweet humming, but she looks trapped."

"Here, you hold her. I have to attach her spirit pouch."

"That is one of my missing tobacco pouches," Dick says. What once was a plain tobacco bag is now an ornate pouch. Similar to the one that hangs on Sora's neck. A repeated pattern of colorful beads. Cut up porcupine quills intermingled between. A flower design made from seashells.

Small and intricate beadwork. Finest Dick has ever seen since Milwaukee's haversack. The baby's umbilical cord knot centers the flower. Dick suspects another tobacco bag has a bird on it.

"There you have something to look at," Sora says. She finishes tying a knot tight and strong. Similar to the one she secured on Dick's wrist. The spirit bag dangles above the baby's head.

"That is all she can do! Is look at it."

"And it is like your mother's, see," fondling her own spirit bundle. Grabbing Dick's arm, she points out his friendship bracelet. "With same string and beads. Just like Father's."

The girl kicks her feet free.

CHAPTER XXVII

"...I bare the loss of it; of my hand didst thou require it, whether stolen by day, or stolen by night."
(*King James Version*, Genesis 31:39)

Rhythmic, lulling, pitter patter raindrops land against canvas. They cannot induce sleep. By the sounds of it, yesterday's thunderstorm is coming to an end. Unlike the troubles Beth faces. Tears drip onto her pillow. Beth hears Patrick and Fred's steady breathing. Their bodies close and radiating warmth. Unaware of her recent distress.

The day can stay away. There is no reason to face it. Beth fears that today will surpass all others. All those other days, that in an instant kindled change.

A lightning flash illuminates her blessings. A thunder burst accents her fears. Neither can she control.

Beth's midsection cramps, ever so slightly, then slowly subsides like countless times before. Damp stickiness between her legs gives no doubt. A deep heartbreak swallows her up. *This is too much, I can't take any more*, she silently pleads to God. Beth dreads the day's beginning.

"Errt-err-uh-errrr," a rooster's crow encourages the day.

Fred groans.

Beth whispers, "The morning chores can wait." She frets his reaction to another loss. More tears well up.

Fred cuddles close. Vexation quickly wrinkles his face. "You're wet!"

Tears drop like the pitter-pattering rain. They hit the pillow soundly. Beth lifts the blankets to give palpable confirmation.

"No!" Fred's eyes blur with tears. His thumb caresses her tear-soaked cheek. Cupping his hand around her ear, he tucks hair away from streaming tears. They outpour faster than the rain from the clouds. His anguish-stricken face attunes to her heart.

Patrick fusses.

Fred kisses her forehead gently. Then his forehead meets hers. Eye to eye he says, "I will see if your mother will take care of him."

"Stay."

"Believe me, Beth, I want to. Patrick needs a change," Fred hesitates as if to add "too."

"I am not ready to face this," Beth says, suppressing emotional explosion. Holding back sobs.

"I will be right back."

"Please, don't go." Beth grabs his sleeve tightly, hoping to keep him. "Stay just a little longer. I am not ready to let anyone know." Beth wants Fred's comfort. Needs his comfort. She wants to cherish this genuine bond longer. Forever. A craving hope that it will transcend loss.

"I will come right back. You can tell your mother and anyone else when you are ready." He kisses her forehead, again, emotionally, and says, "For right now, it is like any other day." He picks up Patrick. "Besides, you know John will be rushing us along like a herd of cattle to the market," he says, imitating Jack's southern drawl. Trying his best to bring some humor into the situation. But he just sounds like a southern German gentleman. "I will be back most promptly."

Beth forces a smile.

"Besides, I'm not inclined to start this disheartening day," Fred continues, an emotional waver in his voice. He pulls the canvas closed.

#

Why? Confusion muddles Fred's mind. It hurts his head and chest to contain how he feels. *Why, God, why? Why take an innocent child?* He screams internally as he walks.

Fred whispers outside the Hess' wagon. "Excuse me?"

"Yes," Lyna replies, peeking out.

"I am incompetent when it comes to diapers. And I didn't want to wake Beth." He lies. "Can you take care of Patrick?"

"Sure, my pleasure, always." Lyna reaches out and says, "Come here my little sweetheart."

"Thank you." Fred hesitates too long.

Lyna face furrows with seriousness. "Is something wrong?"

"Nein," Fred flatly denies as he returns to Beth.

"She's not sick, is she?" Lyna voices worry. "With the cholera? She did spend too much time with Amanda for my comfort."

"Nein," He states, firm. Saying no more as he continues to walk away. *Cholera would be worse*, thinks Fred. A loss of a child is hard enough, but Beth as well. He can't bear the thought. He finds it in himself to understand his father. Suddenly, Father's actions make sense. Father must have believed that if you don't love or care, you cannot feel the pain when it is lost.

Fred can hear Beth's sobs get more intense as he gets closer. Longing to comfort, but fearful. Beth may have come to change her mind. Realize the freedom this allows. Freedom to abandon him and Patrick. He barely opens the canvas door. *Does she still want him?* He wonders.

"What's wrong?" Lyna interrupts, sneaking up behind him.

Startled, Fred releases the canvas. Forsaken awareness may have cost him precious time with Beth. Perhaps even to console any doubts.

"Elizabeth Magdalyna Hess," Lyna says. "Are you sick?" Lyna scrambles up into the wagon bed to see for herself.

Beth lets out a huge despairing noise, like the cry his father made alongside mother's limp side so many years ago. It brings back the emotional memory. It adds further sorrow. Standing hopeless and feeling great loss. All alone, Fred becomes a spectator as Lyna takes control. "I am sorry, Beth."

"A mother knows," Lyna says, looking right at him, then back at Beth. "You will learn this someday. This is only a bump in the road."

Or like a huge rut in the trail, thinks Fred.

Lyna discreetly hands him Beth's wedding quilt. The pattern reminds Fred of one that wrapped Eldora. A tear forces its way out and down his cheek. His back hand wipes it away. He can smell the blood, but no blood shows.

"Don't just stand there. Go wash it before everyone is awake. No need to announce it before Elizabeth is ready."

Fred's body complies. Leaving behind his wife. Sadness overwhelms and clouds his mind. Sadness for Beth, himself, and Patrick. Dreading what this day brings.

#

Fred puts the shovel down. Takes off his hat. Runs fingers through his hair. The prim and proper appearance that Beth admires every day from Fred, rain or shine, is missing. Something Beth has come to view as refreshing amongst a sea of those lacking it. Whiskers and mustache not neat and trim. His pocket watches perfectly placed half loop chain doesn't dangle out the lower right vest pocket. The vest unbuttoned. Shirt tails hang over his pants. Fred looks disheveled as he tucks the hat under his arm and patiently waits.

Beth's palm holds a lifeless tiny fetus. The little girl smaller than the potatoes harvested almost a year ago. Rampant thoughts replay. *What did she do wrong? Why? What will people think? What will she do now?* Looking down at the peaceful little body, Beth thinks, *you will never grow up. You will never play in the dirt.* Beth looks at the hole in the mud. *You will never squash mud between your toes. Get married. Have children.* Beth pauses, swallows. *Feel the rain or snow on your face. Or the wind blow hair tickles across your cheek.*

Beth wraps her kerchief delicately around the fetus. "May you rest in peace, little Elle." Beth kneels and places her gingerly in the muddy ground. A tiny hole no bigger than the width of a shovel.

Fred kneels and invites Beth into his arms.

She leans into his chest. Drizzle droplets fall on her cheek. There is no rush. Even the wagons are not moving in this muck. This day is much too miserable.

Fred replaces his hat and bends over, providing a partial canopy. "And Jesus said, Suffer the little children to come unto me, and forbid them not: for of such is the kingdom of God."

Beth adds her own bible quote, "For behold, the days are coming when they will say, 'Blessed are the barren and the wombs that never bore and the breasts that never nursed!'"

"Don't say that! You are still a young, vital woman."

Beth pushes away. "What are you proposing?"

"Nothing. Just stating the fact." Fred stands. "Shall I." He picks up the shovel.

Beth regrettably nods.

Fred pats mud. It leaves a small, watery pool. Fred digs into his pocket and pulls out a rock. Kneels, saying, "For you, little one." The water surrounds it. "May a garden encircle you."

"That is the rock Christina gave you."

"Ja." He kneels beside Beth. "Christina didn't know I planted it in her garden to find."

"How sweet." Beth smiles. "I like the stripped pink and grey layers. It is very pretty."

"I look forward to someday meeting you, little one," Fred says, adjusting the rock ever so slightly. "'But now he is dead, wherefore should I fast? Can I bring him back again? I shall go to him, but he shall not return to me. And David comforted Bathsheba his wife, and went in unto her, and lay with her: and she bare a son, and he called his name Solomon: and the Lord loved him.'" Fred grabs Beth's hand. "These past three months have been a pleasure with you by my side. You have helped me more than I can say. I have grown to love our friendship. I love you."

Beth squeezes his hand. "I love you too. You should know that. I cherish our friendship so much."

"Just know, I am here for you. Whatever you need. I owe you more than I can repay."

Beth lays her head down on his thighs. "You owe me nothing." She wants to tell him about Eldora. How she feels responsible. Now is not the time or place. There may never be a proper time or place. Beth instead embraces Amanda's sagacious words. *You cannot blame yourself for the course life takes.*

#

"Come join me," Fred requests. Beth attempts an exit, faltering. Fred whisks her into his arms. "Let me assist you." Gingerly he places her under an awning. "Sit here. I will get a blanket."

"Thank you."

The blanket is damp just like everything else. He wraps the blanket around her anyway. It should still provide warmth. "There. Dinner will be ready soon."

"You are making dinner? You didn't have to. I am sure Mama or Disa would have plenty to share."

"They did offer and requested our company. But I didn't feel like company tonight. Thought you might feel the same."

"I do. But I am not hungry."

"Do I need to repeat King David's words."

"I am not fasting."

Fred cracks some eggs over sizzling potatoes.

"I thought you didn't like potatoes and eggs together?"

"I don't. But you do. So, I reckon I'd get used to it." Adding a southern drawl to his words.

"You reckon, do you," Beth mocks. "Where's Patrick?"

"With Disa. She insisted. More like demanded."

"I suppose it is best."

"She still grieves for Eldora and finds Patrick a comfort." Fred knows it will be hard on Disa when they part ways at Fort Bridger. Fred and Beth and the Hess' will be going north to Oregon. The rest will go south. Hildago tagging along with Albert and Rosina towards California. Phillip and Disa plan to pan for gold alongside farming. Phillip states that one shouldn't put their eggs all in one basket. So, Disa values this precious Patrick time.

Missus Olson solemnly approaches and whispers, "So sorry to hear about the baby. But it is for the best. A man can't be expected to treat another man's baby the same way they treat their own."

Fred suppresses anger at the blatant disregard for keeping a secret only a few had privy to. Fred wishes the Olsen's were somehow detained in New York or Independence. He tired of their prattle on the boat and has really become weary of their nonsense.

Missus Olson sits beside Beth and slaps her thigh, saying, "Sorry you lost your baby. Losing a child is very difficult." Folding her hands, looking pompous. "I know, I lost my second child, Caroline, to cot death. I was out hanging the laundry and came in to check on my sweet girl. She wasn't breathing." Slapping Beth's thigh again, she adds, "Anyway, I hope you have plenty of other children, like me, to fill the void. Besides, the child would have been a constant reminder of the unpleasant past. You must believe that it is God's will."

She gets up and leaves before Fred reacts.

"That pernicious bitch," Fred says under his breath.

Beth hangs her head and stares at the smoking coals. Fred fears she will flee into a cocoon like she did on the boat, never to emerge. Fred places a log in Beth's sight.

"Where did you get wood?"

"That unpleasant woman's cowardly husband traded his night-time shift watching animals for it."

"I think your time is worth more than that one log."

"That is why I didn't settle for less than four." Fred points to the other three. It should keep the dampness at bay tonight."

"Here, Bethie, dear, I made some raspberry tea with a touch of milkweed." Lyna gently presents as she sits beside her daughter. "Hope you are alright. This should ease the pain of a birth your body believes occurred."

"And milkweed to ease my mind," Beth says. "Thank you, Mama. I suppose later you will make some rose hip tea to ease cramps."

Mama's eyes twinkle. She exhales a burst of air, smiles and says, "I can hear Mister Gabor saying it would be a waste to use rose hips for anything else but palinka."

"Maybe palinka is what I really need," Beth says.

"This tea will do just fine." Mama kisses her head. "Blessed are those who mourn for they shall be comforted." Mama quotes scripture.

Mama disappears as Beth brings the hot beverage up to her lips and blows warm steam into her face. Fred's impression is that Lyna's concern does just as much for Beth's health as the tea.

Fred stirs the potatoes. "How can a God-fearing woman like Missus Olson, who knows what you have been through, say such things?" Missus Olson's words still sting. Fred should have responded. *It isn't God's will to give sickness. It isn't god's will to let people die. To be violated. To deny a child to suckle a mother's breast.* Grease spats hit his hand, changing his focus. He fills up a metal plate and tops it with hard tack, thinking, *she will need tea for that tough, solid cracker.*

"I agree. It isn't right for her to be so insensitive."

"It can't be God's will for her to be so heartless." He hands her the plate and says, "Here, eat," and sits beside her.

"I don't want any." Beth refuses.

"You need to eat." Fred takes the tea, and reiterates, "Eat some." Beth reluctantly takes the plate, placing it on her lap. "I didn't want to mention it while your mom was here, but I have some of Mister Gabor's palinka. You eat some," pointing at the potatoes, "and maybe I will share."

Beth forks the food about and pushes the hard tack aside. She treats her meal like little Christina would, showing repugnance. Finally, she pierces a potato and nibbles off a piece. "Not bad." She finishes that piece and forks another.

Fred half fills a cup with Gabor's Hungarian alcohol. "Here you go."

"Well, that goes down better than tea." Beth takes another gulp. She turns and places the back of her hand on his whiskers, and says, "Thank you."

He grasps her hand, moves it to his lips and gently kisses.

CHAPTER XXVIII

"Hatred stirreth up strifes: but love covereth all sins."
(*King James Version*, Proverbs 10:12)

The morning air is stale like the view. The wagon's seat bounces to Bobby and Ingrid's in step rhythm. The movement prevents reading or embroidery. Beth stretches out the crocheting on her lap. The scarf looks more like a crooked bull snake that swallowed too many mice. Frustration forces her to unravel and abandon the effort. The unpleasant past day's events cling onto Beth's heart. Like the hot humid air makes her blouse cling. Bobby and Ingrid's rhythm motivates a dull song. "Ingrid and Bobby, move fast and slow, together as one. Friends to the end. Their rhythm always flows with pooh, stinky, stinky pooh. Yet they stay friends forever more," Beth sings. "They never fatigue on their offensive, boring journey."

John rides up alongside, saying, "I have been meaning to talk with you two."

"What about?" Fred's eyes forward.

"I am sorry to hear about your loss yesterday. Was busy all day trying to keep things dry." He rests his forearm on the saddle horn. "You will find it easier to travel without its hindrance."

"Whoa." Fred commands. The oxen stop. "I reckon you believe all these children collecting buffalo chips are hindrances too."

John straightens, making his saddle creak, and rides on.

"Coward," Fred mutters. "Get up!" He instructs. The ox team calmly recommences.

Beth puts a hand on Fred's thigh. Beth dwells on their losses. Losing a child is the hardest to bear. A child who will never experience this world. A baby they cannot hold in their arms. The trail is not easier without their baby.

"This is some curious land," Fred states.

"Yes. Yesterday I thought Courthouse and Jailhouse Rocks looked like someone dumped mud and formed a citadel."

"Hmm, I can see that. They have let it dilapidate. So, Chimney Rock, I won't mention its Indian name, could be Rapunzel's tower." Fred smiles. "I doubt it has a garden, though."

"Yes! You know the story?"

"The story was one of Christina's favorites."

Flat prairies surround the huge pillar as far as Beth's sight can reach.

"Ja. You would think erosion would expose more durable formations. Covering the land with more citadels to see. Making it hard to travel," Fred says. "I suppose it is just like people. Some are durable to withstand trials and others are not."

"I am not sure I am durable enough to handle any more."

"Ja. I have had my fill."

Henry runs by and jumps into the back of the wagon.

"Careful of Patrick," Beth pleas.

Henry maneuvers past Patrick without waking him. "Mama sent me to tell you some news. It is not good news," he says, plopping down between them.

"Tell me what?"

"Franny has the cholera."

Beth internally screams, *"No! Not little Franny! Not Amanda's baby!"* Feeling the wagon jostle side to side. Aware of the motion. Not much else. Beth wants to be anywhere but here. Go back in time. Back to the Motherland. Maybe, yes, Romania. To take flight. Hide. Scream. Definitely, scream! Loud and long. But Beth cannot muster what it takes. She just sits. Emotionally motionless.

Beth barely hears Fred ask Albert, "When is our next stop?" Their voices sound a hundred miles away. Their words slur in the distance. She sits. Unmoving. Barely aware, not caring.

"Just around that bend." Albert points.

"Good!" Fred says. "Can Beth ride Daisy?"

"Of course, I welcome the change," Albert says. He hands over the reins and dismounts.

"Beth, you should take Daisy for a ride. Beth, you want to take Daisy for a ride?"

Beth stares at oxen butts. Immersing herself into the tiny hair detail. Partly hearing the distant question. Partly aware of her surroundings, but totally unable to answer. Beth disallows anything and everything entry into her state of mind. Remaining comfortably numb. Refusing to be a part of the cruel world around her.

"Beth!"

Beth is lost. Deep inside. Only one other time did she freeze like this. The swab closet. Eons ago. While Shaun's hand clasped her mouth shut. While staring at a latch. Only seeing the latch. Like now, Beth can only see Ingrid's back side.

"Henry, crawl back and fetch a rag. Dip it in the water barrel," Fred commands.

Henry brushes Beth's arm but it doesn't jostle her free from her stare.

"Whoa, Bobby," Fred encourages the team off the trail. "Whoa! Bobby, whoa,"

"Here, Fred." Henry hands him the wet rag.

"Here take and water Daisy."

The rag feels good on Beth's forehead. Fred's caressing awakens her to his care. Bringing her back to him.

"I think you should take a ride with Henry. Get some fresh air and a new view." He turns Beth's face towards him and looks at her with those deep blue eyes. "If you feel up to it."

Fred's concern eclipses her sorrow. So will a ride. "I would like that," Beth says, finding the words. "It will be a better view." Right now, Beth admits to herself, it will be better than this wagon train and all the badness it contains. So much better than succumbing to nothingness.

Fred smiles.

Beth lavishes Fred with kisses on his cheeks, on his forehead. He saves her again. "Thank you, we won't ride long." Beth kisses Fred's lips.

"All watered up," Henry returns, averting his eyes.

"I trust you will keep view of the wagons." Fred jumps down and offers a helpful hand.

"Of course." Beth softly hums the previous tune and sings, "Goodbye butts of poo,"

"What?" Fred briefly flusters. He looks at the oxen butts, then smiles back understanding.

#

"Henry! Use that telescope of yours and see if that woman is okay." Beth slides off Daisy's back and assists Henry.

"I don't see her moving. See for yourself."

Hate and anger floods her, briefly. Holding the telescope brings back Shaun's exploitation. A flash memory of a closet's latch. She brings it up to her eye and struggles to focus until she finds a reference point. "There," she says, finally obtaining a view. A half-built cabin semblance sticks out of a side hill.

"Did you hear that?" Henry nudges her view away.

"Henry! It took me a long time to see anything through this contraption." Beth points to the small circular hole.

"Sorry."

"Waaaah! Waa!" Piercing cries echo in the wilderness.

"There it is again."

"I heard it this time. Sounds like a baby."

"Or a dying rabbit!"

"That's not true. Rabbits don't make that noise."

"Yes, they do," Henry says, standing strong and confident. "Jack taught me how to do that noise to attract coyotes and wolves." Henry screams a mimic cry demonstration. So similar to the cry they hear and turns his face red with the effort.

"Whatever for? Please stop."

"To bag those varmints," Henry says, calmly, "so they don't come and eat Rosie's chickens."

She lifts the scope once again. This time anchoring a thumb against her temple. It challenges the focus attempts but allows her to pinpoint objects faster. She looks past poultry netting and nervous chickens to something leaning against the cabin entrance. Beth turns the focus knob too far and the object blurs. Slowly reversing the knob direction, it becomes clear. It is a cradleboard! She remembers seeing such a contraption at Fort Kearney.

"It helps to tuck your elbows more," Henry offers.

Beth surveys slowly around the area, incorporating Henry's suggestion. It takes less time to see a woman lying face down. Not moving like Henry said. Something is wrong. Seriously wrong. Handing the scope back to Henry, she says, "You're right, she isn't moving. You and Daisy go get Papa."

"I won't leave you, alone, again. Remember last time."

Beth lifts him onto Daisy. "I will be alright. You mind me and hold tight!" She gives a quick slap to Daisy's hind quarters.

"Lizbeth," Henry's distraught voice trails off into the distance.

The evening shadows and the woman face down encourage haste. Beth walks briskly. Buckbrush tugs her dress. The woman's position indicates it is too late. Her head lies unnaturally twisted. Roof sod dangles precariously above the body. Beth gasps! A ladder rung sticks out of the woman's back.

Baby's wails get louder and stronger. Movement catches Beth's eye, just beyond the child. Slinking cautiously. Bigger than coyotes. Much bigger! Their approach eerily intimidating. *Wolves!* Beth realizes. The baby's cry must have summoned them. Beth runs and runs hard. Her fast pace stops the wolves' advancement. One wolf menacingly glares. Amber eyes glint like fire in the sunset. Beth snatches the baby and the contraption tight and lifts the door handle. Her shoulder hits a hard, solid impact into the door. It doesn't budge. *Harder, she must do it harder*. Beth slams her whole body into it. It budges free and flies open, throwing her forward into the cabin and almost onto the floor. Juggling for balance, she maintains composure long enough to kick the door closed. *Safe!* She plops on the rocker in exhaustion.

"WAAAH!" The child was having none of it.

"Can't you give me a minute. I just saved your life."

"WAAAH!"

Beth rises. She looks out the only window, just an opening above the sink. Wolves sniff the mother's body. One brave wolf licks blood and growls the others away. Beth grabs the first object available, a wooden spoon, and flings it. "Get! Go on! Get away from her!" Her aim skims across the brave one's back. It causes a chain reaction flight. "Good! Stay away!"

"How do we get you out of this contraption?" Beth says to the infant, laying the contraption and baby down upon the table. "You are all bound up. Let's see." She loosens a knot close to the baby's exposed feet. With each strap pulled free, the baby kicks. More and more skin visible. Buck naked, to Beth's surprise. "You are a little girl, aren't you?" She picks her up.

The girl reaches for Beth's breast. "I don't think that will provide anything for you. Let's find something else." Beth's breasts ache to oblige. Beth hums and bounces. Debating what will satiate the infant. "Observe!" She animates, "A dishrag!" Waving it about. Cries subside. She dips a corner into a milk pitcher. The girl ravenously sucks the cloth dry. Over and over again until she abandons interest. Reaching. "I am too tired to argue," Beth says, making herself comfortable on the rocker. "We will try." She cannot loosen her blouse fast enough. The baby latches tight. Painfully tight. Suckling with zeal. "Oh, dear!" An engorged breast welcomes the infant's gusto.

Beth tries to remove what appears to be a brass tube in the baby's hair. It is woven into the tiny fine strands. "What is this? How do you even have enough hair for that?" The child ignores Beth and settles into a soothing rhythm.

A large bang amplifies the room. "Are you alright?" Fred asks as the door slams the wall. Worry floods his face. "You promised to keep the wagons visible."

"I made no such promise. I am all right. Look what I found."

Papa enters, scolding, "You shouldn't have," he pants, "gone off, alone," he puffs out air, "like that." Papa puts his hands to his knees. Gasping. Hunching over, catching his breath, He chastises, "Elizabeth Magdalyna Hess, what were you thinking?" He asks, inadvertently forgetting her married name.

Beth ignores them both. The little child wraps her fingers around Beth's pinky and her heart.

#

Fred cannot stand to look at the sight anymore. Beth is radiant and happy feeding a child. Reminding him of the child that was just lost. Not his child, but a child he looked forward to holding. Fred can imagine that this is how Beth would have looked caring for Elle. When Ludwig arrives, Fred takes that time to exit.

Beads tinkle when John overturns the woman's body. John's head shakes negative. "The ladder somehow punctured her."

"Did she fall off the roof? Or did the ladder give out on her?" Fred asks.

"I am not sure," John answers.

The sun sets brilliant color in the sky. Fellow traveler's voices a quarter mile away echo in the valley. Clear, distinct talk. Preparing for the night. Fred feels an eerie, empathetic sadness towards his father. A sort of kinship loss. One he recently learned all too well and that this child's father will soon come to feel. An emotion that touches his heart and inundates with memories. A pain that tugs deep into his soul.

John instructs two men that road in with him to bury the woman deep. "There is wolf sign. Use her necklace to mark the grave. We wouldn't want any Indians looking for her amongst us."

"Why? What would be the harm?" If it were Fred's wife, he would want to question anyone who would know how she died.

"Most Indians will shoot first and ask questions later."

"That's ridiculous! No one would be alive to answer." Fred gives John an incredulous look.

"Indians are hard to understand. So are fur trappers. Why they marry these squaws is beyond me."

"How do you know she is married to a trapper?"

"She wears a wedding ring. That is not the Indian way," John says as they carry the woman away. "And those oval frames over there," pointing, "are fur stretchers." John's voice turns harsh. "Is your wife inside this makeshift, half-built, hovel?" He walks up and peers inside the cabin. He squeezes Fred's arm solid and firm. "This is bad."

"What is?"

"The child," John states. "I am unfamiliar with this squaw's tribe. Chances are they will have the notion to act out badly once they learn that white people have one of their own. The child will have to stay with its mother." John wraps his hand around his pistol grip.

"What do you mean?" Fred cannot believe it. Beth and Ludwig's joyful expressions surround the infant. "What are you proposing?"

"A dead Indian raises curiosity. Possibly more death. Where a kidnapped child will certainly provoke violence and death. I will not have that child bring us trouble. The baby stays."

"Surely you don't mean what I think you mean." Fred wants clarification.

"I think it is very clear what I mean." John unholsters his gun. "I will not have that child ride amongst my wagon train." John attempts entry, his face showing determination.

"No!" Fred breaks free and stands, blocking progress. "It is only a child."

"Don't stop me from what must be done."

The child admirers look at Fred, wondering. "It's not right to kill an innocent child."

"Get out of the way."

"No, I will not," Fred says, firmly. "We will stay with the child."

"Yes, we will!" Beth confirms, lighting up like a Christmas tree and standing up next to him.

Fred wraps his arm around Beth's waist and in solidarity, they stand firm. Consensus against John. A proud decision against a man who has spun boundless stories about limitless pioneer hardships on the prairies. Looking past John, Fred can see this country, this place, is indeed alone. Yet, he feels safe and secure. Confident. Fred can live with this decision. "We will stay!" Fred repeats, pulling Beth closer. Wondering how anyone can purposely take a child's life? Destroy a living being. Fred is proud to be married to a woman that also believes as he does.

"Well, you are making a huge mistake. And be warned, you are asking for trouble. Someone will come for this baby and will not hesitate to kill for it." John holsters the gun. "You know not of what you ask for. It doesn't belong in the white man's world, and it doesn't belong in the Indian world. It is a doomed half breed."

"The child is an American." Ludwig speaks up behind them before Fred can voice the exact sentiment.

"A girl." Beth informs.

A girl! thinks Fred. *"How serendipitous,"* he replies, looking for Beth's understanding.

"Yes," she lifts her brows and smiles.

John approaches Fred. Eye to eye. "Bring your wagon and all your belongings here," pointing to the ground, "immediately!"

"Consider it done." Fred wants to slap a 'sir' to the end.

"And stay away." John looks directly at Beth. "Unless you change your mind. And it would be best that you do." He harshly glares at Fred. "Without it!" His eyes flicker towards the precious bundle Beth holds.

"It will be my pleasure keeping this baby away from you."

John sighs derision. "Mark my words, you will regret your decision."

As John leaves, the tiny girl reaches for Fred. Without thought, he complies. There is no doubt this is the right action. The baby tugs on his mustache. Who, now, can separate him from this little one?

#

"Oh, the poor child," Lyna says, wrapping her arms around Beth and the child.

Fred swoops to save the baby from an engulfing strong squeeze, leaving Beth free to hug her mother long and hard. No one, but God, knows when they will be together again.

Lyna stands back and says, "Here." I made you a brauche bag, placing a knotted kerchief around her neck. Lyna caresses the knot. "It contains charms and herbs to keep you safe." Lyna sniffles. Her hand gently touches the baby's head. "She is all alone in a world not of her making."

"No, Mama, she has us," Beth says.

"Ja!" Fred confirms.

"You two take good care of this little spud." Grabbing Beth into another hug. "As well as I know you can."

"Yes, Mama."

Pushing herself back, Lyna adds, "Plant yourself in the soil you find yourself standing on. And remember, Elizabeth Magdalyna, you are always in my heart." Lyna kisses her daughter's cheek.

"I will," Beth clears her throat.

"Now, now, you two. Both of you knew this day would come." Ludwig barges, demanding a hug. "Who knows the plan God has envisioned? Remember, home is where the heart is. Keep your heart pure, my dear."

"We will join the next wagon train," Fred tries to pacify.

"You cannot guarantee that," interrupts John. "Hurry this along." He points to Fred, saying, "I will send a message to Jack and have him check on you. I just hope it is not to bury your sorry asses." John rides off, yelling, "Wagons Ho!"

"Well, this might be goodbye, Albert," Fred says. "You will be heading south soon."

"Yes. Soon the trail splits and leads me to my riches. John is going to let me be second lead till then, since he is letting Hildago stay behind with you."

"Ja. John believes we need protection. So, you're moving up in the world! You have proven worthy of more than dishonor and shenanigans." Fred smiles. "Conrad and Father would be so proud."

"You mean surprised!" Albert chuckles.

Fred offers his hand, "Well, good luck, little brother."

"Thank you!" Albert bumps his shoulder against Fred's, gesturing a small, half hug. "You as well!" He turns and rubs the baby's hair. "And you too, little screamer." Kissing the little child's forehead.

"Don't be calling her that," Beth requests.

"Got to call her something. That is what she was doing when you found her." Albert says. "And all last night. The whole caravan heard her wails."

"The child just lost her mother," Rosie gives Albert an admonishing slap. She hugs Beth and whispers, "I hear that California isn't much farther than Oregon from here."

"Hildago," Albert demands, shaking his hand. Don't you dare let anything happen to my big brother and sister-in-law."

Hildago grips tight, vigorously shaking hands. He smiles and says, "It will be my honor and pleasure to keep them safe."

Fred worries Hildago only wishes to keep Beth safe.

Henry slams into Beth after patiently waiting his turn. Wraps his arms around her hips. "I think I will miss you most awfully."

Beth composes herself and kneels, holding his hands. Looking up at a fine young man, she says, "Let's hope and pray it won't be for too long."

Henry hugs with all his might. Tears well up in his eyes. Finally, he pushes back and says, "I have a present for you." He slips the telescope off his shoulders. "I want you to have this." Presenting with both hands. "So, you can keep a lookout for trouble."

"No, I can't!" Beth refuses.

"I really want you to have it. Please," Henry pleads.

Beth's eyes water as she says, "I will return your telescope when we see each other again."

Fred wishes it were that easy to look out for trouble. He hopes trouble never comes.

CHAPTER XXIX

"If I be wicked, woe unto me; and if I be righteous, yet will I not lift up my head. I am full of confusion; therefore see thou mine affliction;"
(*King James Version*, Job 10:15)

Dick dismounts Sally, unintentionally startling a man pushing a wheelbarrow, "Seems we are headed the same direction. Do you mind if I walk with you awhile?"

The man gains composure and says, "it will be my pleasure."

"Thank you. I was getting tired of Sally's non-responsiveness to my storytelling. You headed to Oregon?"

"California eventually," the man stops. He takes off his leather gloves and offers a handshake. "The name is Jack."

"Dick," accepting the man's blister bleeding hand, "pleased to meet you. You plan on wheeling that all the way?" *That would be an arduous goal*, Dick thinks. *Especially with those hands*.

"Nice to meet you as well. No. I don't plan much farther. Where are you headed?"

"About a few days walk down the road. I have a place just south of the trail."

Jack doesn't wince as he puts on his gloves. He turns the barrow around and walks with it behind. "I have about a day, perhaps two before I lose my load."

"If my memory serves me well," Dick knows it did, "there is nothing between here and the first out-thrusting rock formations ahead." He can barely see the tops in the distance.

"You mean Courthouse. Yep. Not much out here."

"Is that where you're heading?"

"Yes. My wife's grave overlooks the Platte to the North and Courthouse to the west."

"I'm sorry you lost your wife. That must be somewhere around Pumpkin creek?"

"Amanda didn't make it to the creek. I had hoped she would. The cleaner water would have done her good. But that heartless disease, cholera, took my dear Amanda like a thief in the night. And our sweet little baby girl soon after."

"I can't imagine losing a wife and a child."

"I learned of my daughter while at Fort Kearney obtaining Amanda's grave marker."

"That is what you carry? That is a heavy burden. May I?" Dick reaches to take the handles.

"No, thanks, I have it. It is my burden to bear."

"Please, let me." The memory of Jack's sore palms urges Dick's insistence, nudging. Jack's refusal nudge back shows spunk and resolution, something Dick admires. Not wanting to seem too pushy, he eases off. Maybe later Jack will change his mind. The wheelbarrow leaves a notable trail behind, indicating Jack's wife was cherished. Enough to validate this man's determination. "You must come and meet my wife. We live just after Chimney Rock and before you head south to California."

Jack looks at Dick directly. "I have instructions to check on some people just on the other side of Chimney rock."

"Whereabouts, exactly?" Dick knows that land harbors no inhabitants. It was the main reason he chose it. Sora gave approval by saying, "A house here would hide in plain sight and the view is endless." Nearby there is access to many trails. North and south, east and west. Dick hopes their view has not been hindered by these new neighbors. Dick awaits an answer. Jack's continuous steps give worrisome apprehension.

"These people are friends of mine. I'm told they are held up in a cabin built into a side hill."

Dick's heart sinks. It can't be? But it must be. "That is my place." Dick stops.

Jack stops and says, "If so, you need to know," lowering the load he carries. "They found a child."

"And the mother?" Dick stands firm, staring at Jack.

"They buried the mother."

"She's dead?" Saying it like a question, but his confusion wants an exclamation.

Jack hangs his head. His gloved hands fidget.

No! It can't be! Dick's mind battles what he wants to be true and what is more than likely true.

"I am sorry you had to hear it this way."

"Do you know any more? How did she die?"

"I was told she," Jack hesitates, "she died from a fall."

Jack's hesitation indicates he is holding back.

"Please, don't spare me. Tell me what you know." Dick wants to know anything and everything.

Jack slowly says, "She fell onto a ladder rung."

Dick is speechless. *It was his fault!* He should have known she would try to fix his messy chinking job. He should have known she would use the ladder he didn't fix. Where was Dick's mind? Where is his luck? Shiny stars falling out of the sky many years ago lied. There is no luck. Only bad luck.

"Your daughter is alive. Mister and Missus Klucke, friends of mine, are taking good care of her I assure you. They will care for your girl as if she were their own."

Why would they do that? Dick refuses to believe it is out of the kindness of their heart. He leans more towards believing that those Klucke's found a ready-made haven. One he built for Sora and himself. That they found it the perfect place to give up the rough trail life. Dick prepares to ride Sally as fast as possible home, even though nightfall is upon them, and Sally is tired.

"You might want to wait." Jack points. "Two is better than one." A man approaches from the east. "Tis the time of night when highwaymen cause trouble. You ready?" Jack's gun is in hand.

"No need," Dick says, halting Jack's alarm with an open hand.

"A friend of yours?" Jack cocks the gun.

"Relax, Milwaukee is harmless," Dick says. *And his timing impeccable*, Dick thinks.

"I am more worried about two men getting too close. I'll have you know I will put up a fight like a polecat. I'll also inform you that I carry nothing to fight for. All I own is headed to California except this headstone."

"Simmer down. You think we conspired to rob you."

"I don't know. Did you?" Jack is ready to shoot.

"Whoa! Wait a minute. Any fool can see you have nothing to steal." Dick broadly smiles.

"Is everything alright, Dick?" Milwaukee hollers.

Dick lowers his voice, asking, "I don't know. Is it Jack?"

Jack uncocks the gun and lowers it. "I reckon it is."

Dick states again, "We reckon that everything is alright, Milwaukee." But, of course, it is not. And will never be. Dick will have to tell Milwaukee Sora is dead.

#

Milwaukee pours some cornmeal into a cup and fills it with hot water and stirs. "Here, drink."

"What I really need is some white bark juice. Sora said it cures anything."

"It will not heal a heavy heart, my friend," Milwaukee answers. "Only a new season can do that."

"Or a slew of seasons," Dick states.

"In due time." Jack adds. "I reckon this season of my life will pass. Can't imagine what that will feel like."

Dick wants a past season. Where Sora is at home, waiting. The urge to get on his horse and ride like the storm inside him is strong. Not practical, but strong. There is nothing he can do that will bring Sora back.

Milwaukee sits next to him. "I must tell you of a vision. Many days back."

Dick stirs the corn mush.

"I made my bed under a big evergreen. Laid down and looked up into the branches."

Dick doesn't care.

"I was as cozy as a bug. Soon, the branches became intensely detailed. Each needle sharp. I stared deep at just one. I heard baby cries. I closed my eyes and saw the baby. I knew the baby. I did not know the white woman soothing the child. I felt a need to visit Sora."

"Why did I leave them?" Dick's fingers massage his head.

"I believe this to be true. Your baby, Sora's baby, is safe and happy in a white woman's arms."

"How can she be happy without Sora?"

"Fred and Beth will do everything they can for your daughter. They will take good care of your child," Jack says, repeating himself.

Dick cannot see anyone taking care of their child but Sora. Many things roam his mind as he watches the fire glow. Without Sora, there is no one to help raise their child. He can't do it alone. Taking a child to Taos will only raise questions. Sora would hate seeing her daughter being brought up by city folk. Dick rubs his brows. The thought horrifies him. Surely, he can learn to comply to city's restraints if it were the best thing for his girl. He crumbles a buffalo chip and throws pieces into the glowing ambers. *The girl is also Potawatomi*, he thinks, adding doubt. City life will crush her Potawatomi spirit. Fearing she too, will have to comply. Dick also fears living among the Potawatomi may steal his full devotion. Making him forget his Taos family altogether. He cannot bear that. Nothing seems right. Nothing feels right. His child belongs in two worlds. Just as Sora and himself planned. The glowing ambers deteriorate as he searches his mind for a possible resolution.

CHAPTER XXX

"Then shall the virgin rejoice in the dance, and the young men and the old together: for I will turn their mourning into joy. I will comfort them, and give them rejoice from their sorrow."
(*King James Version*, Jeremiah 31:13)

Beth enters the main room. "It feels so good!" Twirling before the fireplace. "So good." She leaps into Fred's lap like a happy child. Beth clasps her hands together behind his neck.

"What does?" Then Fred realizes. He can feel very little clothing between them. He readjusts her away from a sudden arousal.

"All this!" Her hand sweeps gently down her side, accenting her figure. "The freedom! To roam about in my nightshirt. The children are sleeping." She gives him a hug and multiple kisses. "I'm just comfortable."

Fred resists the urge to ease her to the floor. Return her affections and more.

Beth whispers into his ear. "I'm not wearing any undergarments."

Fred reacts abruptly. He stands with Beth in his arms, ready to proceed. Suddenly alarmed by the shocked look on her face. A look he saw once when she busted out of a swab closet. Fred is unsure she is ready for him to break the promise he made. He gains lost senses and places her in the chair they just shared. He lies to her, saying, "I forgot to do some evening chores." It is his turn to take flight. The sticky door refuses his retreat. Fred struggles the door free. The stubborn thing refuses to close behind him, making his exit almost comical. But Beth isn't laughing. Neither is he. Fred puts fixing the door on a mental chore list as he finally slams it shut.

"Trouble in paradise?" Hildago comfortably sits outside by a cozy fire. Just like the one Fred left inside. Fred feels stuck like the day Hans wanted to talk. Not wanting to be social. But not able to go back inside.

"Come join me."

Walking towards Hildago's roost reminds Fred of past needless worries. Despite Fred's conflict right now, things have been copasetic. It is clear Hildago respects the sanctity of his marriage, even though it doesn't stop the side glances. Sometimes Fred catches himself enjoying Beth's movements. *Enough of that!* Fred refocuses and says, "You look settled in for the night watch." Watching for a father's return that may never come. Over two weeks now they diligently take turns watching. Fred sits down on an overturned wooden feed bucket. He pushes his worries away.

"Just settling with my thoughts. How about you? Bedroom trouble?"

"None of your business." Fred prepares a cigarette, thinking on his love for Beth, Patrick and, yes, even little Christina. It grows more and more with each passing day. A bond too comfortable to break. The past proves that with comfort comes loss, sometimes great loss. Like Eldora. Like their baby. This comfort cannot last. Something always takes it away.

Hildago offers a lit stick. "So, why are you out here instead of indoors caressing that lovely woman?"

"Watch your words." Fred puffs the cigarette into life.

"You have a fine woman, a son to follow in your footsteps. What could be troubling you?"

"Nothing."

"What I can see is a woman looking for love and appreciation. If you cannot appreciate her, someone else will."

"Like you?" Fred's anger flares momentarily.

"No, she rejects me. I repulse her, I guess. She wants you. I see her love grow and blossom for you. You grow in love as well, no?"

Fred blows another puff of smoke into the summer's air. Hildago's words give his mind conviction. There is deep love for Beth. No one else can love her as much. So why does it bother him so much to show it? To really show it. He will allow her advances and be as gentle as a puff of smoke.

#

Sleep is not something you typically think about. Thinking keeps you from sleep, but that is all she can do. Think. *Why did he reject her?* Beth can only wonder and speculate. Does he think she is too forward? Not attractive? Will he always push her advances away? In order to keep a promise! Beth thought they were past all that.

Damn the arrangement. She wants a new one. Husband and wife. A family. Patrick, Christina, and Fred. Surely Fred can see this! Unless all he sees is how she affects his life. Or perhaps how without her how it affects his life. Or how Christina affects both their lives. Doesn't Christina bind them together? What will they do without Christina in their life? Will the man they call squaw man return and change everything? She cannot fathom the day. Her heart will be broken. And to continue with their arrangement will break her farther.

Beth's immense love kindles a need to change how Fred sees her. Not as someone to care for the children. Not as someone to put food on the table, clean dishes and the house. But as a wife! How dare he toss her like one of Mags' rag dolls? Like she means nothing. Treating her like nobody. Beth has lost too much. She needs Fred's love and companionship. Yes, she must help him see her more than a helpmate, companion, confidant. He must view her a worthy spouse. Capable of fulfilling his carnal needs. Fulfilling her needs.

'She is spoiled goods. She has lost her bloom.' Are words that echo in Beth's mind. They take root deeper than a seed potato.

That's why! Beth convinces herself. No one, no man, wants hand-me-downs. She muffles a scream into the pillow.

#

Fred pushes at the door. It slightly budges. Trying again, it swings and hits the wall. "Bam!" Same when closing. "Bam!" He walks up to the fireplace, squats and pokes the fire into night-time coals. All is quiet, but the fire poker's small scrapping sounds. A slap on the knee and he stands. Walking slowly, pausing at the bedroom threshold. He hears Beth's snuffled breathing. He didn't mean to hurt her. Fred whispers, "I'm sorry." He wants to hold her. Wipe away her tears. Explain why.

Receiving no acknowledgement. He eases himself onto the bedside and unties both boots. Taking them off. One by one they thud to the floor.

Beth lies still, hardly breathing.

Fred stands and removes his pants and hangs them on the peg. He hangs his shirt on top. He slips into bed beside Beth. The bed creaks as he shifts his weight to be close. Close enough to feel her warmth. Close enough to smell her tears.

"Don't! Stop!" she snaps.

"I am sorry, really I am."

Beth turns and faces him. She loudly proclaims, "You tossed me, without care. All I wanted to do was express how comfortable and happy I was to be your wife."

"I know." He caresses tears away. "I should not have treated the woman I love so poorly."

"No, no, you shouldn't!"

"I am just afraid."

"Of what?" She lowers her voice.

"Losing again."

"Oh, Fred," she states, rubbing her nose against his. "Can't you see that I am very fond of you. It would be impossible to leave you. I love you!"

"That is not what I am afraid of." Fred chokes out the words. "I am afraid of you dying."

Beth showers him with kisses. "We should only worry about today."

"You mean tomorrow."

"Perhaps, I mean tonight."

Fred embraces tight, never wanting to let go.

CHAPTER XXXI

"When a man is newly married, he shall not go out with the army or be liable for any other public duty. He shall be free at home one year to be happy with his wife whom he has taken."
(*King James Version*, Deuteronomy 24:5)

Beth scrapes some hot coals into a pile and places an iron tripod trivet over them. She carefully puts two logs, just so, on the remaining coals. She puffs and blows air unto the coals until the logs catch on fire and manifest exuberant flames.

Every morning, these past few weeks, Beth deems this cabin perfectly comfy. This morning it has an additional homey feel. Patrick sits gnawing on a pathetic crocheted toy shaped like a dog. Christina leis on a blanket, contently kicking. It feels like home.

Looking out the small kitchen window, Beth finds peace in the early morning light. One simple lever allows water down a wooden trough incline to the percolator. An ingenious system that brings a smile to her face. A barrel collects rain and gravity provides utilization. All without carrying or pumping. Unless there is no rain. Fortunately, there has been plenty of that. Amazing, methodical planning, including a way to dispose of the used water. Gravity brings the clean water down and gravity moves water along. Right out to the garden. Nothing like they do in the big city, but still amazing and efficient. She wants to live here forever.

Hildago lifts the poultry netting and drags it into a new spot, letting the chickens out to roam freely. Allowing him to gather eggs.

"Now none of that," Fred says, walking by the window.

"None of what?" She innocently replies.

"Looking at other men while they work." Fred hands her a bucket of milk through the window.

"Here are some eggs." Hidalgo adds and states, "And what makes you so sure she was watching me?"

"Maybe I was watching the chickens run free," Beth expresses, taking the eggs and placing them in a bowl. She carries the bowl of eggs and coffeepot to the hearth, hanging the coffee pot above the flames. She throws bacon grease into a cast iron skillet and sets it on the bracketed trivet. She watches the grease melt before cracking eggs.

The door slams against the wall as usual when the men enter.

Fred wraps his strong arms around Beth and says, "I'm fixin' to fix that door right after breakfast."

"You think you can fix the stubbornness out of it, do you?" Beth kisses him.

"Enough of that you two," Hildago says. "Not in front of the children."

"I don't think they mind," Fred comments. Picking up Patrick, saying, "Do you?" He nuzzles his stomach, making him laugh.

Yes, it feels perfectly comfy, thinks Beth. *It feels like home.*

#

"Hildago, do you see them?" Fred closes and opens the door smoothly.

"I have had my eye on them."

"How long have you been able to see them?" Fred is glad Hildago observes. Rasping the top door edge just a little more. Most of this days awareness was diverted to the task at hand.

"Not long. They just left the trail." Hildago scopes them out.

"We have company coming, Beth."

Wiping her hands on a dishrag, she stands at the threshold. "No, no. NO!" She whips the rag over her shoulder. "It can't be. I don't want it to be," she says, wrapping herself around his chest.

"It must be." A man pushes a wheelbarrow. Another holds a spotted-horse's reins. They walk with purpose towards Beth, Hildago and himself. The great view benefits them, giving ample time to consider a course of action. Fred feels safe here. At home. But it may be time to pack up and move along.

"Three men," Hildago says. "Here, look for yourself. I don't think they pose a threat."

Fred uses the telescope to survey and must agree. Henry's gift proves to be worthy.

"I was hoping this day would never come," Beth says.

"We both knew it would."

"I will put the kettle on and set the table. The stew is almost ready. I guess the cake I made was for company."

"Well, that is something to look forward to," Fred says, trying to lighten the sadness. Many nights, staring into the darkness, watching, Fred's thoughts were on this day. Keeping him awake. There was contentment when another day passed. Each new day hopeful. Melding together a family. *His family!* A family who will, once again, feel the pains of losing a child. And hear the words *"it is for the best."* It is nothing to anticipate. But cake is!

"Let me look again, please." Hildago requests. "Yes. I see a familiar walk."

"Who do you think it is?"

"Jack!" Hildago walks, then strides towards them.

"Jack!" Beth's excitement booms from inside the cabin.

"Ja." Hope cautiously returns.

#

"Hello Fred, you sure are a good sight for sore eyes and tired feet." Beth hears Jack's southern drawl. "I met up with these fine gents on the road."

A man with a wide brim hat drops horse reins and proclaims loudly, "My name is Dick, this is my home!"

Through the window, Beth sees him walk past Fred. Beth's heart quickens with refusal and fear.

"I'm sorry. I didn't have time to introduce him first," Jack apologizes. "Dick is the father. This is, the uncle, Milwaukee."

Dick enters and politely takes off his hat. "Excuse me, ma'am, where is my daughter?" Without waiting for an answer, he quickly tosses his hat on the antlers above the fireplace. The tall man, after a hasty assessment, ducks through the bedroom door. He swoops up Christina and holds her tight while she cries. While he cries. Rocking back and forth.

"Come join us. Beth has prepared a meal. I hear we are having stew and biscuits," Fred says. "And Beth made a cake."

"Yes, I did!" Beth captures Jack in a long hug.

"Hildago, can you take care of the horse?" Fred requests.

"My pleasure. I'll tie this beautiful creature next to Daisy. The two girls can have a long chat."

"Ja. Thank you! We will hold dinner for you." Fred motions Milwaukee to enter. "Come. Sit."

Beth rattles off questions, holding Jack tight. "Nice to see you! Did you get the tombstone placed? Have you heard about Franny? Do you know if your family is well? Is my family well? Is there any news?"

"Nice to see you too!" Jack takes a step back. "Let me see your baby bump," he hesitates, "Sorry. I didn't know. You lost the baby?"

"It was the day before we found his child." Beth points to Dick, who now speaks soothing words to Christina. Christina whimpers uncertainty, not sure if the man holding her is all right.

"I lost Franny. I should have been there for her. Franny didn't even make it as long as her mother," Jack informs.

Beth hugs him again, tighter. "I am so sorry. You couldn't have known."

"Here, take her." Dick interrupts their reunion. "I am not able to pacify as well as her mother," he says.

"What's wrong, Christina?" Beth says, "It's all fine."

Dick's eyes get big. "Christina?"

"We had to give her a name. It didn't seem right to keep calling her baby girl," Beth responds.

"Who is the other young one?" Dick asks.

"Patrick."

"Seems like he could sleep through a stampede," Dick says. "Did I hear there was going to be cake? I like cake."

"Yes," Beth answers, "it won't be long."

"Milwaukee, don't just stand there, come, sit." Dick insists, sitting down at the head of the table and pulling a chair out for Milwaukee.

"Ja, please, come, sit." Fred motions and reinstates.

Beth perceives Fred's discomfort. It mirrors her own awkwardness in offering. "Yes, please." She hopes these formal gestures will end soon. Fred coaxes Christina out of her arms.

Milwaukee pulls the chair further from the table.

"None of that, my friend, up to the table," Dick demands.

Milwaukee complies.

"So, you have come to call my little squirrel Christina, have you?"

"Ja. She is spirited like my little sister," Fred answers. He takes a chair next to Dick.

"A very fine Christian name. I don't know how Sora would have felt about it. What do you think, my friend?" Looking at Milwaukee.

Milwaukee nods and smiles.

"Cat got your tongue, does it?"

Beth pours them all coffee.

"If I remember right, there was to be a naming ceremony in the future. Until then, I like the name. It is better than little squirrel." Dick hyper articulates and tickles under Christina's chin. She smiles. "Come here, little squirrel," he coaxes.

Surprise fills everyone's faces when Christina doesn't hesitate.

"Seems like she likes the name little squirrel," Milwaukee states. "It is custom to have ceremony."

"I believe she does! Don't you, little squirrel?" Dick says sweetly. He bounces her gentle like a man who has experience with children.

Patrick cries and Fred jumps up. "My hands are free I will get him."

"Thank you. The cake is ready. We are just waiting on Hidalgo," Beth announces.

"I'm here and it sure smells good." The door barely makes a noise as Hildago closes it. "That is a fine job, Fred," Hildago commends, looking around. "Where is Fred?"

"Probably struggling with a diaper." Beth pulls the stew off the coals.

"Appears to me that he doesn't have any trouble with doors," Dick adds. "I have been fix'n to do that. Always found something more worthy of my time."

Fred emerges successful and asks, "Shall we say grace?"

"May I?" Dick offers. No one objects and Dick makes the sign of the cross and says the Lord's Prayer, adding, "And thank you, Lord, for these fine folks who have graciously taken upon themselves to care for my little squirrel and home. Amen."

#

Circles of smoke rise above her head. Christina reaches and swats. Dick blows more and listens to the conversation. Learning more about these generous folks.

"I have been meaning to tell you, Beth, how appreciative I am that you befriended my Amanda." Jack tells Beth.

"It was she who befriended." Beth clearly makes known.

"Nevertheless, her last days were better because of you," Jack says.

"So, you have been walking all these days?" Fred asks Jack.

"No. It took the stone carver a couple days."

"This man, God bless his soul, walked carrying a heavy tombstone all the way from Fort Kearney," Dick says, adding, "nearly 200 miles. Insisted he carry his burden alone."

"And a hard man to keep pace with," Milwaukee adds.

"A man with a mission," Fred says. "I remember the day Jack set out determined to obtain a marker, even at the cost of his position on the wagon train." He looks down at his son. "I only wish the opportunity was available for my wife. Eldora deserved a memory marker. I think I would have done the same, Jack. If I had the chance."

"I don't understand," Dick says. "Beth isn't your wife?"

"I am," Beth says. "Just not his first."

"My first wife died giving birth to this little man." Fred musses Patrick's hair.

"Three men who have lost wives in the same room together." Dick clenches the pipe between his teeth. "What are the chances of that?" Dick lifts his girl. "Here, Go to Uncle Milwaukee." She accepts the transfer by admiring Milwaukee's beads.

"The odds are not as small as one might think," Jack states. "A sad state of affairs these days. But meeting these men on the trail made my journey more pleasant. Their stories helped pass the time."

Beth smile and says, "I remember, you too, had a good share of stories,"

Beth's smile lights up the room like Sora's used to.

"Tell us about the buffalo you raised!" Jack insists.

"I find that a good story should never be told the same way twice. Thus, if I commence to telling, you and Milwaukee will have to bear with me and my additions." Dick warns.

"I look forward to the enhancement," Jack says.

"I have had many adventures, more than most will ever have. In my adventures I have witnessed buffalo pushing snow away to get to the grasses below. The cow would rather starve than do that." Dick puffs smoke into the air.

Beth refills their coffee cups and starts another pot.

"One day I saw two buffalo calves frolicking and decided to introduce them to my cattle. Just to see what might happen. Yes, I had a ranch."

"You raised them and eventually yoked them to a wagon," Jack adds.

"Now, now, don't be pushing my story along." Dick pushes his pipe forward. "Yes, I did coax them to accept the yoke like oxen. They took to it as well as the oxen, maybe better. I trained them every day. When they were ready, we went to town. Well, I don't have to tell you what a spectacle that was."

"I can't imagine the stares," Fred smiles.

"Heads certainly turned. All eyes were on the man brazen enough to roll into town with two buffalo yoked up to a wagon. It is worth more than money can buy." Dick chuckles. "Really! I couldn't drink all the free beer that was offered. Just so they would have a chance to ask how I did it. The buffalo got jilted. No beer for them." Dick chuckles hardier, getting everyone else to laugh.

Beth takes Christina into her arms like a loving mother would do. Christina suckles at her breast. Beth plays with her fingers and hums.

Dick puffs smoke clouds above their heads and continues. "Those two calves were so easy to train that I got the idea to breed them with cows. Cattalo is what I called them. I thought they were a good breed, but others did not. They found them harder to handle. I found them hardier. But I tired of people complaining and wanting their money back. So, I sold the ranch. Went back to trading furs. Spent so much time at forts they recruited me as a market hunter. A real passion for me. I am leaning towards starting my own trading post down in Taos."

"You will be taking the girl away?" Milwaukee voices concern.

"I don't know." Dick goes to the hearth and removes a brick. He pulls out libations and pours some into his coffee. He offers it to everyone. Seeing no takers, he places it back into its hideout. Sitting, he explains further, "I'm not able to sit still for very long. Sora knew this. She was the only one who could make me sit at all. Without her, I am lost. Without purpose." he pauses, gulps coffee. "I don't know what to do."

"Take care of your child," Fred speaks up. "That is what you do."

"I am a wandering man," Dick says. Tears well up into his eyes. They slowly dissipate as he continues, "I have worked cotton and tobacco fields. Hunted and trapped for others and myself. I had a ranch that was profitable but too much work for me. I roamed about searching abandoned mines after the Mexican war. I fought wars. But I have never cared for a baby." Dick takes his cup and swallows the rest. He removes the brick again and fills his cup.

"Did you find anything in the mines?" Hildago is curious.

"Not a thing, they were always picked clean. Nothing has given me value until I met Milwaukee and his family." Dick grasps the cup, both hands, and looks down.

"I lost a wife, too. It is a pain I shall always carry." Fred takes a sleeping Patrick to bed.

"Losing a wife is something that lingers deep within," Jack reiterates. "It makes you relish what you have."

"I do cherish that little girl. But I do not know how to care for her." Dick doesn't want to inform them all of his other family in Taos.

"You can learn," Milwaukee says. "I am family. I take little squirrel to village. You come and see her when you can. Even stay. We find you another wife." Milwaukee offers.

"No. You and Nanoke are getting old with age." Dick points out.

"The village will help," Milwaukee confidently says.

Dick does not doubt it. "No. It is not what Sora and I want," Dick corrects himself, "wanted." He cannot leave his little squirrel with Milwaukee's people, and he doesn't want to leave her with Delores in Taos. Christina needs both worlds to influence her inner self. Sora believed that. Dick wants nothing less. His love for Christina, this cabin, and this land forces him the bravery to say, "I will consider accepting your offer Milwaukee."

Beth hands Fred Christina and offers, "we could take care of her."

Dick clears his throat. Quietly he says, "excuse me, I have to relieve myself." Dick goes outside. The night air calms his anxiety. Still, he doesn't know what to do or what to think about these strangers and their kindness. Dick needs to withdraw and think.

CHAPTER XXXII

"A gift is as a precious stone in the eyes of him that hath it: whither soever it turneth, it prospereth. He that covereth a transgression seeketh love; but he that repeateth a matter separateth very friends."
(*King James Version*, Proverbs 17:8)

The night is fitful. Sporadic, thoughtful considerations keep Dick awake. He readjusts his feet on the hearth and leans back in the rocking chair.

A white silk scarf wraps around his hands. It is as soft as Sora's skin. A tear wells up and escapes. The scarf helps wipe it gone. He will never again see Sora's eyes light up at the expectation of receiving a gift. Dick wraps it around his neck and ties it like a gentleman's cravat.

Taos is where Dick needs to be. Delores and the children deserve a husband and father. But Christina needs a father too. But Christina represents infidelity and dishonesty. Sins that can't be forgiven. The truth will not help Delores understand. But perhaps it is worth the consequences, for Christina's sake. Time to own the past and accept all his responsibilities in one place. Taos, where he belongs.

But that leaves Potawatomi influence unreachable. His little girl will suffer for the lack of it. Yet, Milwaukee and Nanoke's clan will only keep his little squirrel bundled up and secluded. *That is not what Sora wanted.* Which is partially correct, Sora did tie little squirrel into that contraption. Which Nanoke will surely do. But truly, Dick cannot deny them access.

He did promise to raise their child in both the white man and Indian ways. So, Christina's home is here. In the house Dick built.

Nothing in him wants to raise a child on his own. He stokes the fire and ignites his pipe. Blowing smoke puffs into the air, remembering Milwaukee saying smoke travels ahead of requests.

Can he accept Beth's gracious request? Where does Fred stand on the issue?

"How did you all sleep?" Jack questions, rolling onto his elbow.

"Satisfactorily," Dick answers. He takes a double puff and blows out smoke.

"You lie, you toss, you turn, you not even sleep." Milwaukee tells the truth.

"Not unusual these past few days," Dick responds.

"Good morning," Beth says as she enters the room.

Dick worries that she may have changed her mind during the night.

Fred follows close behind, holding Patrick. Before Dick can respond to Beth, Fred says, "Good morning!"

"Morning!" Dick can't add good to it. Sora isn't here to enjoy the morning with him. Her death has sucked the good out of everything.

"Morning," Jack says.

"Good morning!" Milwaukee also greets.

Christina clings onto Beth's shirt, comfortable in her arms. "Christina has taken a liking to you." Dick's feet hit the floor, rocking himself forward. He stops on the front tips of the rocker and says, "I don't mind if you folks stay on a while." Surprised looks request clarity. Dick turns the rocker without getting up towards them. Not sure how to convey his true proposal, choosing his words carefully. "I propose that you stay as long as you like. Continue being Christina's wet nurse and help make this place a home." Dick eases into what he really wants is for them to stay forever. Take on the responsibility and care of Sora's precious gift.

"There is no need to prolong goodbyes," Fred says.

"I think it will be hard enough as it is." Beth puts the kettle on.

Little squirrel kicks wildly, reaching towards Dick. *She sure knows how to warm his heart.* "Maybe stay the summer and through the winter. I will personally escort you on to Oregon or California whichever you prefer."

"Well," Jack springs into action like a man ten years his junior. "That is something to think on the next three days. Captain Smette's caravan will be coming through then. He said you were welcome to join up."

"That will also give me time to convince you to stay." Dick stands and holds out his arms. "May I?"

"Entertain your papa while I make breakfast," Beth says, handing Christina over.

Hearing the word 'papa' makes his decision harder to swallow. Holding firm his ground, he states, "Christina needs more time to adjust to the situation."

"Is it possible, Fred?" Beth twirls around.

"I suppose anything is possible," Fred answers. "Let's get Jack squared away with breakfast and a few supplies. Then we can discuss it. Like Jack said, we have about three days to figure it out."

Beth gives Fred a loving hug.

"Good!" Dick rubs Christina's stomach. "That is all I ask."

Fred sits at the head of the table with Patrick. Dick is glad to see Milwaukee join him. *This may be the most comfortable option after all. At least shaping up to appear so.* He looks at Christina's big brown eyes. The same deep brown as Sora's. He rubs her cheek. She grabs the bracelet Sora gave him the first time they met. Suppressing emotion, he joins the others while she clutches tight.

Hildago opens the door. The now quiet door, thanks to Fred. He presents a hat full of eggs and a milk bucket, filled to the brim.

Beth ladles some milk into a bowl and says, "I hope pancakes will fill you up for your journey."

"I propose," Dick says, clearing his throat and looks at Fred. "That you also consider staying on permanently."

"I do not understand," Milwaukee queries.

"How would you like Fred and Beth to be your Madre and Padre?" Dick lifts Christina into the air. "That is, if they are willing?" He looks past Christina to view their reaction.

"You will let these strangers take care of your girl over me. Sora's girl?" Milwaukee strongly questions the decision.

Fred looks at Beth. Both obviously find his proposal favorable. "What do you think, Christina?" Dick purposefully ignores Milwaukee, giving him time to understand.

Fred and Beth simultaneously sweet talk, "say yes."

"I think it is best for Christina to have a mother and a father. Here in this cabin. The cabin Sora and I made for our child."

"You are father," Milwaukee states. "We will find you another Potawatomi woman to be the mother."

"I don't want another wife." This Dick is sure of. It would surely complicate things further. Dick doesn't desire any of that. Dick elaborates, "I loved Sora. No other can compare. Yet Sora was unable to still my wandering feet for very long. If I would have been here instead of roaming, Sora may still be alive." He cannot escape the guilt he feels.

"You do not know that." Milwaukee points out. "You don't have to love another wife. We will find a woman who understands."

"I know that is true, my friend, but they will not want to live in this cabin alone when I find I must meander. Without Sora, I feel there will be more of that."

"Then they can go with you or come to the village."

"I like to go on my own as you do," Dick says, handing Milwaukee Christina. "I fear she will become more Indian and less a part of the changing world."

"What harm is that?" Christina cries in Milwaukee's lap. He takes his beads off and dangles them. "For you." She grabs and promptly slobbers on the beads. "She is Indian. You should worry that she will become more white and less Indian."

"Yes. I don't want to take that from her. First and foremost," Dick directs, "I must come and go as I please. You Milwaukee, also, may come and go as you please. We are family. This is our home. Christina's home," Dick commands. "If you decide to stay, Mister and Missus Klucke, you have to stay here. Where we can visit and watch Christina grow. Close to where Milwaukee and I like to roam."

"And Nanoke?" Milwaukee requests.

"Ja. You are always welcomed, and anyone you choose to bring along," Fred firmly says.

Beth flips another pancake and says, "Of course."

"As you must come visit our village." Milwaukee insists. "It is important."

"That is doable," Fred assures. He places a plate full of Beth's cakes on the table.

"I am expecting that you do visit Milwaukee's village. I need to make sure she is exposed to the Potawatomi way," Dick insists.

Beth quickly wraps arms around Dick's neck, begging, "Yes, please!" Beth's exuberance seals the proposal like wax stamped on an important letter. "We can, can't we Fred?"

"Ja. It will be a pleasure."

"I want her to call me Uncle."

"I am Uncle," Milwaukee corrects.

"Yes, my friend, you are."

"I think that this arrangement makes Christina one lucky girl," Jack says.

"Lucky these fine people found you when they did." Dick rubs Christina's head. "Lucky that this place is all yours, Christina," he says. "In your care Fred."

"Can we have breakfast now?" Jack requests with a smile. "Hildago and I have many miles to cover."

"Yes, let me say a prayer," Fred states. "Thank you, dear God, for renewed life, and the blessings of new friends and family!"

"Amen." Dick whole heartily agrees.

CHAPTER XXXIII

"In the day shalt thou make thy plant grow, and the morning shalt thou make thy seed to flourish:"
(*King James Version*, Isaiah 17:11)

Fred pats the ground and presses firmly around the rose cutting. "There!" He stands. The recently built corner fence points north towards the trail. Future roses can grow in plain sight of the kitchen window. Fred stands back and admires. *Perfect!*

"I think that is a great placement for that stick," Beth jokingly says, looking out the window.

"Do you like the corner fence?"

"I don't see it giving much support, presently." Beth smiles.

"I will plant more rose bushes around it. Someday you will not even see the posts the roses will rely on for support." Much like he relies on her. "It is a lovely night, come, join me outside."

They sit leaning their backs on the house. Fred says, "They're yellow roses, you know."

Beth brightens and says, "Our first kiss!"

Fred kisses her and says, "Not the last." He takes the silver engraved cigar tin holding his bogarted cigar out. He smiles at how the vest fits better thanks to Beth's stitches. "May I?" He politely asks. The aroma reminds him of the day Patrick was born. That day there was no celebration in his heart.

"Yes, please. I don't mind. Papa used to smoke cigars occasionally. I miss him. I miss all my family. Henry the most."

"Maybe, when the children are older, we can make the journey to see your family."

"I don't think Dick and Milwaukee will approve."

Fred looks at the fine red glow of the cigar as he puffs and says, "We don't need their approval. Just need to tell them where we go and how long we plan to be gone."

"Maybe they could join us."

"Perhaps. That would make things easier. They know the paths people take and could show us the way." Fred puffs. "For now, we have a new family. One you, hopefully, won't have to ever miss." Fred relishes the smokey flavor lining his mouth before he exhales. Fred grabs the jug full of his first brew made in America. He pulls the cork and takes a good, long drink. The cool beer mingles with cigar and renews his palate. *Things have changed!* Fred thinks of all he has lost and all he has been given. Taking another puff, thinking, *So many losses.* Another swig. *Some experiences distasteful, like a poor brew.* At this moment Fred is happy for what has been given, a good batch more precious than pure gold.

#

"Here! Take a puff. Just don't inhale." Fred offers.

Hesitant, Beth says, "No, that is not for me."

Nudging her he says, "It is to celebrate Patrick's birth. I haven't felt like celebrating until now."

"Like prost or noroc?"

"Yes, very much like that. We should, also, celebrate Christina becoming family as well."

Beth takes hold, looks at it and takes a little puff, but not further than her mouth. She thinks being a mother and a wife with this fine man at her side is the best for her. She coughs. But not cigars. She hands it back. "May I wash away the taste?" She requests.

"Ja." Fred hands the jug over.

Beth takes a sip. Unsure that the taste is any better than the cigar, she takes a larger sip. "Not bad," is her final decision.

"Can you taste the rose hips?"

"No." Then again, she just had cigar smoke touch her taste buds. A thought runs through her mind about roses. The thorns are the things that hurt, but the petals and fruit heal. Beth hopes and prays that time will heal her grief. That her family will mend the pain of loss. "Where did you get rose hips?"

"From the prairie roses by the river. Take another swallow, this time smell it. A beer is more than taste. Tell me if you can smell anything else added."

"It smells a little like a rosebush next to an enormous pine tree," she says after a whiff. The beer's flavor is more pleasurable this time. "It tastes like nothing I have ever tasted before."

"Juniper."

Beth takes another gulp. "Yes, there is a hint of that pungent berry." Looking past the small fence that keeps no one in or out, Beth sees a caravan of people settling in for the night. She suggests by asking, "Do you suppose the people who camp over there would be interested in your brew?"

"Hmm, never crossed my mind. That is a great idea. I could set up a make-shift table with barrels close to the trail and sell beer, bartender stye. Most travelers are plum out by the time they reach here."

Beth smiles. "Yes, most are plum out."

"They won't even care what flavors I add. I could boldly experiment."

"Not sure juniper beer will sell," Beth says.

Fred holds onto a big inhale of cigar smoke and then releases it into the breeze.

It isn't the first time Beth realizes how fast things change, like a puff of smoke. Here, one moment, gone the next. Beth wants this moment to last forever. She wants to always have Fred, Patrick, and Christina to love. And one day have her own children. Fred's children. Curiosity asks, "How many children did you say you wanted?"

"Don't remember saying, but we will take all that the good Lord will provide."

"Yes," Beth agrees. She cannot wait until next year when the roses bloom. A foreground accenting a beautiful horizon. The horizon that brings a magnificent sunrise almost every day. A view she can share with all those she loves. Beth wiggles bare toes in soft, fine dirt. A view that makes all they have gone through more bearable. A bucolic view that reflects how she feels, alive and well, ready for what comes around the bend. The quintessence of it provokes Beth to hum one of her favorite hymns as she leans lovingly into Fred's arms. She looks up at the big blue sky and spots an eagle effortlessly soaring. The evening summer sunshine warms her face. She is happy and carefree.

While sifting through her ancestral background, Katherine found interesting stories that fueled a passion to write a historical novel. Katherine loves to travel and explore the vast world we live in with her husband DeVane and, on occasions, with family. She is a mother of two daughters and grandmother of two grandsons. Katherine currently lives in her home state of North Dakota.

Katherine Murie Webster

at:

https://Facebook.com/kmuriew
https://Amazon.com/author/kmuriewebster

Facebook

Amazon

Made in the USA
Columbia, SC
20 September 2021